FIVE GOLD RINGS

KRISTEN BAILEY

Ebook ISBN: 978-1-80508-413-6
Paperback ISBN: 978-1-80508-414-3

Cover design: Emma Rogers
Cover images: Shutterstock

Published by Storm Publishing.
For further information, visit:
www.stormpublishing.co

ALSO BY KRISTEN BAILEY

Sex Ed

Five Gold Rings

Souper Mum

Second Helpings

Has Anyone Seen My Sex Life?

Can I Give My Husband Back?

Did My Love Life Shrink in the Wash?

How Much Wine Will Fix My Broken Heart?

Am I Allergic to Men?

Great Sexpectations

For Nick.
Who I married on the twelfth day of Christmas.
Even though he hates Christmas.

ONE

23RD DECEMBER

Eve

What does Christmas look like to you?

My vision of a perfect Christmas dates back to when I was a child: brand new flannel pyjamas, hot chocolate with squirty cream, a living room fizzing with anticipation (or maybe that was the sound of Dad's dodgy Christmas lights). A tree so big we pruned it back to watch the television, rammed with decorations. No branch shall remain unbaubled. There is no colour scheme here. It's decorations made out of pasta shapes and half a tube of glitter. It's tinsel that the tree wears like a disco scarf; pieces of string weighed down with cards from aunties we never see; badly wrapped gifts lying on a carpet of Christmas tree needles; hands rustling through tins of chocolates. Mum telling Dad not to put the wrappers back in the tin. Does he listen? No. But she can't be angry with him. He throws a wrapper at her that gets caught in her big mass of curly hair. Noel, my brother, has nabbed the good armchair, and wears a Star Wars dressing gown thinking he's a Jedi when he's not. He knows he has the good chair and sticks his middle finger up at me. I pull a face back, and he laughs so hard, he snots on himself. There's a Christmas film on the television. I can't even tell you what it is but there's snow on the screen, falling in white blankets, resting on someone's eyelashes. It's a festive warmth you feel in your chest. Because this is joy, this is a huge colourful shiny version of what love looks like.

That is what Christmas looks like.

It should look like that.

It shouldn't look like a blonde woman on her knees noshing off your boyfriend of three years in the shower.

'Shitshitshitshit...' Chris mutters. Unfortunately, this does not deter the girl on her knees who assumes his swearing to be associated with impending orgasm. He tries to pull out. She tugs on his balls. I stand there, speechless, waves of shock pinning me to the spot, drowning me. Seriously? He turns off the shower. Yes, do that. Save the water and our energy bill, at least. The girl turns around and her eyes widen. The two of them stand there, looking like they're expecting me to throw them some towels. No such luck.

'Eve... This isn't what you think it is...' Chris says, pushing his hair back from his face. 'I thought you weren't coming back until this afternoon.'

That wasn't the sentence to lead with.

The girl grabs a robe next to the sink and wraps it around her body. My robe. I know the girl. Her name is Allegra, and she works in his department on accounts. She's wearing my robe. The bitch is wearing my robe. She bows her head in shame, looking for escape, but this is a small bathroom and I'm blocking the only way out of here.

'I got an earlier train so we could buy the last of your gifts for your family.'

I hear my voice wobble and pause to take the deepest of breaths. Don't give him the satisfaction of your tears, Eve.

Never. You've given him three of your best years, don't give him an inch more.

'You should have texted,' Chris adds. He's not doing well here, is he? His body starts to shiver. I hope he freezes. Am I giving him a towel? Hell, no.

'I was online this morning and saw a lamp in John Lewis and thought your sister would love it. I've reserved it. Thought we could go up to Oxford Street and get all the last minute bits. We've got nothing for your aunt and uncle yet either,' I say, trying to focus on something else, anything else except what's happening in this room.

Allegra, in my robe, stands there, looking slightly unnerved. I turn to her. She's pretty. Polar opposite to me, with my brown wavy hair and brown eyes. She would have been Mary in the nativity for sure, while I would have been the innkeeper's wife, maybe a townsperson.

'Hi. Allegra, isn't it? We were going to spend Christmas with his family in North London. All the family. Massive turkey. You should see it, it's like they fed it steroids.'

I turn back to Chris, who has now lost his hard on. Water drips from the tip of his bell-end. Drip, drip, drip. 'Eve...'

'I've been in Bristol. I was presenting a paper. For a conference. A law conference,' I tell Allegra, the details irrelevant but I need to fill that awful, empty silence. 'I was scheduled to get in later, but I thought I'd surprise my boyfriend. Surprise!' I exclaim drily with added jazz hands. This is a surprise. God, I have questions. How long? Why didn't I see it? When I caught the train, bleary-eyed at 7 a.m., I imagined slipping into our house, stripping down and crawling under our duvet, slow morning sex, a coffee under our Christmas lights. Talking about our Christmas plans – all our plans. I exhale a slow pained breath.

'Can we talk about this?' he whispers.

Talk? No, we can't. I am suddenly enveloped by rage.

'Every Christmas since I've known Chris, I've spent it with his family. I made them the priority. Not mine. Christmas day itself is always themed, Allegra. I've worn red, and tartan, and fur. Not real fur, obviously, as no one should wear real fur, but I joined in. I ate his uncle's dry ham and played charades and plaited his niece's hair...'

'I know, but Eve...' Chris pleads.

I turn from the door and march into the living room. By the tree is a pile of bags and gifts ready to be loaded into the car, wrapped in twine. Biodegradable fucking twine. I open the window to our third-floor flat and start flinging things out. The first gift is the most expensive and that's his mother's hamper, full of cheese straws, organic oat biscuits and Christmas nuts. There are going to be some bloody happy squirrels out there.

'EVE! DON'T!' shrieks Chris, scrambling to reach for a towel and following me into our living room.

Too late. Cashmere throw for Granny Clara. GONE. I hope it gets run over or adopted by a stray cat. His dad's books on naval history are next. Au revoir. Sail away into the bitter winter air, expensive hardbacks. Allegra at this point has scuttled towards our bedroom where I can see they've slept in our bed. My robe is on the floor as she tries to pull a dress over her head and locate her knickers.

'Oi! Oi!' I hear from outside the window and I pop my head out.

'I'm sorry!' I yell. 'Just caught my boyfriend getting sucked off in the shower by another woman.'

The postman, weighed down with Amazon parcels, pauses for a moment then salutes me. 'As you were, love!'

'You're acting like a madwoman,' Chris interrupts.

Chris is really not redeeming himself in any way here. I pop my head back inside. There is no contrition, angst, no regret. Who is this man? He thinks I'm mad? Maybe madness is lying.

Telling your girlfriend of three years that you spent the night in, binge watching property shows and eating fried chicken.

'This isn't what it looks like... It was just the one time.'

I give a hollow snigger under my breath. Mainly at Allegra who stands there with her arms crossed letting me know that is also a lie.

'How long?' I ask her, tersely.

She has tears in her eyes. She knew we were together, there's a photo of us on the bedside table that would have watched over proceedings last night. She could at least do me the courtesy of telling me the truth now I've caught them in the act.

'Since the summer...' she mumbles.

'Allie!' Chris exclaims.

She has a nickname. I pause for a moment, and a bottle of clementine gin destined for his cousin drops to the floor, shattering into little shards of alcohol, fruit and heartbreak.

'Chris, we should go. Get some clothes on. Give her some space.'

'But my stuff... I... I...'

'You have stuff at mine. We can buy stuff.'

He has stuff at hers? I'm staring into space, mesmerised by the lights of the Christmas tree and all the deception bubbling to the surface. Chris scampers next door, pulling on tracksuit bottoms and a hoodie, grabbing his big parka, no socks, the trainers he uses for the gym, none of it matching. There's a Fair Isle theme to his family do this Christmas. We would have matched in cream and forest green. I bought him a jumper, hidden in the back of the wardrobe. But I don't say a word.

'Eve, it wasn't meant to be like this. Shit. You weren't supposed to find out like this...'

'How was I supposed to find out, Chris?' I enquire.

'I was going to...' he spurts out, panicked.

'Christmas day itself? Was it my gift? Were you going to get

"I'm a big shitting cheat" put on a mug?' I reach below the tree, digging through packages to find that gift. 'Here's my gift.' It's in a snowflake bag with a card:

Eve, With all the love in the world, C x

Inside the bag is a small red velvet box from Caspar & Sons. I pause. I know that place. I work there. I laugh. Seriously? I open up the box. I can't breathe. It's a ring. I stare at it for a moment then take it out, playing with the gold band between my thumb and forefinger, the diamond catching the light and casting its rays across the room. Solitaire, round cut, gold ring, low clarity. Allegra is struck silent by it.

'A ring! You old romantic,' I say dryly, my tongue rolling along my teeth, before flicking that ring and everything it meant out of the window.

'EVE! What have you done?' Chris cries, running to the window and looking out into the hedges, grabbing handfuls of his sandy brown hair in his hands.

Was it expensive? Good. Fucking ace. I hope he never finds it. Ever.

'Get out. Now,' I say.

And with that Allegra grabs him by the arm. The ground crunches as he steps over shards of glass. He doesn't break my gaze the whole time; my jaw is clenched so hard I think my teeth may shatter. As he turns, I think about the number of Christmases I've spent with him, the money and time I've wasted on gifts, the number of times I said, 'I love you'. My heart feels like stone inside my chest – grey heavy stone, everything that Christmas isn't. I shut the door behind him and rest my forehead against it.

I hear the murmur of their voices in the hallway. 'Crap, I've left my phone in there.'

'You idiot. You can't go back in there.'

'She knows my passcode, she'll see everything.'

'Everything?'

I place cold hands to my temples and try to rub away my frustration, my confusion, my hurt. I walk to the bedroom. His phone is charging next to his side, as usual. I dial in the passcode and open up his messages. Filtered pictures of his genitals, messages about hook ups and hard nipples, a whole complement of emotional devastation on his new iPhone 14. I open our bedroom window that opens out on to the street. I throw that out, too.

Joe

Hey, Eve. You OK? So, as it's Christmas and it's a time for giving, I thought I'd give you this. Yes, it's that thing. I know, I know... It's a bit cheesy and last year I literally just gave you a chocolate reindeer, but I wanted you to have it. Is that weird? That's weird. It's just I've known you now for nearly two years and I think you're great. Really great. And I know you have a boyfriend, but I guess it can't hurt to hear that someone else out there thinks you're amazing. I mean, I love you. That's a lot, isn't it? That's a strong word. I like you very much. I like you, strongly. I've made my feelings for you sound like a questionnaire now. What I mean is, I just like being around you. You make everything better. Merry Christmas.

I look in the mirror. That's a really bad monologue. I can't say that to Eve. Firstly, because it's Christmas but also because it's a proper Hugh Grant ramble and she'll laugh in my face. The pure facts are she has a boyfriend and I have to respect that line, that unwritten code of not being that person who breaks up a relationship. Maybe I should just post this to her. It's just a gift. Between friends. At Christmas. 'Tis the season and all that. Do I crush on Eve? A fair bit. Perhaps too much. Instead of bouldering my way in there, though, I offer her friendship, I buy her the occasional drink, I admire her from afar like some doe-eyed puppy. I distract myself with flings and date other people. People who just aren't... her.

Her boyfriend is Chris, he works in publishing, he has a proper job and does grown-up things like play squash and has a car that works. There is no question who's the better option. I met the boyfriend once at a works drinks do. Did he speak down to me, highlighting the size of his car engine like a dickhead? Yes. But I saw the way that Eve leaned into him and how much she adored him. In that moment, I knew sabotage was not the way forward because it would likely just lead to heartache for me.

'That is a *lewk*, Joe Lord,' Gabriel, my housemate, says from the doorway of our shared house.

'Too much?' I say, turning to him.

'I'd argue, not enough. You look like a mixture of Superman and Santa's Little Helper. It's frankly hurting my eyes,' he says, shading his view. 'The shorts are very...'

'Tight? Can you see my...'

'Candy cane?' he says, laughing. 'Joe, you're a buff butler. They probably went a size down so you could give all the ladies something to look at. You're all chiselled, tall and handsome. They'll want to get their money's worth.'

'Look at? I've done this gig for too long now. They get gropey.' It's a part-time gig I got into by mistake. I thought I was applying to be a real-life butler. I thought I'd be helping someone like Bruce Wayne fight crime in smart tailoring. I didn't realise I'd be wearing shorts so tight you can see the outline of my crack. That said, I need the extra income and it's easy money. Except when they get gropey.

'But the tips...'

'Keep the lights on. I know.'

'Yes, I know that sounds awful as your housemate, asking you to whore yourself out to keep a roof over our heads, but needs must.'

I look at myself in the mirror again. Even I can't believe the rates I get paid at Christmas. I get paid stupid money because the rest of the world has plans. Christmas plans involving drinks, carolling and getting ready for the coming of the big man in red. Normal people have already blocked work out of their hearts and minds so yes, I work because no one else wants to. If my agency wants me to pour shots into ladies' mouths at a bottomless brunch, dressed as an elf with bells on his shorts and don a fur-lined cape like some sort of Christmas pimp then so be it.

Gabriel looks down at the gift on the bed. 'When are you going to do it then? Not today, surely?' he asks.

Gabriel is party to the knowledge about Eve because I told him once when I was drunk. He knows about the crush, but the advice is awful. He told me love is a competition, and I need to access my baser instincts and put myself up for contention. Like silverbacks trying to win the mating rights of a lady gorilla. Gabriel watches too many nature programmes.

'No. She's busy today, she has Christmas plans. You know, I may not even give it. It's a stupid idea.'

'Dude, no. That's a cute gift. You've put thought into it. I hope you've put that much thought into my gift.'

I got Gabriel kitchen gadgets because that's how he gets his kicks. What I've got him will blow his little mind and I can't wait to see his face when he opens it.

'Find her tonight, dressed like that, with some mistletoe. Keep it all on theme,' he continues.

'Not today,' I say resolutely, shaking my head.

Gabriel pouts, another plan of his rejected. 'And not with that speech either...' He smirks.

'You heard that? Was it shit?'

He nods. 'I've never even met this boyfriend she's with but even I know you're a better option. Maybe keep the focus on you and how you feel about her. Like don't tell her about the time you got drunk in that chicken shop and you told Mustafa and all his staff how much you loved her and he felt sorry for you and gave you free chips,' he says, joking, even though he was the person who ate those free chips. 'Just tell her how much she means to you.' He glances over to the bed again. 'You're very good at wrapping. Can you wrap the rest of my gifts?'

'I am. And no.'

He looks over at the tag and the handwritten note. 'You old romantic. If I wasn't straight and with a girlfriend, I'd marry you myself.'

'I want a ring before I commit. I'm not sharing you.' Gabriel was one of the first people I knew in this crazy city when I moved here for university. We bonded over study breaks where Cup Noodles and naps featured heavily, and he has since been my saviour, letting me rent his second bedroom and looking after me like one would do a very large pet. That might change when his girlfriend eventually moves in but for now, it's preferable to living with randoms who label their food and eat in the bath.

'You missed a bit of fake tan by the way, on your thighs.' Gabriel looks down at his own thighs in comparison. 'I would help but I don't love you that much.'

'Thanks, buddy. Do you need a lift to work? I head out in about half an hour.'

'You're going in costume?' he asks, confused.

'I'm driving. I don't want to get stuck there later looking for public transport and taxis at Christmas. Plus, this might get us in the mood. I'll chuck some Christmas tunes on?'

'Then you, sir, are a saint as well as a disgustingly handsome elf.'

I laugh then scan over to the gift on my bed. Not this Christmas, Eve.

TWO

Eve

The only guide I have about how to react when you've caught your boyfriend cheating on you comes from television, films, soap operas. In this moment, I am sure I am expected to sob uncontrollably without any consequence to my eye make-up, call an army of friends to come round, wrap me in a blanket and tell me I'll find love again and that he's not worth it, set to a montage of diva power pop.

This does not happen.

The forty-five minutes that follow are pure chaos, driven by full on mania, that starts with me marching to the bedroom, staring at my robe on the floor. Do you know how hard it is to find the perfect robe? One that provides warmth, coverage, that has pockets and an inbuilt sash. I can never wear this robe again. And I can't sleep on those sheets again, so I strip the bed. But then I notice something tied to the bedpost. Oh. I can't sleep in this actual bed ever again, so I obtain a power drill from under the sink and start to take the bed apart, bit by bit.

Standing there looking at piles of wooden posts and molehills of dirty sheets and clothes, I then tear at pictures, toss relationship memorabilia and all of Chris' belongings onto the floor. His clothes end up in a massive scrapheap. Everything from the socks with the holes to pants to work shirts to old hoodies that I occasionally wear because they're comfortable. Do I inhale a hoodie like some heartbroken saddo? I do. But then I feel anger. I feel the need to rip it up. Except I'm not a wolf with superhuman powers so instead I throw it out of the window which seems to be my big power move today. I throw it all out of the window, hoping for scenes on the streets where people steal the clothes and Chris is left naked, exposed forever.

As I scoop everything up, I then see a condom wrapper. But where is the condom? Shit.

I run to the bathroom to throw up. Squatting next to the loo, I look at the shower where I caught them doing the do. I spray bathroom cleaner everywhere, as if it can exorcise the memory of what I saw them doing in here. Do I spray too much so it's all I can smell and then throw up again? Yes, I do.

I head to the kitchen to get a glass of water. I down it and realise I need to eat. There is no food in the house. I orchestrated that much because I knew we were going to be out a lot over Christmas. I don't have the sanity or patience to cook something from frozen, so I head to the gifts below the tree again. A tree that sparkles, almost mocking me with its twinkle, looking all hopeful. Don't do that or I'll throw you out of the window, too. I rip open a wine and panettone gift set that was destined for Chris's aunt with the big hair and the doll obsession, and I claw at that Italian sweetbread with my hands and just eat it, downing stodgy clumps of it with Rioja at 9 a.m.

As heartbreak has no good sense or reason, I also do the very healthy thing of going on social media to track down any patterns of things going wrong. In the summer, they went for that team building exercise in York. Is that when it started? A few drinks at dinner, an invite to a hotel room, a habit they couldn't break? A month later she posted a meme about love on her Insta with winky faces. A dinner table laid out on a Saturday in October where she was waiting for company. I check my phone calendar. That was the weekend he told me he was on a lads' break playing golf in Essex. Balls and holes. I can see why he could have maybe got the two confused. After that weekend, he bought me flowers. He never buys me flowers. But then it gets too easy to replay every moment, doubt everything he ever said, wonder why and how I was such a fool.

I'm not sure what to do next. Next to me is a tin of short-bread that was destined for Chris's great aunt that I start to eat with wild abandon. I may need to get in more food before this wine kills me off. I dig through gifts thinking about what other treats I wrapped up. I bought his aunt a selection of jams. Can I just eat those with a spoon? My phone ringing switches my attention. I have to answer this.

'Noel,' I whisper.

'Evie, Eve, whatcha doing? It's Chrrrriiiiiistttmas!' my brother wails down the phone.

'Are you drunk?' I ask him, hoping he's not as drunk as me.

'I'm just excited. How was Bristol? How are you and Chris getting there tomorrow? You want to share a cab?'

I take a deep breath, trying to ensure my words don't shudder down the phone to hear his name. We were supposed to be going to Christmas Eve dinner tomorrow with my brother. 'Yeah, about that... I don't think I can?'

'WHAT? C'mon, sis, you're actually flaking on me, at Christmas?' he says, his tone changing.

'I think I have flu. It's pretty bad.'

He pauses for a moment. I should have gone with another excuse. Like I don't have a heart anymore, it's in tiny pieces on my floor. That or diarrhoea.

'Then pop some pills, I won't see you all Christmas otherwise...'

'A little sympathy would be nice.'

'I'm sorry for wanting to spend some time with my actual sister this Christmas.'

I pause for a moment. It's nice to hear I'm important to someone. But I can't tell him. Noel would rage for a start. He would not react well. He would choose violence. As much as I adore my brother, I don't know if I have the mental capacity. I also can't show up to a restaurant in trackies, my hair swept back from my face, sobbing about the state of my love life. I don't want to ruin Christmas. But if I see him, I can't not tell him. I will break to have to sit there in a French restaurant staring into my onion soup and the whirling abyss of my emotions. This is not a good idea.

'I just can't. I'm so sorry. I'm really not well.'

'Evie, seriously? You've got time to sleep it off. See how you feel tomorrow? At least just come for a drink? It doesn't have to be a late one.'

'I don't know how to tell you this. I... I...'

'You're a flake?'

'Noel, don't be a dick.'

There's silence on the other end of the phone. He's angry. I can hear his eyes rolling from the other side of London.

'You're my sister, my only sister. You are my person.'

I sob silently on the other end of the phone.

'You're abandoning us at Christmas again to spend time with your boyfriend. I get it.'

But he's not my boyfriend anymore. Tell him. He's Noel, your Noel. But I can't. The shame, the sadness is too strong, and I don't want to share that with someone I love so dear.

'I'm sorry...'

'Fine. Both of you will at least show your faces on Christmas Day though, right?'

'Noel.'

'Eve!'

'Noel, I can't...'

'I can't do this. Just make sure you at least explain yourself to Dad.'

He hangs up and I take a massive glug of wine. God, that was awful. I never lie to Noel, ever. I do flake out on many a social occasion with him because he's the sort who doesn't plan. He'll send a quick text to say, 'Hey, I have festival tickets? I'll pick you up in half an hour!' without even thinking he may have to bring a tent, some wellies and a change of underwear. I can't share this with him. I just can't. I can't share it with anyone because, unlike my boyfriend, I fear I may have empathy and when you're downing Christmas drinks and getting into the rhythm of the festive season, the last thing you want is some sad sack on your doorstep looking like a loveless orphan. Maybe I'll hide out here, tell him on Boxing Day. In the form of a meme and a YouTube link to a sad song – he'll get it because he's my twin and that's how we communicate, via the power of noughties rock ballads. I miss him now. I miss his reassuring hugs. I think back to the time I got dumped at university and he came to find me with a banoffee pie, a shopping bag full of alcohol and an offer to 'find the douche who'd dumped his sister and sucker punch him.' I declined the offer. We drank all the alcohol.

I sit there blankly. Maybe I should call Noel back? But it's only then that something catches my eye on the coffee table nestled in a pile of paperwork: a printout for tickets. Ice skating at Somerset House, bookings for today, a 10 a.m. session followed by a champagne brunch in the oyster bar. A full-on Christmas date. Just not with his girlfriend because I was scheduled to come back here for 4 p.m. So a date that was going to be followed by him playing happy families with me, and a proposal? He was going to ask me to be his wife. Like, part time? When was that proposal going to happen? What was he going to do? Get on his knees? Like her? Or was the ice skating his parting gift? The blowies in the shower have been fun but I'm off for a life of domestic bliss now. I picture Chris and Allegra ice-skating. She's in one of those big fur Dr Zhivago hats, the snow falling lightly around them, and giant, glamorous trees twinkling in the background. They cling on to each other, skidding all over the place. He wipes a snowflake off her cheek. They kiss. I look at the booking confirmation. He's a liar and a cheat but not a very clever one. I scan the QR code on the booking. I cancel the booking. They have a twenty-four hour no refunds cancellation policy, am I sure? Yep, very sure.

And as I click the button to confirm, a tear curves down my cheek ever so slowly. Because cancelling a reservation is not a hugely gangsta move. But also, because in all that paperwork, I also see a receipt. £725. For an engagement ring he bought in early December. Lovely. I hope someone found that ring. Hopefully that old lady who wears the orange beanie and a thick tweed skirt and spends a lot of time walking between Lidl and the bus stop on our street. I hope she pawns it in and buys herself the biggest fucking turkey you've ever seen.

Why do we give each other rings? These small, metallic circles that are supposed to cement a relationship, that are supposed to be lifelong symbols of commitment. I'd have worn that ring. I'd have worn it with pride, with hope, and all of it would have meant nothing. Absolutely nothing. I have nothing. So, I cry, desperately wanting to hold back the tears but it's like someone's turned on a tap. Flashbacks flooding into view of moments, words, promises that really amounted to nothing. I'm just here, alone at Christmas. I don't even have a bed anymore because I dismantled that. And through my tears, in the corner of the room, I see a red velvet ring box from Caspar & Sons on the floor where I threw it. *Solitaire, round cut, gold ring, low clarity.* At least he went to my place of work to buy that ring. I glance down at the empty box. I need to get out of this flat. I need answers. I need to go there.

Joe

'I'M GETTING MARRIED, BITCHES!' our future bride shouts at the top of her lungs across this crowded bar, at a volume usually reserved for people stuck at sea trying to flag down help.

The bride's name is Tiffany and I reckon she might be eighty percent alcohol at the moment. Whoever she is marrying will need both luck and carbs to sober her up ever again. A group of her friends squeal in reply, and they all gather in a collective twerk around Tiffany to Destiny's Child's *Eight Days of Christmas* so even though it borders on obscene, it is at least festive. A Christmas twerky, one could say. One of them twerks with such velocity that she actually loses a chicken fillet from her bra, so one half of her bosom looks slightly deflated. There is no way I can fix this situation, can I? I stare at the fillet on the floor as someone steps on it. Too late.

'Do you want to see her ring?' one of her friends shrieks at me, staggering, slurring her words, her hand on my chest. Another friend cackles in reply at the euphemism. I'm fine with seeing neither but I smile because that's part of the job and the tips are what will keep me going today. 'I'm sure it's a beautiful ring,' I reply and one of them falls off the velvet banquette she was sitting on. I offer her an arm so she can rejoin us at the table.

'What's your name?' she asks me.

I never give my real name. I learned this the hard way when I was stalked online a year ago by a bride's mother who sent me unsolicited pictures of her breasts.

'Douglas.'

'Hi, Douglas, I'm Bianca,' she says flirtily, a penis straw in between her lips. The maid of honour (the bride's sister, who has already visited the bathroom five times since we've been here) has gone hard on the penis motif this evening: there are penis games, penis drinks accessories, the bride even had an inflatable one on her head before, like a hen unicorn, and people threw rings at it and cheered every time she caught one. Willy hoop-la. Bianca does not seem undeterred that I have a very unsexy, imaginary name. It was the name of one of my uncles who ate a lot of meat that came in tins. I think he died of gout.

'Are you single, Douglas?' she says, uncrossing her legs and pushing her chest forward. Bianca is classically beautiful but there's a ferocity to her that scares me, and that's just in her eyebrows.

'I am an elf, so we have a very strict non-dating policy in the North Pole. Santa doesn't allow it.'

Bianca cackles so hard, a bit of cocktail shoots out of her nose, not that she'd notice it. 'Oooh, roleplay. Well, you're down south now, Douglas. I won't tell Santa if you want to be a bit naughty.'

'But Santa will know,' I reply, diplomatically. 'I like my job.'

'Do you make toys?' another one of the hens asks.

'I do.'

'I have some toys I'd love to show you...' replies Bianca.

I try not to think about where that woman's toys have been. This is not my first hen do. If we're keeping a tally, then we're on about twenty-five. I have had women eat sushi off my naked body (someone tried to pick up my penis with chopsticks...), women have painted me in the nude, I've roleplayed all sorts from firemen to Vikings (which I don't mind as the fake fur keeps me warm at least). I went to a tennis hen do once and had to wear a sweatband and there were many jokes about the bounce of my balls. Is this a forever job? No. Just a little side career that keeps me afloat and pays the bills whilst I meander through my mid-twenties thinking about what I really should be doing with my life. For now, I am here for the cold hard cash, my dignity parked outside with my battered old Mini.

'Shots, shots, shots, shots,' one of the hens starts to chant and they all join in. That's the problem with hen dos. If my dignity is outside, then so are their inhibitions. I reckon Bianca is a respectable primary school teacher in the day but here, with her tribe, she just wants to roar into the night, expressing an appetite for alcohol, and, well, penis. I get it. I have three older sisters so sometimes you do have to own the night, you need to gather your womenfolk, dance to absolutely any damn thing by Beyoncé all in the name of saying down with the patriarchy. They're still chanting about shots. That's my job. This is a bottomless brunch. I'd rather they got their money's worth with the food, but I think salad bars and sliders are the last thing on their minds. I grab at bottles of vodka and cranberry and put a boot to the table, refilling the sea of shot glasses, aware of someone's hand grabbing one of my butt cheeks. I think that's an aunt who was initially told that today was going to be a nice Mexican meal. Yes, Aunty Celeste – that's a different sort of burrito you're trying to grab. She told me something about her South Pole a while ago that may scar me forever.

'Dance, dance, dance, dance!'

This is not usually part of my job description. You have to pay extra for the dancing and even then, it's not really dancing. These ladies have all seen Channing Tatum, and they expect full on thrusting gymnastics. We have a grinding expert at the agency called Julius who is known for his flexibility, even though I know that he bulks his pants out with socks. I look over at Tiffany who puts her hands together in a prayer position, possibly begging.

'But it's Christmas!' one of them squeals.

That it is. I hope Aunty Celeste is carrying cash. I try to just think of the debt this will pay off, the gifts I can buy all my nieces and nephews. I can upgrade their chocolates to Lindt, actually put things in a savings account. I start to shimmy which is a pleasing advancement to proceedings for all of them as it also makes the bells on my shorts ring. I'll just shimmy and thrust then. Aunty Celeste puts a tenner in my arse crack. I should keep going.

'Tiffany, get a picture next to his schlong!' Bianca screams, like it might be on view. It won't be on view because this isn't that sort of club and that sort of behaviour will get us thrown out. Tiffany bends over in a fit of giggles. 'Like you're sucking him off!' I fake a smile, inwardly begging them not to simulate that sort of action, here, now. People are eating. Tiffany looks less keen as well, but Bianca reaches over and pushes her head towards me.

'Bianca! Piss off!' she shrieks back at her. Looks like we're at that part of the brunch already. There's usually a fight at these things, usually over cliques, past beef, laced with jealousy, and the girls bare their nails at each other. I just didn't think it would happen so soon. Tiffany's head bounces off my thigh but as she pulls her head away, there's a scream that echoes through this place. I mean, I work on my thighs at the gym, but I hope they haven't given her concussion.

It's only then that I see it. A chunk of her hair, stuck in one of my bells.

'Hold up, don't yank it!' I tell her, trying to detangle her, putting a hand to the top of her head as she panics, moving her head back and forth. Bianca is in hysterics and snaps away on her phone.

'You stupid bitch... Stop taking photos!' Tiffany says, a perfectly manicured taupe nail pointing in her direction. Someone tries to stop Tiffany as another girl comes over, her face in my crotch trying to free her friend. 'Has anyone got any scissors?'

I flinch for a moment at the thought of something that sharp down there.

'How are these bells attached?' Tiffany squeals at me.

'I don't know, I didn't sew them myself...' I reply, apologetically.

'You call yourself family. You've always been jealous of Tiffany and now it shows...' Tiffany swings her head around and my crotch goes with her to hear Aunty Celeste having a pop.

'Oh, shut up, Aunty Celeste. You're only here because we mixed up the invites. Dried up old—'

Bianca doesn't get a chance to finish that because Aunty Celeste gets up and hits her with quite a sizeable handbag. Someone claps. Ouch. That will leave a mark. The table suddenly becomes a sea of arms and spittle and high-pitched insults, and I notice the tears forming in Tiffany's eyes as she crouches beside me, her hair still caught in my bells.

'Come with me, there's a disabled toilet over there... Can you maybe shuffle over with me?' I ask her. She nods, in a strange crouching position and we sidestep over tentatively. A line of people waiting by a chocolate fountain clock me and burst into hysterics. I flip them the finger. As we enter the toilet, I close the door behind us.

'I grew my hair out for the wedding,' she says, tears rolling down her cheeks, one of her fake lashes giving up on her and trying to leave her face. 'Do you think we'll have to cut it?'

I look down, the throbbing music outside the door and sweat in my eyes not helping me or bringing any calm to this situation. 'So I'm going to suggest something. I don't want you to think anything of it, but I think it'll be easier if I take the shorts off. I have underwear on underneath and then it'll be easier to see what I'm doing.'

Big, drunk eyes look up at me and she nods. I'm grateful at this moment for an elasticated waist, trying to be gentle as I step out of the shorts, which are left hanging there off her head of hair. And I am here. In my underwear. I reach over to the sink.

'I'm just going to use some hand soap to try to loosen the hair and... Please don't cry...' I ease my fingers over where her hair is trapped, thinking back to a time we had to do this with my sister who had gum in her hair. I may have put the gum there. The shorts finally fall to the floor.

'See, no cutting needed,' I say, relieved, hurriedly redressing, watching her run her fingers through her hair. She collapses to the floor and sits there, backed on to the door.

'I'm so sorry. What a bloody disaster of a day.'

'But we detangled you...'

'I mean the drama out there. Bianca being a total lech...'

'It's part of the job. I'm frankly a little more scared of your Aunty Celeste, she's a handsy one.'

She giggles through her tears and I pass her a bit of hand towel to blot her face.

'Your name isn't Douglas, is it? The agency told my sister different.'

'I'm Joe.'

'Well, thank you, Joe. I am sorry.'

'I've seen much worse.'

'Really?'

'I was on a party bus once and someone's maid of honour got so drunk, she tried to step off the bus while it was still moving. She broke both her legs.'

Tiffany guffaws, still crying, snot flying out of her face with some velocity. She wipes it off with the back of her hand.

'I'm such a mess...'

'It's allowed. It's your hen. What's your groom up to today?'

There is a sudden flicker in her eyes when I mention him, and she beams at me. It's a warming change of emotion.

'He's having a weekend on a boat in Marbella. His name is Robbie.'

'And when's the big day?'

'Sixth of January, the twelfth day of Christmas. It's all themed. All the tables are named after a part of the song.'

I want to make a joke about maids a-milking without

sounding coarse, but I do like how talk of Robbie and her impeding nuptials brings her happiness, calm.

'He also chose you an excellent ring.' Tiffany looks at me strangely and I point to her hand. 'May I?' She extends it for me, and I take it in mine. 'Marquis cut, incredibly clear diamond, classy with the rose gold, too.'

'You know rings?' she asks me.

'I work part-time in a jewellers'. That is a ring from someone with impeccable taste but then look at you,' I tell her, despite the make-up falling off her face and her hair starting to foam where I put the hand soap. She beams at me and then reaches into her bra. Crikey, lady, I was just being nice. She pulls out one hundred quid in notes.

'Here. You are really nice. Take this. Please go.'

I shake my head. 'But you have me for another two hours,' I explain.

'Mate, I'm going back to my hotel. I'll leave them to fight it out, but I am going to get a Nando's and go eat it in bed and pass out,' she says, still swaying slightly from the booze. I like how it's still the afternoon and this is the plan.

'Can I call you an Uber?' I ask.

She grabs both my cheeks. 'Sweet Joe. The politest bloody stripper I've ever met in my life. You're so lovely. You're very good looking, aren't you? You look like a young Zac Efron with better eyebrows.'

'My mum tells me that, but she's biased.'

'Your mum is so right. But I am relieving you of your duties,' she says, grabbing my chin with one hand and all at once, I like that she's not seeing this as a moment to have one final fling with singledom, that behind those drunken eyes is a girl ready to get married, whose heart belongs to another. I open the door but as I do, a man dressed all in black puts an arm around me.

'Alright, Jingles?' he says menacingly. 'This isn't that sort of establishment, mate. Out you go.'

Tiffany widens her eyes, slinking away before they can get to her. The group by the chocolate fountain cheer loudly. Oh, knob off.

'This isn't what you think...' I explain, reaching over to the table where we were sitting, grabbing my bag.

'Yeah, yeah... Were you taking turns to have a wee? Admiring the flooring? I've heard it all before...'

As I'm escorted out, I glance over and see that Tiffany and her hens are still mid-fight. Aunty Celeste radiates with rage, one is asleep under the table and Bianca is sobbing over a broken phone. Tiffany catches my eye and waves.

'And she's getting married,' the bouncer says, shaking his head, casting his judgement a little too vehemently.

I shrug his arm off. 'I'll walk myself out. Don't mind me.'

As I exit the venue, I get a couple of wolf-whistles from the line of people waiting to go in.

'Alright, Dopey!'

Leave it. 'Dopey was a dwarf, I am an elf,' I say, re-educating them.

I get out my phone. It's only 3 p.m. On the 23rd December. I may as well go home. Time to find my car and maybe treat myself to a decent Deliveroo to see in the season. I remember I have money in my pants. That's the difference between a meal deal and Wahaca. But it's then that my phone starts to ring. I reach around to get it out of my bag, glancing at the screen, confused as I look at the name of the caller.

'Mr Caspar?'

'Oh my, Joe. I am so glad you answered,' he says, sounding surprised.

'Is everything alright? I wasn't due in today.'

'Could you get down to the shop though?'

'Now? Why?'

'Yes. It's just... Eve...'

THREE

Eve

'Eve. My love. Why are you crying? Please don't cry. Can I get you anything? Soup? Has someone died?'

Mrs Caspar takes my face in her crêpe-like hands as she ushers me into the back room of their tiny jewellery store in Hatton Garden. Compared to the bright modern designer shops that surround it in white marble and glass, I always think their shop looks more like a quaint French patisserie shop, elegant gold cursive lettering on the signs, brass fittings on the doors and all the jewellery on show on red cushions with handwritten price tags, all behind misted windows. I like how people stand outside looking at the rings as if they're drooling over fancy macarons.

'Is Mr Caspar in?' I ask her, trying to pat down my face. I am crying because, well, my heart has been smashed into splinters like a bauble that's crashed to a cold hard floor but because I'm also quite drunk from having downed a lot of the Christmas alcohol I had planned to gift to Chris's family. I can feel it swishing about in my stomach now, wine on Baileys on fruity infused gin. It's not a good mix.

'He's with a customer. What on earth has happened?' she says, wrapping her arms around me. I rest my head on her frail shoulder and let all the emotion burst out of me. I don't for a moment suppose that the reason I took on this part-time job was because of the Caspars. I needed money for London rents and getting through the last of my MA and this job seemed much better than slaving it out in restaurants. When I came for my interview, it was like walking into Geppetto's workshop. Mr Caspar was the last existing Caspar, the son in Caspar & Sons, and it was less an interview, more a cuppa and a chat. They just wanted someone to trust, someone who believed in the idea of selling love to other people, love in the form of very expensive jewellery. We had tea and cake and halfway through the interview, Mrs Caspar raked crumbs out of her husband's beard, which to me was the sweetest act of love I'd ever seen.

'Christopher. Did he come in here to buy a ring?' I ask her, tearfully.

'Your boyfriend, Christopher? Yes. Oh dear, did you not like it? I thought he said he was proposing at Christmas...?' she explains, pulling up a chair and encouraging me to sit down. I pout my lips, hating that Chris would have come in here and pulled the wool over this sweet couple's eyes, too.

'I mean, I know you aren't keen on big jewellery. You're not flashy or about big stones. Did you not like the ring?'

'The ring was fine. I just... I found out Christopher has been cheating on me. This morning. I found out this morning...' I mumble. It's the first time I've said it out loud to anyone and the words tumble out of me. I can feel my face wear the shame like a veil. Mrs Caspar steps back from me, her forehead burrowed into a hundred lines, and she takes that in, her breathing slowing down. It's that sort of transformation you see in vampire films when the nice little old lady is a decoy. Really, behind the velvet dress and wrinkles is killer rage.

'I will KILL HIM!' she shrieks, gripping on to the side of my chair. I appreciate the rage but I'm not sure this is good for her angina. I stand up to try to pacify her. 'HOW?'

'Did he cheat on me? I'm not sure if you want the exact details, Mrs Caspar. It was in our flat...'

She puts her hand out. 'No, I mean, how could he do this to you? You sweet girl...'

'I don't... I just...'

I have no words, no train of logical thought. It's probably why I ended up here. After I saw the receipt, I felt I needed to come to the scene of the crime, ask the Caspars some questions. Did he choose it himself? Was it specially made? How long did it take him to choose? Did he mention someone called Allegra? Who likes to wear my robe? Is he in love with her?

'I hope you've thrown him out!' she exclaims.

I shrug in reply as she puts her hand in mine, studying my very sad eyes and the paleness of my skin. I don't know how to tell her now that soup would actually be the one thing I need now. Is it chicken?

'Call his mother. Go on, tell his mother. I don't have a child but if one of mine did this to another human then I'd give him a beating.'

'I don't think I can do that, Mrs Caspar.'

'Put it on the Facebook!' she commands.

'Frankly, I'm too embarrassed...'

Her tone changes. 'Eve, you have nothing to be ashamed of. This is him! All him! You caught him in your flat. He brought this into the place where you live, where you sleep. The boy deserves to feel all that shame tenfold. I can't believe this...'

For a moment, I think about just inviting Chris to this shop to let the Caspars on to him so they can give him that beating he needs. I'd watch that and enjoy it.

'I have Facebook! I'll do it myself!' she shouts.

'Mrs Caspar…' I whisper.

She looks at me and shakes her head to see me tearing up again.

'You know the jewellery shop three doors down is run by some dodgy ones. We can ask if they can do us a favour? I'd pay…'

'Mrs Caspar, NO!' I say, cry-laughing, half wondering how she knows they're dodgy. Is this something to do with their Thursday bridge nights?

A maroon curtain suddenly gets pulled back from the main shop and Mr Caspar stands there, impeccable in his three-piece tweed suit, checking the time on his pocket watch. There is something very grandparent-like about the both of them, the old-school way in which they write us actual cheques to pay us and always have boiled sweets about their person. 'What on earth is the commotion here? Eve? What on earth?' he says, looking at me.

'It would seem young Christopher has not been exactly honest and faithful to Eve,' Mrs Caspar explains as delicately as possible.

It takes Mr Caspar a moment to take in the meaning of that, and he stands there, glasses perched on his nose, frowning. 'Oh, Eve, really? But he came in here and he bought…'

'A ring, I know…' I tell him sadly and he lilts his head to one side to take in what that all means.

'I'll KILL HIM!' he suddenly says, eyes bulging. Not you, too. Think of the stress. You have diabetes.

'Mrs Caspar has that covered,' I inform him, trying to crack a joke but failing miserably, just some exasperated version of myself, not knowing how and why I even got here, in this shop.

His gaze returns to me, a deep furrow to his brow, like he's trying to recall events. He then goes to a box on the desk in his back room. As much as we've attempted to persuade the

Caspars to go online, they still prefer a paper receipt that they can file away.

'1st December was when he came in. I remember we joked about advent. I suggested a calendar of jewellery.'

I smile as he says this, thinking about how he takes such care with his customers, the times I make him cups of tea and he never drinks them because he's busy chatting with people and finding out their life stories. His thick fingers flick through the papers and the bell at the front of the shop rings.

'Estelle, I think that's the courier. Just give him the yellow parcel under the till.' Mrs Caspar shuffles out of the room as he reads the receipts carefully then takes pause. 'It wasn't just a ring. It was earrings. For his mother. Sterling silver hearts.'

I stand there for a moment to take that in. We got his mother a hamper. I'm pretty sure everything in there was edible. I wrapped it carefully in cellophane and I made a label with one of those snowflake cutters and used my very best writing. I threw that hamper out of the window. He bought earrings. Not for his mother, that much I know.

Mr Caspar grabs my hand and looks up at me from his desk, knowing that I never saw those earrings. 'I am very sorry, Eve. I feel responsible. I should have known it when...'

'You knew?' I ask him, tears still blurring my vision.

'I didn't. But I had a feeling when he just chose a ring out of the display, like he was choosing a muffin in a coffee shop. "I'll take that one." He'd done zero research, even when I tried to turn his head to the other rings. I know you've always adored emeralds. I'd have gone for something with far greater clarity in the stone, but no... He didn't take the time to think about it, to think what would suit you, what you would love. Maybe that's a sign...'

I stand there for a moment to feel the situation heavy in my chest, wondering what he was thinking – why he even wanted to propose – and I think about how he could have just gone down the high street and done the same in any shop. But then I realise why he came here.

'Did you give him a discount?' I ask.

'I did,' Mr Caspar says, scrunching his face up. 'I am so sorry, Eve.'

'Please don't say you're sorry. You have done nothing wrong,' I whisper, my tears now streaming down both cheeks to see this lovely gentleman so mortified to have played a part in this somehow. He reaches up to hug me and I hug him back. Mrs Caspar re-enters the room and joins in, too, in this group hug of velvet, tweed and tears.

'Is there anything we can do, Eve? What are you going to do for Christmas? Weren't you going to spend time with his family?' Mr Caspar asks me. 'Did you want to come to ours?'

We all part from the hug. 'That's very kind but I think I'll go see my dad and my brother...' I say, lying. I'm going to get drunk on my own, watch Christmas films and cry until I look like a giant prune.

Mrs Caspar holds her hands to my face again. 'Such a beautiful girl. I always say that, don't I, Rudy? Sometimes people just have a kindness in their face, that shines out of their eyes. That boy doesn't deserve your good soul.' She kisses my forehead, and my eyes start to water again.

'Maybe I can help you here for the rest of the day while I try and work out what I'm doing? Do you need help? You don't have to pay me. I just... I could sort out the boxes at the back or do some invoicing. Just anything to take my mind off things?'

They both nod at me resolutely and, for the first time today, I feel I'm at least in a safe place where two wonderful people will look after me.

'Anything you want,' Mrs Caspar tells me.

'That bottle of rum you keep out the back. We can hit that, yes?'

They both nod. 'Why, it's also Christmas, too,' Mrs Caspar says, smiling.

I think that might be what hurts the most.

Joe

There's an undeniable glow about London at Christmas that I don't normally take in via car. Usually, I'm on a Tube or a crowded bus, or running between jobs so, for a moment, it feels a bit magical to be sat on Oxford Street at these traffic lights. It's a dusky winter's afternoon, the sort London does so well – where the cold can freeze your features but the faint sunlight brings them a rosy glow. Shoppers weave in and around my car, the lights festooning the streets, as far as the eye can see. A fierce tapping on the bonnet takes me away from the moment.

'Mate, bus lane. You absolute plank!'

The man glares aggressively at me on a food delivery bike, and I am reminded why I don't drive in London. I don't know how to respond so put a thumb up in the air to almost thank him for the insult, secretly hoping the pizza on the back of his bike ends up in a gutter. I'm going to get a fine, aren't I? That'll be my sexy elf money down the pan. I try to navigate my car around a theatre-bound family all wearing antlers and apologise to everyone as I'm doing so. I think even that five-year-old is chuckling at me, or maybe my car? Who knows anymore? I'm not sure what I'm doing. Mr Caspar was very vague on the phone. Eve is at the shop. She's not well. I thought she had plans with her boyfriend so I'm not sure why she's even there. I'm all too aware I do quite a bit of heavy lifting in that shop so maybe I'm being called to move boxes. But Eve is there. Her name carries me to that place, that's all I know.

As my car pulls up to the back of the shop, Mrs Caspar keeps watch at the door and waves at me with both hands as she sees me. When I step out of the car, though, there is the inevitable laughter as she sees my outfit.

'Joe! What have you come as?'

I give her a mandatory twirl. 'This is my casual Christmas look, Mrs C. Don't hurt yourself laughing,' I tell her, wondering if it's the cold or the comedy making her dentures clatter together. 'I have other jobs, too.'

'Involving that outfit? Traitor,' she tells me, narrowing her eyes.

I took on the weekend job at Caspar & Sons to fill a gap during the days when I'm not being a semi-naked butler. I went through so many job ads online and it was all telemarketing, sales and estate agents. So, when I saw a handwritten note in a corner shop one morning looking for a reliable, well-spoken person to work for a family business in Hatton Garden, to make the world sparkle, it intrigued me.

'You look skinny. Have you eaten?' Mrs Caspar asks me, reaching up for a hug. Such is the warmth of the Caspars that they treat all their employees as if they're family. Mrs Caspar hates that all my family are down by the coast and has taken on the role of surrogate mother, asking me about my nutrition and commenting on my haircuts.

'I'll eat later. Eve? You said Eve was ill? Is everyone OK?'

Mrs Caspar blocks the door for a moment which isn't great as I am quite cold.

'Eve is single,' she says in a loud whisper. 'She's not with her boyfriend anymore. He cheated on her. In the shower. He's an absolute shit.'

I take a sharp inhalation of breath. It's a lot of information to process at once. Plus, Mrs Caspar never swears. She's not with the boyfriend? Eve is single? 'What did she find in the shower?' I ask, thinking she may have found an earring or a strand of hair. The plot thickens.

'Him. And a girl...'

'That's awful,' I mumble, stepping back for a moment to take in the horror and magnitude of an event like that.

'Well, it's not awful. For you,' she says, with a knowing grin, moving her shoulders from side to side in excitement.

'I have no idea what...'

'Joe,' she says, smirking.

I stand there, mouth agape. Is she hinting at what I think she's hinting at? I was too obvious in how I crushed, wasn't I? We've worked together in this shop for about eighteen months and over that time, a person reveals their true self to you in a number of ways. They show you how kind they are with people, that they're self-deprecating, funny, intelligent and they suddenly become the most flawless thing in that shop. That's cheesy. I can never tell her that. I never have. Instead, I just stand across from her in that shop and pretend I'm not crushing.

'Mrs Caspar, what are you insinuating?' I say, trying to act casual.

'Oh, Eve – I bought you a coffee and a pastry,' she says, mimicking my voice.

'That's not what I sound like... I'm just nice.'

'You never buy me a bloody coffee.'

'Because Mr Caspar says it gives you palpitations...'

She beams at me. 'Don't be coy, young man. It's the little things you do for her. It's very sweet. Like you don't just buy the coffee. You make the coffee man put random names on the cups to make her giggle, you walk her to the Tube station if we're in late, the looks. I know those looks. I've been around to know when someone has a crush. We all seem to know except Eve. You're gorgeous but you're not subtle, Joe.'

My face starts to scrunch up in horror. I just wanted her to know I was nice, not some lusting schoolboy loser.

'Mr Caspar looks that way at lamb chops,' she laughs.

'Do I stare a lot? She'll think I'm strange.'

'She doesn't think you're strange. She's always very complimentary about you. So maybe this is your chance...?' she suggests.

'Or not? That's a terrible idea. Is that why you called me? The timing is off – you want me to swoop in when she's vulnerable and just witnessed something completely awful and tell her I like her?'

'YOU DO LIKE HER!'

'Keep your voice down,' I tell her, trying to peer through the door. 'So why is she here?'

'He bought her a ring. From here. It's like the final punch, the fact he was cheating and going to propose. We were here sending out the last deliveries before closing up for Christmas. She came in to ask about the ring and she's stayed. It's all a bit of a mess. We've fed her alcohol and she's a bit teary. Mr Caspar and I feel awful.'

My shoulders slump at how devastated she must be. I wasn't keen on the shitbox boyfriend, but she was loyal to him and gave so much of herself to being with him. I also know what alcohol the Caspars would have fed her – it's the rum in the back room and that stuff could strip paint. Mrs Caspar opens the door slightly and I can see Eve maniacally hoovering the shop. If anything, this does not feel like the moment to swoop in and declare feelings.

'Even if this isn't your moment, she needs a friend. Take care of her, take her out for the evening. Mr Caspar and I are far too old for all of that. Just keep her safe?'

I nod as she links arms with me and leads me through the door.

'LOOK WHO I FOUND!' she announces to the shop floor, a little unconvincingly, like I may have been hidden away in a cupboard. Mr Caspar's confused frown tells me everything I need to know about his opinions on my outfit. Eve turns around, trying to smile, her face a shadow of what it normally looks like, and it makes my heart slump for her.

'I see good news travels fast...' she mumbles. 'Is the costume for my benefit?' she says calmly, looking me up and down.

'Well, it is Christmas. I was headed to the North Pole for elf duties but, well, the Caspars rang so I came straight here instead. With my bells...' I shimmy a little and immediately regret it.

'What did Santa have to say about that?' she asks.

'He's cool. You're on the good list so he thought it more important I help you out... The children and gifts situation can wait.'

The smile she replies with is something I don't recognise. It's something she forces out and it breaks my heart because normally that smile lights up this place.

'That's if you need my help. If you'd rather be alone then that's also fine. I can change, too. You don't have to go around London with me dressed like this...'

We all stand there for a moment while she decides what she wants to do but she doesn't say a word. She comes over and hugs me, nestling her head in my chest. I wrap my arms around her, to feel her body so sad against mine. Oh, Eve. Whilst you're there I should tell you that I don't usually smell like coconut or shimmer, that's just the tanning oil I use for work. Mr Caspar issues a thumbs up behind her back, and I shake my head at him. As Eve holds on to me for that bit longer, he scampers away with Mrs Caspar to the back room, no doubt so they can spy on us through the curtains. My chest starts to feel damp with tears and I realise she's crying. I have to think of something really nuanced and clever to break this ice now.

'You've done a good job with the hoovering,' I say. Smooth, like peanut butter.

'I just needed to be somewhere else that wasn't my flat, do something that wasn't throwing stuff out of the window.'

'You threw Chris out of a window?' I say, confused. She lives in a flat. Is she on the run?

She gives a sad little laugh. 'Of course not. Just his stuff. You think I could do that?'

'I have no doubt. Adrenaline can make you super strong in the moment. Like parents who find they can lift cars to save their kids after a crash.'

I should stop talking about car crashes. She still clings on to me tightly.

'I'm sorry, Eve. I really am.'

'What has Mrs Caspar told you?'

'Enough. They're worried about you. I think they called me as back up. They're closing soon.'

She glances over to the pendulum clocks on the wall and wipes at her face.

'Oh. I... just didn't know where else to be... I'm such a mess,' she says, sobbing again, and I clutch her tightly. Please don't cry. It's breaking my heart.

'I'm sorry he didn't realise your worth.'

That's a good line from me. I need more of those. I hold on to the moment but am also quite aware that the fumes from her drunkenness radiate off her and she sways slightly, taking me with her. It does mean my shorts make a noise.

'Your balls are a-jingling, you should see a doctor about that.'

'It's my best party trick.' I think I hear a tiny giggle and the sound is a complete relief. For some reason, though, I think this is a reason to unleash my own brand of quite awful comedy. 'What's a monkey's favourite Christmas carol?'

'I don't know...'

'Jungle Bells.'

'That's less funny.'

'Well, I'll keep trying.'

'You should.' I will.

The sound of the telephone in the shop suddenly bursts into life, preventing me from having to jingle my balls again or attempt to remedy the situation with my bad jokes. We wait for the ringtone to end but when it does, we can hear Mr Caspar in the back room having quite an animated conversation on the other end of the phone. Eve and I look at each other, slightly concerned, and head to the back room to see what the commotion is about.

'What do you mean? The parcels should be cufflinks. Five sets of mother-of-pearl cufflinks. I checked them myself. There should be no rings in that package.'

We all hear a raised voice on the other end of the phone and I watch Mrs Caspar's face drop in horror as she wanders out to the shop front checking under the counter for receipts and paperwork, lining it all up on the glass top. She puts a hand to her mouth and I glance at Mr Caspar, who's watching her carefully.

'Can you give me a moment to double check the inventory and what went out today? I will call you straight back.' He hangs up and turns to us all in the shop as Mrs Caspar goes under the counter and retrieves a blue bag.

'Estelle, that was the bag. With the cufflinks.'

'No, you told me to give the courier the YELLOW bag, Rudy.'

They both look at each other, confused, angry. Something has happened here which old age, cataracts and I think possible colour-blindness can explain.

'How on earth can you get yellow and blue wrong?' Mr Caspar says, mumbling something in his native language under his breath.

'Don't you dare, RUDY CASPAR! You told me yellow, you old goat...' This is the first time I've seen them have a domestic and I worry that I may have to hold one of these sweet old fragile people back in a moment.

'What was in the yellow bag?' Eve asks slowly.

'Rings. All sorts of rings. To be delivered straight to venues and addresses because of last minute adjustments. Christmas proposals, festive weddings, all sorts. The cufflinks were for an event, this evening... How?' Mr Caspar says, confused.

Eve puts a hand to her mouth, slowly recalling events. 'This was all my fault. I distracted you when I first came in. I was emotional. The courier came in and you were looking through your paperwork... This is all my fault.'

I don't quite know what to say so stand there shaking my head, putting a hand to Eve's shoulder. 'This is not a disaster,' I say, trying to be calm. 'I have my car. I can deliver the cufflinks now, get the rings and bring them back to the shop. Is it all London based?' I ask, trying to provide a solution to the panic.

Mrs Caspar offers me a grin at the suggestion but still manages to sneer at her husband.

'Could you do that?' Mrs Caspar asks me. 'Surely you have plans?'

'Well, it's Christmas. I'm an elf. I was obviously sent here for a reason,' I tell the room, knowing that my plans tonight mainly involved a takeaway in front of my television.

'We can reimburse you for petrol and pay you for your time,' Mr Caspar explains, his tone full of relief and gratitude.

I downplay it and watch as Eve looks at the receipts and paperwork on the glass worktop. 'Mr Caspar, were *you* going to deliver the rings?' she says, eyeing up the addresses on the receipts.

'Well, yes. I sometimes like to deliver the last few rings before Christmas. It's a nice thing to do, gets me into the season,' he says boldly. 'It's all Central London.' Given Mrs Caspar has to do Mr Caspar's shoelaces for him, this feels like a mission. I glance over the receipts with Eve. He has to deliver a ring to a boat?

Eve puts a hand to Mr Caspar's arm. 'Look, maybe there's another solution here? I feel really responsible and I don't want to mess up anyone's Christmas. Let me help. I'll go with Joe to get the cufflinks and then we can ensure all those rings get to their rightful owners. It is Christmas, after all... Joe, that's alright, yeah?'

I hesitate at the suggestion. Mainly because this did come from her, not me. A suggestion that we spend some time together in my very little car on some sort of Uber rings service. Mrs Caspar takes pause, too, considering her offer, and I see her eyes bulge open to see a plan may be emerging, born from our previous conversation.

'THAT is a very good, kind but also wonderful idea,' she says excitedly, unable to mask her joy, elbowing her husband. 'Rudy, you're getting far too old to do those deliveries yourself. Joe, does that work for you? Could you do this together?'

I was just going to pick up cufflinks. Mrs Caspar is thinking beyond that, she's plotting. You can use the magic of Christmas and the forced proximity to heal her sweet broken heart and then get her to fall in love with you. This is awful, transparent and I'm already sweating at how this has somewhat evolved because ten minutes ago, I thought I'd just take her out for some food and make sure she got home safely.

'Did you have Christmas plans over the next day or so?' I ask Eve.

'I did, but not now, obviously.'

I cringe slightly. Oh yeah, the boyfriend and the shower. I forgot.

'Did you?' she asks me.

I'll have to make an awkward phone call to my family, but I can delay my trip down south. I shake my head, a large gulp sinking to the back of my throat, like she's just said yes to a date. I have not thought this through. I'm dressed as an elf.

'Then let's do this together. It'll be a distraction, keep me busy.' She pauses, looking lost in her own emotions. 'I don't want anyone else's Christmas ruined either so let's do something... good. You in?'

As she says it, I smile because that's very Eve. Some would want to burn the world down after her morning and drag them into their suffering but everything she does is steeped in kindness. I'm in, I'm there, *so* there, but I have to keep my cool. Mr and Mrs Caspar, who moments ago looked like two small dogs hating on each other, have come together, linking arms to watch us.

'I'm in,' I say as casually as possible.

Mrs Caspar claps her hands and comes over to give us a collective hug. 'I love this. Thank you. This is an excellent plan,' she says, nodding her head excitedly at me. No, Mrs Caspar. Please, no.

FOUR

Eve

'So how are you doing this?' Mrs Caspar asks me as I grab at pieces of paper and stuff them into my handbag. 'Joe just texted – he's parked out on one of the side streets.'

'Well, we deliver the cufflinks and collect the rings. Then we work through all these deliveries.'

'We will message the customers to explain you're on your way. I'll send you the details so you know when they need to get there by,' she tells me, holding me close as we head outside. 'Don't try to do them all today! Get some rest tonight. Do you have anywhere to stay? Room at the inn can be hard to find this time of year?' she jokes.

'We'll work it out. Have a little adventure. We can do this.' We must do this. I like a challenge, but something tells me I volunteered for this to make me think I can achieve something, to save this craphole of a day and have something else to remember it by.

'Well, have fun,' she says, winking.

'Did you just wink at me, Mrs Caspar?'

She stops for a moment. 'It's a twitch, I'm very old. I mean, Joe will make it fun. You're in safe hands there with the handsome elf.'

I smirk as she says this. 'I know. I am sure we will get our fair share of attention given his shorts, too.'

'Yep, his jingle is very impressive.'

'And there was me thinking it was mostly baubles.'

Mrs Caspar cackles and throws her arms around me. 'Go well into the night, you two. Keep me posted. We adore you both.'

'I wouldn't do this for anyone else. Thank you for looking after me today. I don't deserve you.'

'You do.'

She blows me a kiss and I go in search of Joe. As I approach the car, I think about what Mrs Caspar just called him. The handsome elf. He's the sort of man who might catch your eye, he has kind eyes, light brown hair and a hint of stubble and chisel. But maybe I've just never looked at him like that because my gaze was always looking the other way. Joe and I have known each other for nearly two years now, the part-timers at Caspar & Sons. As much as it pains me to say it, he's just a nice guy; the sort who'll suggest a quick drink before home, the one who'll cover for me when I'm late or ill and buy me the occasional coffee. He displays that sort of buddy behaviour that restores your faith in people. It's a relief to see him today because he's like a security blanket; his friendship feels sincere and genuine.

'For the love of sweet baby Jesus,' I say, as I open the door.

Our noble steed on this quest is Joe's battered old green Mini. I may have grabbed a lift in this motor before. The heating rattles and a door handle doesn't quite work without a shake and a shuffle. I think I've also pushed this car down the alley behind the shop to get it working. Please don't make me have to do the same today mainly because I'm drunk and haven't eaten properly all day.

'You've been in my car before?' he asks, slightly insulted.

It's like walking into a grotto on wheels, like Christmas threw up in here. The whole inside of the car is bedecked in fairy lights, there's a little mooning Santa on the dashboard, Christmas music blares out of the stereo. 'I've been in your car when it's been less... festive.'

'I like Christmas, shoot me...' he says, unapologetic.

'I didn't have you down as the sort.'

'Well, I hope I didn't read miserable Scrooge?' he says, pouting, as I strap myself in.

'Nah, it's just I know Christmas people. I thought you'd be more of a low-key Christmas dude. A sensible jumper and mulled wine kind of man.'

'I'm novelty jumper, all the way. I Christmas hard.'

'Favourite Christmas song?' I ask in a quickfire way.

'*Driving Home for Christmas* by Chris Rea,' he replies with no hesitation. 'Yours?'

'*Jingle Bell Rock*,' I reply.

'Classic. Favourite item of a Christmas dinner?'

'Pigs in blankets. Yours?'

'Brussels sprouts.'

'I'm leaving the car now.'

'Have you had them roasted with bacon? And then I use the gravy and cheese sauce as a dip.'

I look over at him and laugh.

'Don't mock it till you've tried it, Eve,' he says, pulling out of a junction, leaning over the wheel, his frame far too big for the size of this motor.

'So this explains the outfit then. Is it just a range of Christmas shorts and robes until New Year's?' I ask.

'I wish. I was at one of my many other work gigs: a festive hen do as an elf waiter.'

'That sounds like fun.'

'It was carnage. I was allowed to leave early which is good because it means I can be here instead of being groped by someone's Aunty Celeste.'

I laugh as his car chokes slightly, like it has a winter cough, and instinct tells me to reach for a grab handle.

Joe looks over at me. 'I don't know whether you're judging my driving here.'

'It's just the car. Am I allowed to ask if it's roadworthy?'

He seems insulted by the remark. 'Cheeky. It is. It's a relic, I know, but it has sentimental value,' he tells me, stroking the steering wheel.

'Go on...'

'My dad bought it for me as a first car and we did it up together. She's seen me through many a road trip. I just don't have the heart to get rid of her...'

'Her? Your car is female? She has a name, doesn't she?'

'Olive. I know that is sad. Don't judge me.'

'It's strangely endearing...'

There is a moment of silence, Joe's Christmas music filling the space.

'I am really sorry to hear what happened with Chris. You know that, right?' he mutters.

I force a smile. 'What did Mrs Caspar tell you?'

'Bits. We can talk about it if you want but if you'd rather shelve it then we can do that, too.'

'It's not your problem, I don't want to burden you.'

'Maybe, but perhaps I'm far enough removed from the situation to remain impartial. And it's important to chat about it. Don't pent up that emotion. If you want to listen to trash rock and scream, then go ahead.'

'You have Christmas trash rock?'

'I have Spotify, we can do a search. I am sure there is some punk rock band out there who've done angry Christmas before...'

I try to raise a laugh because that was funny.

'Can I ask a question though?'

I nod.

'Did he really bring her back to your flat? Where were you?' he blurts out. 'Apologies if you don't want to talk about it.'

'I was in Bristol for a law conference,' I reply. I think about that trip, a mixture of panel-watching and lectures, but I'd also presented a paper and it had all gone well – so well, that my fellow departmental mates had tried to drag me out for a Christmas jolly-up of turkey churrascaria with unlimited cocktails. But I refused. I wanted to jump on an early train and get back to Chris. I didn't want to face a hangover with Christmas wrapping ahead of me. So I returned to my accommodation. I went to bed with Cup Noodles and Netflix on my tablet, messaging Chris, not realising he was, well... otherwise engaged. The memory of that makes me shiver slightly.

'Oh, the paper on protest rights... How did that go? I know you were stressed about that.' Joe's comment brings me back into the car. The extent of our conversation at work is always polite chit-chat, peripheral details about each other's lives to fill the silence when the shop is empty or we're dusting the shelves. But it's surprising and comforting that he remembered that much. It's nice that in all of this drama, someone has asked about that.

'It actually went really well. People said it was very well-researched. I even did a PowerPoint.'

'With animations?'

'Many.'

'Well then, that's awesome.'

'I guess...'

'I'm trying to help find the positives here,' he tells me. The song changes on the stereo. It really is all Christmas, isn't it?

'Perhaps. I think I'm still too angry to be positive. I just want to...'

'Go on, tell me...'

'I want to vandalise his car. He has golf clubs in the boot. I want to bend them.'

'OK, Superman,' Joe says, half laughing. 'I mean, we can trash his car, but I'd need some sort of face covering because I value my personal freedom.'

'Or I thought before about shagging it all out. Get drunk and get on Tinder.'

'Really?' he says, white with shock. 'I don't know how to help with that...'

I giggle. 'But also a stupid idea. That's a sure-fire way for me to feel worse than I do. Mrs Caspar said I should call him out on Facebook.'

'We can do that, too,' he says, seeming relieved.

I put a hand to his thigh as a gesture to say thank you for listening to me rant, but his leg flinches and he swerves the car slightly.

'Whoa, hold up there. Sorry...' I say speedily.

'You... You have the coldest hands, ever,' he says, blushing. 'I thought you were drunk. You're supposed to be all toasty warm when you're drunk.'

'I am. I think I've had a year's worth of units in one day. I don't even know how I'm operating. I think I'm just being carried around on a wave of adrenaline.' I blow into my hands and hold them to the crackling heaters in the car.

'Well, you know what they say... cold hands...'

'Warm heart?'

'Need gloves... There are some in my glove compartment along with...' He stops for a moment.

'A gift?' I say, eyeing a package in there wrapped in holly paper and a red ribbon.

He backtracks all of a sudden. 'That's for my mum. I was

going to say there should be some sweets in there if you need something to add to your heightened state.'

I don't say no and watch as he mouths the words to the Christmas song on the radio. 'Sweet?' I ask him.

'Throw one over,' he says opening his mouth. He catches it, I cheer.

'You're a good catch.'

'It has been said,' he replies, the Christmas lights in his car reflecting off his face in a million different colours.

Joe

I was not ready for this in any way, shape or form. Back at the shop, I had to make excuses about locating my car because I had to fling things in the boot and brush down the seats and make sure there were no strange smells lingering. I had to stand there in the cold, my chest on show, wondering if I could do this. If I could be in a car with her and take on this Christmas ring challenge. Now she knows my car is called Olive, and she's talked about shagging randoms to get over her ex, then touched me and I nearly rear-ended a UPS van. What do I tell her? Don't touch me because I'm in love with you and we have a job to do? By the end of this evening, she will think me a certified freak.

'It's this road on the left, number five...' she tells me, studying the house numbers on the dimly lit street. First stop tonight is to deliver these cufflinks that have not reached their intended target. There is no plan despite Mrs Caspar's best efforts. We drop them off, we hang out, we come up with a reasonable system for delivering these rings that I hope will involve a change of clothes for me and well, I'll never turn down food. As we pull up to the house though, a whirr of music, lights and cars and a very fetching inflatable dancing Santa greet us, and we peer our heads through to the driveway of this very impressive gated home.

'I'm assuming this is what the cufflinks were for?' Eve mutters as I park up. 'I'm completely underdressed for this. I'm in a hoodie.'

'And I am an elf. We could just put them through the letterbox?'

'We need to get the rings,' she tells me, looking in a mirror trying to smooth down her hair. Her hair looks fine but I won't say that out loud. She puts a hand in mine. 'Let's both go so we can cancel each other out. Team effort, right?'

I take a moment to register the fact she's holding my hand. 'I guess,' I say cautiously, getting out of the car. I'm not sure if it's the alcohol in her system but she walks up to the party confidently, and I follow a little more gingerly waiting by the gate, trying to work out the occasion. It looks black tie. I don't know what category my costume falls under but it's definitely not that. We stand there for a moment to try and figure out the best way to tackle this.

'Are you both from the agency?' a voice suddenly booms from behind us. We turn to see a man in a tuxedo and a winter coat, holding an iPad and wearing a headset. I've been around the service industry long enough to know who this man is. 'Wait staff are supposed to convene in the kitchen and leave all personal belongings in there. Did you not get the memo? We will report this back to the agency... NAMES?'

'Steve...and...'

'Joanna'

'Why are you dressed up?' he asks. 'Wait staff in black and white. And you look like you've come from the gym. You look ridiculous,' he says without any hint of regret that he could be insulting us. 'Oh, hold up. Are you the fella jumping out of the ice sculpture?'

'Yes?' Eve replies and I swivel my head towards her. Alternatively, she could have said, no, we're here from the jewellery shop and we're here to give out some cufflinks, but the man starts walking which we take as a sign to follow. Eve shrugs her shoulders at me, looking far too relaxed. I feel there are easier ways to do this but at least we can get in the house through the back and not be seen, rather than have to spoil this party by entering with the fancy guests.

'How do you jump out of an ice sculpture?' I whisper to Eve as he leads us through a back door that opens out into the kitchen.

'Carefully?' she says, sniggering. 'Just don't lick the ice or your tongue will stick to it.'

I burst into laughter. Why would I lick the ice? Headset man turns, looking Eve up and down. 'We'll have to keep you behind the scenes in the kitchen. We can't have you out in front of the guests.'

I notice Eve slightly deflate at the comment.

'She's actually from the catering company – the accounts manager. If the client, Mrs Kohli, is available, she'd value a quick word.'

'Well, stay here and I'll bring her down.'

He eyeballs us both and shows Eve into a downstairs utility area that's storing boxes of orange juice and champagne. Headset man glares at me, signalling that I still follow him. Really? I widen my eyes at Eve. I don't want to make a scene so stick with him as we weave through the back corridors of this giant house.

'So, this ice sculpture... I wasn't quite briefed. How does it work? Do they want me to say anything?' I say, panicked. Maybe the shorts can do the work for me here. He gives me the strangest of looks.

'No, you come out, sing and then the grand piano is set up for your set.'

Oh, shit.

'Great,' I say, putting a thumb in the air. We turn the corner to find an ice palace contraption on wheels, and I glance beyond it to see a room of about one hundred people milling about with champagne flutes and canapes who in a minute are going to see a grown man elf play *Chopsticks*. I may be ill. I hope Eve has a better plan.

'Well, get in...'

How do I do this? Maybe I can say I need Eve. She turns the pages on my music... but headset man is having none of it and pushes me inside, closing the walls of ice around me. Dry ice wafts around my feet.

'You and you, come and help me push this...'

Oh my Christ, we are moving.

'Ladies and gentlemen, can we have your attention please?' someone announces on a microphone. 'We are so happy to have you here tonight, but I just wanted to interrupt the evening's proceedings with a little musical interlude.'

Fuck.

'My darling wife, happy anniversary.'

A spotlight turns towards me, the ice sculpture opens, and I stand there, not really knowing what to do so I wave at the room. There's a backing track. I may pass out. I know this song, but I can't subject them to my singing. They're old, it may kill them off. I let out the first line and watch as Eve's face appears at a doorway, grimacing. I can't quite tell what that emotion is, but I think I felt that once when I ate a bad oyster. A man with a microphone in his hand looks at me sternly and an older Asian lady in a full length, black sequinned gown, clutching at a champagne glass, raises her eyebrows, seemingly surprised by this gift from her husband: a half-naked, tuneless elf.

'Who are you?' the man says into the microphone, loudly into the pit of silence that is the rest of the room. There's an aunt to the front who is so agape her teeth fall to the ground. Someone put that lady's teeth back in.

'I... I...' I look over at Eve who points to the rucksack on my back.

I look up at Mr Kohli, suddenly flanked by four gentlemen in matching tuxedos and I take a deep breath. I look at the banners and balloons in the room, and a family portrait hanging on the wall. I hope I've got this right.

'Mr Kohli. You think after all these years you can surprise your wife?' I announce, a shake to my voice.

A few in the crowd chortle at the joke. 'A gift from her to you and your... sons? Not me, I'm not the gift but...' I swivel to retrieve the boxes from my bag and remove myself (carefully) from the ice sculpture. 'Cufflinks. Mother-of-pearl, courtesy of Caspar & Sons. An excellent choice, Mrs Kohli. Congratulations on a very happy fifty years.'

Mrs Kohli's disposition suddenly softens, and she smiles at me as the boxes are handed over to the men and there's a collective round of applause and gasps as they crowd around their mother to hug her. Did I save that? I bloody hope so. I know my singing bloody didn't.

'Again, Mrs Kohli, we apologise profusely for gatecrashing your party. My name is Eve, this is Joe – this was all completely unplanned. There was a mix-up with your order, so we came to try and fix things. Mr Caspar also has this gift voucher for you and he says you are very welcome at his shop, any time.' Eve pitches it perfectly in her warm, assuring voice.

I see Mrs Kohli exhale, smiling at both of us in her study, away from the buzz of the party. 'Well, I was just going to give them the cufflinks before the party started. This was a far more interesting way to gift them,' she says, glancing in my direction. 'I am just very overwhelmed that you got them here in time. Let me get the rings for you,' she adds, taking the boxes out of a desk drawer and handing them to Eve.

'Well, we take what we do very seriously,' I say. In my jingling shorts. 'Mother-of-pearl is an excellent choice.'

'Mr Caspar helped me. It was symbolic. We have four sons, and I wanted a pair for my husband, too. The man who helped me become a mother,' she tells us proudly.

'It's quite an achievement, fifty years...' I add.

'Oh, you get less for life these days but they have been a very happy fifty years... I am very lucky. He was the one who suggested we marry at Christmas. He told me it'd be the greatest gift.'

I look over at Eve who looks a bit glassy-eyed and I suddenly realise what a punch in the guts that must be after what almost happened with Chris.

'You certainly entertained us all. Please go to the back, have a drink, something to eat, whatever you want before you go,' she says kindly.

'That's very kind, Mrs Kohli. Happy anniversary. Can I just ask, who were you expecting to jump out of the ice sculpture...?'

She picks up her champagne flute and giggles.

'Someone just told me, Michael Bublé. Fully clothed, I should add. Not sure how he'll follow you, young man. You made a couple of my aunts very happy,' she says, laughing. She looks at both of us. 'How long have you two been together then?'

As soon as the words leave her mouth, I gulp silently.

Eve giggles nervously. 'Oh, we're not together. I don't date elves...'

Mrs Kohli furrows her brow. 'And why the hell not? Are you blind, dear? Look at the calves on the man!'

I blush. 'Mrs Kohli, that's lovely but you are married...'

'Married, my dear, not dead.'

FIVE

Eve

> I'm so sorry.

> Don't hate me.

> You didn't deserve this.

> Can we talk?

> Did we buy anything for my Uncle Bob?

> Did you get me a Fair Isle jumper?

It's like a really bad break-up poem on my phone. Each line trying to appeal to my better nature but at the crux of it, he's most worried about heading to his family do without any gifts in hand, without a Fair Isle jumper or even his phone because that's lying on the street. I hope a bus ran over it.

'Who uses Facebook Messenger anymore?' Joe asks, gazing over from the driver's side of the car.

'Chris. I threw his phone out of a window, so this is him messaging from a computer.'

'Oh. Are you going to reply?'

'I'm going to let him stew, like a pot of red cabbage.'

'Wise.'

'But cruel?'

'Rethink who's the cruel one here...'

'True...'

I glance over at Joe lip-syncing the words to Nat King Cole on the radio. I like how he's some sort of voice of conscience. I feel as if he's in my corner. The perfect partner to have amidst all this distraction. I put my phone down for a moment.

'Am I allowed to say that was kind of fun? The sneaking into a party and doing a good thing. I feel... I don't know the word, energised, maybe?' I tell Joe.

He raises an eyebrow. 'Easy for you to say. You weren't the one in the ice sculpture. I am just glad I made the decision to stop singing. I'm hoping Bublé can redeem that for me. That was awful.'

'Yeah, what was up with the singing?' I ask.

'Can't hold a note. I'm quite terrible. Really bad. Any longer and the ice would have shattered, and the party would have made the news. *Singing man shatters ice sculpture and kills couple celebrating fifty years of marriage.*'

I laugh. 'You're not even singing now. You lip-sync the words to songs, like you're whispering them.'

'Because I can't sing,' he says plainly, not even embarrassed by this revelation.

'Everyone can sort of sing. You must have sung Christmas carols at school.'

'No, I was told not to sing because it was disruptive.'

'Do you have hearing problems?' I ask, turning to him, amused.

'No, I'm just not blessed in that department,' he replies. 'I'm told I sound like a rabid crow.'

I giggle. 'Well, it's good that you compensate for that by being blessed in the calves department then.' Joe swerves the car a little and laughs nervously. I like how he's mildly embarrassed by the comment given that's his line of work, but we've all noticed the legs in general. Today, it's been hard not to miss them. 'Mrs Kohli liked them.'

'It's the older lady opinions that always mean the most. You know they've seen a lot more calves, so they have a larger frame of reference. They know what's good...' he says jokingly, his red cheeks telling me he doesn't quite believe what he's saying.

I smile broadly in reply. The humility he has about his own looks is warming but at the same time, I think about Mrs Kohli's comments assuming us to be together. It's almost laughable to look at us and think that may be a thing, mainly because I'm the biggest of messes. In my current tear-soaked, emotional state, I can't think of a worse partner for this lovely man.

'Do you sing in the shower?' I ask.

'No. I shower in the shower.'

'I feel I need to hear more of the singing to be able to judge.'

'I'm not singing. This is Nat King Cole. He has one of the finest singing voices known to man, let him sing to you.'

I sing along. I'm only vaguely in tune and I don't know the exact words. 'It's baritone, anyone can sing this. Join in, come on... *Jelly tots with their eyes all a-glow!*'

'It's like the spirit of Nat King Cole has entered the car itself,' he says, grinning.

I think the problem here may also be that while Joe is playing designated driver and is completely sober, I still may be a teensy, weensy bit drunk. I downed two glasses of champagne before I left the party and grabbed us a selection of canapes that I have balanced here on my lap in a napkin. I offer him a cocktail-sized samosa. The problem is I've started the drinking so if I stop, my body will go into shock, dehydrate and there's no way I can do tonight hungover. Therefore, the best plan is to keep supplementing my intake so I'm on the edge of functioning and fun.

'Maybe we just need to warm up your voice. I mean, we'll need to sing through this whole ring-delivering mission,' I explain.

'Why would we sing?' Joe looks over, slightly bemused.

'Because FIVE... GO-OLD... RINGS!' I bellow a little too loudly, lifting the ring boxes aloft. I have them all in my possession, my precious, and it's time to get them to the right people. The mission starts now, our road trip of bling. 'I am shocked you didn't piece that together. We're on a quest but we're also on theme.'

He laughs. 'Well, a few rounds of that will surely pass the time. Could be worse... We could be delivering a partridge in a pear tree.'

'Or some geese a-laying.'

'Six randy geese...'

It's not that funny a joke but I still snort unattractively at it. I look down at the ring boxes, opening up each one in turn, all very different, all perfect. At least ten thousand pounds of bling here by my estimation. Everything from glittering engagement rings to sleek slimline wedding bands. Seeing them all makes me feel a strange mixture of emotions, and I think about the ring Chris gave me, and how shitty it made me feel to look at it. I'll never want that feeling for anyone else. I want the owners of these rings to look at them and feel how someone should – proud, loved, special.

I'm aware of Joe glancing over at me looking at the rings, realising I've gone quiet.

'What did Chris go for? When he chose your ring?' he asks.

'Solitaire, round cut, gold band, clarity was a bit shit.'

He looks disappointed on my behalf. 'That's a cheapskate ring, eh?'

I shrug my shoulders. It was the emptiest of gestures. And for a moment I think of a proposal that never was. How would he have proposed? What if I'd never caught him? My breath shudders, anger stirring within to think I'd have been none the wiser and worn that ring and tried to convince myself that was love, that his second-thought ring was a symbol of my worth. Joe looks over panicked, to see I'm lost for words.

'Do you want to stop anywhere? I can take you home if you want?' Joe asks kindly.

I don't reply.

'This is when London really needs more motorway services,' he jokes.

I manage a smile and look over at him. 'What? Those soul-less buildings on the side of motorways where you have to pay for overpriced coffee and queue for the toilets?'

Joe's jaw drops like I've blasphemed. 'Hush now,' he says with a finger in the air. 'Some of my best road trip memories involve motorway services. I went on a stag do once where we left the groom behind in one. They are hallowed places of bad early morning fry-ups, car picnics and the only time I ever have a Burger King...'

I'm mildly bemused by his enthusiasm. The Burger King thing is facts though.

'My favourite road trips were when my dad would come and pick me up from university and we'd always stop at the Pease Pottage Services on the M23 on the way home. We'd have a Burger King, request the crowns and eat like royalty... It became tradition.'

'A happy memory?'

'The happiest... If you open my glove compartment, you'll also see a very healthy supply of condiments that I've acquired from these places, so I won't have a bad word said about them... It's really what London is missing. I could take you to one now and we could roll into Burger King and...'

'I could have a bite of your Whopper?' I add. That came out wrong. I freeze. 'Oh, my life, that was rude. I don't know where that came from. I'm not a biter...' I can feel myself blushing and glance over at Joe to see he's blushing, too. 'I mean, we don't have to share. But yeah... We could share chips, nuggets and other stuff.'

He nods, looking a little worried about how he should have answered that. Please don't think I'm weird.

'We can do that. But seriously, I can drop you home now? We can reconvene in the morning?' he suggests.

I think about what's waiting for me at home and think about how it's the last place where I want to go. 'Can I ask... kind of a favour? I took my bed apart...'

Joe turns to look at me briefly, in shock. 'Like with an axe?'

'Oh no, with a power drill... Can we go to yours? I know you rent a room and your landlord might not be happy, but I can take a sofa. Or go to a Premier Inn. I just don't want to be in my flat...'

He pauses for a moment. This is overstepping, isn't it? At best, I'm a work colleague. I see him twice a week. Maybe he doesn't know enough about me or doesn't want to get further tangled up in my drama.

'My landlord will be fine, but I don't have stuff for you though. Toothbrush. Clothes.'

'We could go to a supermarket? The big one near Earl's Court should still be open.'

Because that's a really exciting prospect two nights before Christmas. However, there is a small part of me that just wants to cling to him for that bit longer. Just so I won't be alone tonight.

Joe negotiates the junction in front of us then glances over at me. 'You're in luck then.'

'I am?'

'I have a supply of reusable shopping bags in my boot,' he says, a little too proudly.

'For occasions such as these?'

'Obviously,' he says, smiling.

Joe

So, things to know about me. No, I can't sing. I remember performing in my grandparents' front room once, alongside a red plastic keyboard I got that year from Santa. Halfway through my song, their dog died from a stroke and it's a long-standing family joke that it was my singing that caused it.

There are so many thoughts running through my head right now, I can't quite think straight. Firstly, we spoke about my calves in the car and I'm not sure if she was appreciative or mocking them. Then I told her how much I love a motorway services. Motorway services are where weirdoes meet to hook up, and families have to stop their cars so little travel-sick toddlers can change their clothes and have a wee. There is no romanticism there. Neither is telling her how much you love a Burger King and then blushing hard when she makes a slightly inappropriate joke about a Whopper. Nor telling her about your shopping bags. Now she thinks I'm both dull and a little bit odd.

But I guess the most important thing in all of that is that Eve is coming to my house. Definitely just to crash. But it still means I need to change the sheets and kick my dirty pants under the bed and maybe give the toilet a bleach and take the five different mugs by my bedside downstairs. If I had known this was happening, then I would have planned this so differently and with a lot more class. Obviously, I will take the sofa, I will be a pure gentleman about all of this and give her space, but I can't have her going off me for life because of my poor house-keeping.

'Big trolley?' Eve asks me as she stands outside the supermarket.

I nod. We're going shopping together, with a trolley. Is it ridiculous that I'm mildly excited by this? Just ambling alongside her doing something that's steeped in normality, like a normal couple. Stop it, Joe. However, I also realise that I am still an elf, out in public again; there will be heckling, there will be the assumption, in this very crowded supermarket, that this is all for attention or that I am staff. I need to make a note to put a change of clothes in the boot next time I do an agency job.

'Put it away, mate, you're putting us all to shame,' a security man tells me, clocking me at the door. Oh good, it's already started.

'Come on,' Eve says, hooking an arm through mine as I push the trolley. I try my best not to trip, blush and look like an idiot. As it's Christmas the usual festive anthems are blasting out at us, and the aisles are an utter madness. People on the hunt for last minute gifts, root vegetables stacked high, a manic look in the eyes of the customers; this is one of the last days to shop, to make Christmas Day perfect, to physically fight people for that last turkey. Eve looks a little wide-eyed to see all the people charging around and holds on tightly to me. I'd like to say I want to protect her but frankly, this is Christmas Armageddon. I don't know how to fight old people over yule logs.

'So, tell me... I don't even know who you're spending Christmas with? I didn't even ask,' Eve asks me as we see people grabbing at discounted boxes of mince pies. If I sound like I'm judging, I grab at a box, too. We will need fuel for our adventure.

'Family. I'll drive down on Christmas Day when we're all done. I just need to tell my sisters.'

'You have sisters?'

'I have three. I'm the youngest.'

'Wow. How did I not know this?'

I shrug. I'm not a huge discloser of personal information but it's also a big thing to tell someone your life is dominated by so many women. Sometimes it scares people off, and if you met them, you'd understand why.

'You have a twin brother, that much I know... Noel?' I reply. Eve nods in surprise. She told me, once, a while ago. I hope she doesn't think I'm weird for remembering. 'I have an excellent memory for these things. So can I ask, does Noel know about Chris?' I ask tentatively.

Her face drops before she answers. 'No. Because Noel would not react well and I'm not sure I can deal with that drama on top of everything. I'll let him know after Christmas.'

I see the sorrow in her eyes, and it makes me want to give her a hug, to reassure her.

'I get it but surely he would want to know, to make sure you're OK?'

Her expression sours as she shakes her head. 'I don't want to spoil his Christmas, too. He'll find out soon enough. I just don't want to share that sadness or wear that shame tonight.'

'Chris's shame, not yours.' I frown, realising that what she's said suggests she's planning to spend Christmas alone. That's not right, and I want to say something but she's already giving me a long, hard look. I don't know if she thinks I'm telling her off.

'So, I also need clothes...' she tells me, heading into the clothes concession, trying to change the subject. 'I'm thinking if we're going to attend these grand proposals and weddings then we need to look the part and I may need to be without my Air Max.'

I nod as she throws a multipack of tiny knickers into the trolley. Don't look at the knickers.

'Do you have a suit?' she asks me.

'I have a dinner jacket. Is that too much? Will I look like staff?' I ask her.

'We may as well go all out. Is it a proper dinner jacket? Or do the trousers have Velcro on the sides so you can rip them off?' she asks, sifting through a rack of black strappy heels, chuckling.

Is it terrible that I love that she's mocking me? 'Excuse me. I also have normal everyday clothes,' I say unconvincingly in my elf garb.

'Red or green?' she asks me, picking out two dresses from a rail and holding them next to her. She could wear either and carry them off, but I need to look cool and constructive and appreciative of the female form without sounding like I fancy her.

'I think the neckline on the red is a little low for a wedding. And the green' – will go with her eyes – 'has a more suitable hemline...'

'Spoken like someone who has sisters,' she says, throwing it in the trolley. 'Now do I go with the big tinselly Christmas tree earrings or something a little more demure?' she asks, picking out some earrings from a stand.

'The Christmas tree earrings are a statement but let's go demure, because if memory recalls, you don't do bling,' I tease her, raising an eyebrow.

She looks at me and smiles. It was something she once told me. I always thought it was funny that she worked in a high-end jewellery shop but never coveted anything in there. She was almost the very opposite.

She puts a gold stud pack in the trolley. 'Ooooohhh...' she says, her attention is suddenly caught by the rail of clothes next to her, and she starts to sift through the labels on the items. 'Joe. Christmas pyjamas. They're only four pounds a pair.'

I stand back for a moment, watching her so excited by this Christmas bargain.

'Let's get you some!' she squeals. 'They have your size. It'll be fun?'

'Are you still drunk?' I look over at the pyjamas. They're very red and the Ho-Ho-Ho motif is strong. This is maybe not the time to tell her I sleep in just my pants. Perhaps I should cover up if we have company.

'I mean, I haven't got you a gift. This could be my very bad novelty gift to you? We're here for me but, I mean, we can pick up some food, too, some wine for tonight, stuff for the car whilst we whizz around London... On me?'

Her face beams with excitement and I'm not quite sure what to say. This is already a gift, Eve. Spending a bit of time with you. But I can't say that now, can I? I also have got her a gift. It's in my glove compartment. But I can't give it to her. Not yet.

'Well, I will not go through this alone. Only if you buy some for yourself, too,' I say as she grins at me, shaking my hand. As she looks for her size, I notice two young boys standing there, looking through the rails.

Eve looks up and spots them, too. 'Are you boys OK?' One of them is clutching onto a basket filled with assorted gifts and cards. The smaller child nods but the older looks warier of us strangers – especially the one dressed up as the elf.

'Are these really four pounds?' the older kid asks.

'I think so,' replies Eve. 'Are you Christmas shopping?'

'For our mum,' the little one replies, and I notice him tightly clutching some notes in his hand.

'Are you alone? Is your dad not around?' Eve asks, glancing about the place.

'Nah. We don't have a dad,' the kid says, his older brother glaring at him for disclosing such information. Eve and I exchange a glance and I know she's thinking what I am about these two boys who've come in here, on their own, to a large supermarket this Christmas to buy gifts and show someone they love them. It's an act that would melt the coolest of hearts. I restrain myself from asking them how they crossed all those busy London roads on their own.

'So you're both shopping for your mum?' Eve asks, bending down to their level. I peer into the basket and see a large bar of Galaxy and a copy of Take-A-Break magazine. They both nod nervously. The eldest is still not sure about me but I know the look in his eyes. It's a look I have often felt from being the eldest brother of three sisters, standing there in a shop at Christmas and debating whether to go with the comedy fridge magnets or the wine.

'What's your budget?'

The younger brother shows her the notes in his hand. She looks around. I can tell she's doing some quick maths in her head. 'Well, these pyjamas are a nice idea. Do you know what size your mum wears?' Eve asks.

'She's medium sized. Like you but with bigger...' the eldest says, gesturing that his mum has quite the rack. Eve giggles, helping him find a pair and folds them into the basket. 'Do you know if women like those hand cream gift sets?' he asks her.

'I'm not super keen on them,' Eve says, tactfully. I turn to her thinking about the one I've bought my great-aunt Edith. It's lavender. She loves that shit. 'Maybe just get her one or two things she'll actually use. A nice bubble bath, a lip balm. You've made a good start here. I can see your mum likes chocolate and magazines... What else does she like?' Eve asks them.

'Idris Elba?'

'Well, I don't think you can buy him here and so difficult to wrap...'

Both boys laugh and I sigh silently to see her being so natural with them.

'She also likes tea,' the littlest says.

'Then maybe a mug? The best gifts are the ones where someone's really thought about what you like,' she says, and I see her pause again. I wonder if she's thinking of Chris and a ring ungifted and unwanted.

'Your mum is very lucky,' I add, trying to intervene.

The littlest lad looks up at me and stares. There is a look there of complete mistrust which I'm immediately offended by. I am dressed like Christmas. All kids like Christmas.

'Why do you not have a shirt on?' he asks, watching as Eve snaps out of her moment and rises to her feet. 'We saw elves at the grotto in the shopping centre and they didn't look like you.'

'He was warm,' Eve adds. 'He's used to it being very cold.'

'Are you actually an elf? From the North Pole?' the youngest lad asks.

'Yes,' I say animatedly, realising I now have a responsibility to sell a dream here. I need to up my festive game to help the kids still believe.

'Then you know what we want for Christmas?' his brother says, sneakily trying to catch me out.

I panic. 'I don't work in the lists department. I'm in manufacturing, I build the toys.'

'Whatever,' the littlest brother says, suddenly the world's biggest cynic. 'I got a Nintendo Switch last Christmas. Did you build that?'

'No, I work in wood. I build rocking horses and stuff.'

'How old are you?'

'Twenty-seven.'

'What's your name?'

Crap. I need an elf name.

'Jingles.'

'Do you have a last name?'

I panic. 'Jangles?'

Both boys roar with laughter. Loudly. Maybe a little too hard and at my expense. Eve's nostrils flare trying to contain her giggles, too. That Christmas spiel needs work. The littlest turns to Eve and throws his arms around her midriff. 'Thank you. I hope you have a nice Christmas,' he tells her.

I see her grin broadly. 'You, too. What about Jingles, does he get a hug?'

'No, he looks like a right old pervy bell-end,' the eldest one says, and they turn with their basket of gifts and run in the other direction.

SIX

Eve

'YES! See how good we look?' I joke as I walk into Joe's living room, looking at him as we wear our matching pyjamas.

He lunges into the tighter, tapered bottoms and laughs. 'Well, they're at least warmer than what I was wearing before,' he tells me, looking over at the coffee table to see I've grabbed some items from the kitchen and laid out all the food from our supermarket haul.

We did excellent work there. I found a selection of clothes to make me look presentable for the next couple of days, and Joe was gracious enough to walk me around as I grabbed toiletries, make up and all the assorted things that I have plenty of at home but couldn't bring myself to go back and collect. We then hit the party food and wine hard. Happy birthday, baby Jesus, because your birth means we can buy charcuterie platters, ready-made trifles and chocolate treats as a put-together festive supper.

I sit down beside Joe on the sofa and pour myself another

glass of wine as he helps himself to a wedge of cheese. Joe is surprising me in many ways tonight. For a start, I'd never have got Chris in matching pyjamas, but there are little things I'm learning about him today. Like, the man knows how to shop. If this sounds ridiculous, I mean he knows how to check a bag of clementines for rogue mouldy ones before he puts them in the trolley, load a conveyor belt on the tills (heavies first; chilled in the middle; produce to the back) and he spoke to the checkout lady, using her name, asking her about her Christmas plans. Turns out Cindy isn't keen on turkey, she's having chicken. Fair play, Cindy.

I watch him now as he flicks through the TV channels. I'm quite into his front room. There's a heavy bachelor vibe with the computer games and earthy man colours but they've made an effort with a tree in the corner, with multicoloured lights sparkling to a melody I can't hear.

I look up at the top of the tree and frown. 'Why is there a picture of a man on your tree?'

'My landlord and housemate is called Gabriel. Like the angel. It's funny... To us, maybe...'

It is funny and somewhat adorable. I like how someone in the house made the effort to cut out Gabriel's face, attach him to a toilet roll and make him wings and a tiny tinsel halo.

'Well, this is lovely. Thanks for getting it all ready,' he tells me.

'Least I could do,' I tell him, as he looks down at my notes on the table mapping out our route for the next couple of days. 'You sounded busy upstairs?' I ask him.

'Oh... Well, I wanted you to have the bed, so I just had a tidy and...'

'You don't have to do that.'

'It's cool, I'll take the sofa.'

'Is it a double or a single bed?' I say. 'We could always top and tail?' He freezes for a moment, and I realise how that sounds. Oh, I've been dumped in the most horrific of ways. Let's share a bed in our matching pyjamas like it's some awful revenge sex set-up. 'I mean... That sounds dodgy. I just don't want you to be put out.'

'I'm not. I'll take the sofa,' he says, slight panic in his eyes. He shoves some pretzels in his mouth to have to avoid talking about that in any more detail. 'You were good before... With those kids,' he says, changing the subject.

'The ones who called you a bell-end?' I reply, laughing. To be fair, he was called much worse in that supermarket. I thought that people might like the novelty of the costume, but one tutting woman covered her child's eyes, and an older gentleman called him a pervert.

'The very ones,' he says, helping himself to titbits on the table. 'Some stellar gift giving advice there.'

'Oh, I learned from the best... My mum was the best gift giver I know.' He notices how I speak in the past tense, and he hesitates to know how to reply. 'She was obsessed with Christmas. I mean, twins called Eve and Noel...'

'I thought your birthday was in September?' he remarks.

'Conceived at Christmas.'

He stifles a smile. 'How long has she been gone?'

'Three years.'

'I'm sorry,' he says quietly, turning towards me.

'That's kind. Christmas always hits a bit harder. So, you can imagine the events of this morning haven't really helped...' As my words tail off, I still can't believe that all happened this morning. My mild booze buzz has worn off and a sad sobering reality is back in view. I think back to when I first met Chris. It was just after Mum died and I longed to find joy again, to enjoy Christmas again, to love again. But I guess that's now gone. Waves of sadness overcome me thinking how Chris has stamped all over this time of year for me. Tears form in the corners of my eyes that start to roll down the curves of my cheeks.

'Oh, Eve...' Joe tells me, handing me a napkin.

I take a deep breath. 'But then we're changing the narrative, right? We're jumping out of ice sculptures, helping kids in supermarkets. And the next two days will be just that. Weddings, proposals... helping generate some real joy at the best time of year. So I can remember this Christmas for different reasons.'

He nods, still not really knowing what to say but I am reassured that he's still here and not run away in abject horror. The fact is there is so much to say, so much emotion pent up in me and I don't know how to express any of it so instead, I reach over to hug Joe. Given we've been work colleagues up until this point, it feels good to drip feed him details of my backstory, but I feel I have over-hugged this evening. I hope I'm not scaring the poor fella.

'Well, I don't know about you, but I feel we're really bonding, you know?' I joke, trying to change the mood of the moment.

'I didn't want to say. I think the pyjamas have taken it next level,' he replies, my head resting by his collarbone. I close my eyes. It's a good place to be. I realise, though, I may have held the hug a fraction too long. There's a time limit for hugs, isn't there, before it gets weird? I sit back and take a long swig of my wine.

'So, what are we watching?' he asks, grappling with the remote.

I try to laugh away the awkwardness. 'Something without romance. I don't want glowing people with good hair telling each other they're in love under snow and fairy lights. I want violence. Preferably something with guns.'

Joe nods and flicks through the channels. 'I think you're onto an untapped genre there. Christmas revenge horror. Gotcha... *Die Hard* feels like a good choice.'

'I love this! Guns and Bruce Willis in a vest... Nakatomi for the win...'

He seems amused by my detailed knowledge of the film, pulling back the lid on a raspberry trifle.

'Hang on, let me get some bowls,' he says, looking around the table.

'No need. There are two spoons there. Less washing up. Plus, this feels like a better way to overcome my heartbreak, eating it straight out of the bowl...'

'Well, if it will soothe your fragile soul then who am I to get in the way of that? You're not the sort who scrapes off all the custard and just leaves me with the fruit though?' he asks, holding his spoon up, waiting to dive in.

'No,' I say, moving next to him on the sofa, the trifle in between us like a dessert baby. 'And if I didn't say this before, Joe, thank you for making this day a bit better,' I mumble.

'My pleasure,' he replies. He clinks his spoon against mine.

After that, I don't remember much more. I ate a couple of spoonfuls of trifle. I remember Bruce Willis arriving just in time for a Christmas party and falling asleep to the sound of gunfire, parties and angry Germans.

Christmas Eve

Joe

'Joe! Oi! Oi! Wake up, wake up...'

I open one eye to see Gabriel sitting on our coffee table, a mug of coffee in hand, poking a finger into my shoulder.

'What on earth are you wearing?' he asks me, looking down

at my Christmas pyjamas. 'You look so fucking festive.' I feel this is a running theme for my attire of choice in the past twenty-four hours. He chuckles and I sit up, rubbing my eyes and taking the coffee from his hands. Gabriel seems to have got in straight from work having done a night shift at the hospital, a lanyard still around his neck. I can see there is much explaining needed from my end.

'We need a new sofa. This one is very lumpy,' I tell him.

'There's a naked girl in the bath,' he tells me, his eyes wide. 'I assumed it was you in there, so I went to have a wee and then turned around and there she was...'

'You saw her naked?' I exclaim.

'I saw boobs.'

'That's Eve...'

His eyes widen. 'THE EVE!' he almost shouts.

I flap my hands around, encouraging him to keep his voice down.

'I only saw the tops of the boobs, maybe like a flash of nipple. She was very understanding. What on earth? You slept with Eve?' Gabriel says, stamping his feet around the place. The problem with Gabriel is that he also drinks so many energy drinks, he literally has wings. 'This is good news!'

I flap my hands around to try and calm him down. 'No, it's far more complicated than that. She found out her shitface boyfriend was cheating on her yesterday.'

'What? How? That's awful.'

'She found him in the act. Anyway, she needed a place to crash and we're headed out today, too... To do some work Christmas thing.'

'But you're a glorified stripper – she's going to go stripping with you?'

'I am not a stripper,' I retort, slightly insulted. 'The other jewellery-based job... there's a whole side story. I jumped out of an ice sculpture, a kid called me a bell-end, I ate a whole family-sized trifle because she fell asleep, and we both rescued some lost rings for Caspar & Sons that we need to deliver today. I said I would do it with her.'

Gabriel's eyes roll around trying to take in the many details that have transpired over the past twelve hours. 'But weren't you meant to head home today for Christmas?'

'I'll go when we've delivered the rings.'

Gabriel sits there smiling. Yes, I'm doing it because it's Eve. It's far too complicated to relay this level of detail this early in the morning but there is so much to say. But most importantly, she's here. In our bath. A bath I'm glad I cleaned yesterday in an absolute panic. It was a bizarre evening. Did I ever think this was how we'd spend our first evening together? No. Not at all. In my mind, if I was ever going to tell her I liked her, I always thought it'd be part of a sincere conversation over a coffee. I would compliment her hair and her kind nature. Then I would bookend that conversation with a brief presentation of my feelings for her. It would be a calm, collected moment, after which... I never dared think that far ahead. But instead, we have this. A series of moments where I'm next to her, reminded of why I like her so much, like a tightly wound spring aching to tell her everything, but also trying to be a friend, a gentleman, a fellow human, at a time when she needs that.

'Then why is she shaving her legs in our bath?' Gabriel asks.

I shrug. 'We're headed to weddings, nice places where people are going to get down on one knee. I spent most of last night dressed as a sexy elf so we're going to attend these occasions looking classy.'

'So, like a date?'

'Not a date.'

'I've seen you in a tux. You're a handsome bastard in a tux. She'll be into you in a tux. Definitely.'

'That's not what this is about,' I explain.

'But it's Eve. You like Eve. You've just spent a sexy evening together.'

'Gabe, we watched *Die Hard*,' I say, pouting.

'Everyone loves *Die Hard*.'

'I went out with a girl who said it was unrealistic and portrayed the Germans in a bad light,' I say.

'Which is why you're not with her anymore,' Gabriel tells me. 'Look, I don't know half of what you just said. Message me bullet points, but from the sounds of it, there's an opening here, right? To tell her how you feel?'

'Mrs Caspar said that, too,' I tell him. 'It's just not the right time.'

'My friend, it's Christmas Eve. The universe has given you a moment.'

Gabriel binge watches too many sitcoms where people end up together, when really they need to step back from the romance of the moment and analyse the timings, the reasons, the future longevity of their relationships.

'Maybe we'll just spend some time together and she'll get to know me a bit better. That's all it is. I like her too much to rush into anything.'

Gabriel beams at me, looking down at the table at the remains of old breadsticks and dips that we half devoured. 'You're a good man, Joe Lord. Remember, I love you.'

'Love you more,' I tell him, patting him on the back.

The sound of footsteps on the stairs causes me to sit up on the sofa, putting a hand through my hair, hoping I didn't spill any of that trifle down me. I mean, she fell asleep. It had to be eaten. When she puts her head through the door, she's wearing the green dress we selected for her yesterday. You see, she's the sort of girl who can pull off anything, even a chiffon emerald tea dress that we've pulled off a supermarket rail.

'Morning,' she says.

'Merry Christmas Eve... Eve...' I say.

She shakes her head, not quite amused with me.

'You hear that a lot, eh?'

'Possibly.'

'You're wearing the dress,' I tell her.

She throws a little pose with her hand on her hip. 'I am. I mean, I won't be standing next to any naked flames, but it will do. Do I look like a Christmas tree?'

Prettiest tree I've ever seen. I don't say that out loud, of course.

'No.'

'I just wanted to say sorry, too. I'm Eve,' she says, coming over to shake Gabriel's hand. 'And you must be Gabriel from the...' She points towards the top of the Christmas tree.

He puts a hand in the air. 'That would be me. I'd like to say it's nice to meet you, but you've seen me wee so I feel as though we're already friends.'

She laughs and I see Gabriel turn to me, signalling his approval. You're friends because she laughs at your jokes or because she's seen you wee?

'How did I get upstairs?' she asks me.

'I carried you,' I tell her. 'You were out cold.'

If it sounds romantic, then it was far from some gallant knight carrying a damsel into a tower. Drunk people have limbs like lead, so it was a slight struggle. I may have banged her foot against a banister. She was that out of it that she didn't notice. But I got her upstairs, I tucked her in. I left her a pint of water knowing how much alcohol was in her system. I then went back downstairs to finish my film and basically procrastinate over the fact that the girl I've liked for an age was in my bed and what it all meant.

'Well, thank you. Sorry, was I snoring? I do snore when I've drunk a lot.'

Like a bear in deep hibernation. 'A little. But I'm glad you got some sleep.'

'I've made coffee. Sounds like you both need fuel for your adventure today,' Gabriel tells her.

'That would be amazing. And carbs. I need to carb up after yesterday.'

'Well, I can do one better. I will do bacon. The situation deserves bacon,' Gabe tells us, a little too excitedly.

'Gabe... Mate...' I say.

'God, remember the last time we had bacon together, Joe?' Eve tells me.

'The Smoked Trout Christmas Party Incident...' I reminisce.

I pause for a moment. I fell in love with her at that party, despite its dubious title. I always trace it back and I think that was the point I knew she was really cool. Mr and Mrs Caspar hired out a private room in a pub for their six employees. Eve wore a black vest top with a brocade skirt. We ordered exactly the same off the set menu: the soup, the turkey, the Christmas pudding and we both commented on how we'd opted for classic combos. In reality, though, we'd made exactly the right decision because the majority of the party ordered the fish starter and by the time the coffees were served, people were being violently ill. Whether it was the alcohol or the smoked trout we will never know, but they were like scenes from a Halloween film. We then spent the rest of the evening apologising to waiters, ensuring people got home safely and then sat there in a private dining room with its carefully Christmas curated playlist in the background, drinking and chatting, not entirely alone as Mr Caspar was fast asleep and we couldn't move him. But Eve told me about her boyfriend, I told her about my then girlfriend, we talked about the advantages of living in London (the food; the Tube; the energy) and had a whole hour of doing impressions of *The Simpsons* characters. She talked passionately about studying for an MA in Law specialising in human rights. By the end of the evening, we were sat on the floor, eating bacon rolls we specially ordered at the bar, the soft glow of Christmas lights caught in her hair, her swigging at the remnants of bottles of wine. A moment where she sat next to me, chatting to me about her Christmas plans in her best Bart Simpson voice. Me laughing so very hard and realising how much I could really fall for her.

SEVEN

Eve

Ring 1: A square cut, double halo diamond ring in 18k white gold. For Gloria.

'Hold up,' I tell Joe as he walks in front of me on this pier. 'These are supermarket heels, they're not built for running.' I bend down and try to adjust the straps on these shoes, watching as Joe stands there jogging on the spot. Joe is in a dinner jacket and I hate to say it but he wears it well. Some men wear tuxedos like they're playing dress up, but he looks effortless in his, the bow tie actually tied as opposed to a clip on, his shoes polished but not too shiny. It's like he's going to a film premiere but will be the sort to charm all the fans and journalists on his way. As he walks towards me, I remember how last night I fell asleep on him and may have left a big trifly puddle of drool on his shoulder. He's always been nice, but now I can't work out if that's just pity at play. I really hope the Caspars haven't paid him to look after me. I hold on to a railing – these damn shoes – but then, as if on cue, Joe's there next to me and he bends down to help me with a shoe strap. He's suave, gentlemanly, but it's also winter so he starts jogging again. We're by the river Thames which ordinarily would be peppered in lights, fine architecture and appear quite magical. However, the breeze is strong. So strong, it makes Joe squint and clench his teeth, too. 'Feeling the cold?' I ask.

'My nipples could literally cut through glass... I apologise. That's not a festive image,' he says, putting his hands under his armpits.

'Would you like my fur thingy?' I tell him, handing him some random coat thing I picked up from the supermarket that looks like it once belonged on the back of a Muppet. He shakes his head, patting it on my shoulders to tell me I need it more. He may be right. Contrary to what Joe thought, I didn't sleep as well as I'd hoped last night. I must have got four hours solid drunken sleep, but I woke up at 4 a.m. lying there in Joe's bed wondering where the hell I was. When I fell asleep, I was on a sofa. And then I called out for Chris, remembered what had happened and then sat up in the twilight gloom of that room, in floods of tears, just hoping to God that I was in Joe's bed and hadn't blacked out and ended up somewhere completely different.

After that, I got up and stood by the window, watching a house down the road that had enough lights on it to guide aircraft to safety. I watched the mesmerising patterns of the lights illuminate the street, and some robotic reindeer continuously buck their legs but not really get anywhere. *A midnight drink if you need it,* read a little Post-it note next to a pint glass of water. I sipped at it and turned on a bedside light. Was I nosy? Maybe a little. I distracted myself with photographs of Joe's friends, people I thought may be his sisters, a noticeboard of old tickets and postcards. I stubbed a toe on a big medical textbook, I found an old toy monkey under a pillow, I checked out what toiletries he might use. But when that was done, I curled up on his bed and steeped in my loneliness for a moment, allowing sad thoughts to get in the way, praying for daylight so I could have company again. When the time allowed for it, I had a bath, I flashed a housemate, I washed my hair and got a brief thrill in cracking open new palettes of make-up and fresh brushes. I looked in a mirror and put on some sort of mask to try to face the day. Maybe this is what I needed, a quick fix, an adventure, distraction so one day I would be able to sleep again.

'Are you here for the Christmas Eve cruise?' asks a young unimpressed lady with a clipboard, dressed up as Mrs Claus. Even if this is the company, this is a better alternative than being alone in my own thoughts.

'Not quite... We're looking for one of your passengers. Do you have the manifest? Passenger name is Frank Truman. We were supposed to be meeting him here.'

'Eve?' a voice asks from behind me. I turn and instantly smile. It's an older gentleman in a navy suit, dark overcoat, cravat and the wise man that he is, he wears a hat to keep the cold off his head. 'Rudy told me to expect you... Do you have it?'

'I do indeed. Lovely to meet you.' I beckon Joe over who has the ring box safely ensconced in his jacket pocket. He opens it, presenting it to him, the diamonds catching the reflection in his glasses. A grin appears on his face in response that gives us no choice but to be instantly happy for this man we've only just met. 'Is this as you expected?'

'And more. That Rudy Caspar is a genius. We go way back, did he tell you?' he tells us.

'No, he didn't,' Joe replies.

'He's a pain in my general arse but he's a good man. Give him my best.'

'Oh, we will,' I tell him, watching as he nervously scans the people on the pavement, walking along the gangways towards the pier. 'I suppose the ring is for a lady friend today?'

'Yes. Her name is Gloria,' he says, retrieving a handkerchief from his pocket and wiping his brow. 'Now tell me, kids, do I look overdressed? I'm shaking. Can you even believe it? At my age...'

'You look very handsome,' I tell him. 'This is quite the proposal. On a boat.'

'She loves the film *Titanic*. Is it ridiculous?'

I don't know how to tell him that that boat sinks at the end. 'Not at all. We hear of some pretty ridiculous proposal plans in the shop,' I explain. 'Isn't that right, Joe?'

'Yes,' he adds. 'Mainly involving animals. That never ends well.'

He takes a large nervous breath and I hold his hand, looking him straight in the eye.

'Are you here with anyone else today? Did you bring any moral support?'

He shakes his head at us.

'Tell me about your girlfriend,' I ask him quietly as he leans into me.

'Please... Girlfriend? I am not fifteen. She's my best friend. The very best friend I could ask for.' I grin to see his eyes soften to talk about her. 'Gloria, her name is Gloria. She has blue eyes.'

'And how did you meet?'

'The internet.'

Joe coughs for a moment to stifle his laughter and Frank shakes his head at him. 'Oh, you can laugh away. It was my granddaughter who told me to get on there. My previous wife passed away ten years ago, and we thought it was time that I perhaps did something with the time I had left... to give love a second chance...'

I pause a moment to take in his words. *To give love a second chance*. I think of someone broken, love lost and then a heart repaired, ready to love again.

'Did you find her on Tinder?' Joe asks.

'You cheeky sod. It was Match. I won't lie, I met some right sorts on there but then I met Gloria and she's... well, she's everything. She's lovely.'

'Cooo-eeee! Frank!' a voice screeches from behind us. Joe widens his eyes at me. We turn to see Gloria stood there waving at us, complete with Christmas dress and Santa hat. 'You told me this was a Christmas champagne cruise. You're not even dressed for it,' she moans.

He laughs at her, a twinkle in his eye to see her excitement. 'Well, you look marvellous, my dear. Gloria, this is Eve and Joe.' Given Gloria has never met us before or has no idea who we are, she wraps her arms around us, and I get it. I get why you would want this exuberance in your life. 'Don't you look lovely? It's an actual boat! Frank, this is fabulous!' She attaches herself to Joe, linking her arm into his. 'Shall we?'

'Oh, we're not coming on board. We're just staff. Of sorts... Do have fun though,' Joe explains.

'Rubbish. Come on board,' Frank says, clutching my hand. 'Have a drink... My treat.'

'There is room, Mr Truman,' the lady with the clipboard says, appearing next to us. I turn to Joe who looks mildly panicked. But the panic is felt more in the fingers clasped around my hand. Frank is petrified. Of what? The possible rejection? She wouldn't say no, would she? But it makes my heart melt to think that he's so invested in this moment that it's giving him the jitters. You can do this. Just say it, tell her how much you love her, any person would want to hear that.

'Well, maybe we can come on board for a glass of something... Joe?' I suggest. I don't know why. It feels a little presumptuous to get on the boat and be a part of the proposal but maybe there's a small part of me that wants to witness this, to see love get its second chance, to maybe prop up poor Frank who looks a tad pale.

Joe seems to be shaking his head at me subtly, but I can't

quite tell what he's trying to communicate. The grasp around my hand gets a little tighter. This man needs our help. 'Well then, anchors away... Let's get on board.'

Joe

When you come from Brighton, it is expected that you know the ocean, you understand the sea because you've spent your formative years looking at it, living by it, swimming in it. I've done all of that. No problems with any of that. But I live with an unfortunate affliction of not being able to handle boats. Put me on the open water in any sort of vessel and my body does seem to reject the idea quite aggressively. My most searing memory is of being on a ferry to France with my family and I spent the full hour chundering so badly that I knocked myself out on a wash basin and we spent the first two days of that French vacation in a French hospital, treating me for concussion and rehydration. *Madame, I would recommend that we keep your son away from the boats. He has, I don't know how to say this in English, but a sickness of the sea.*

Now, against all my better judgement, this very jolly lady called Gloria in her fur-lined Santa hat is grabbing on to me, and we're boarding a boat. We were only supposed to drop off the rings at the pier. That was the deal. Now we're passengers. Alongside a strange motley crew of people who've come to appreciate the festive wonder of the Thames, everyone from families in matching jumpers to tourists with selfie sticks who've been sold this cruise as part of their package holidays. There's also a Santa. With a saxophone.

'OH MY, FRANK! It's beautiful! Isn't it beautiful, Joe?' Gloria asks me. I nod. Yes, Gloria. There are Christmas trees, holly garlands, lights and snowflake confetti on the table. It's all a dream but all I can feel is the unsteadiness of the floor, swaying from side to side. 'Let's go on the deck, Frank!' she says, parting ways with me, leaving me standing by the bar with Eve, my legs slightly apart trying to keep my balance.

'Are you surfing?' Eve asks me. 'What are you doing?'

I grab on to her arm and steady myself at the bar. 'You didn't tell me we'd be going on the actual boat. This was not the plan. You keep changing the plan,' I say, vaguely annoyed.

'We have time. I didn't think anything of it. The poor man looked so nervous. I thought it'd be nice to offer some support. He's so old... Why are your eyes doing that?' she asks me.

I can't quite focus. 'I'm not good on boats.'

'Are you scared of water?' she asks me.

'No, I get seasick,' I explain, my throat stiff, almost preparing itself for the inevitable.

'But we're on a river... Do we need to leave?' Eve says, panicked. But as we look out of the windows, some gentlemen unchain the boat from its mooring and the lady dressed as Mrs Claus waves us away. Do these things have toilets? They must do. Otherwise, what are you supposed to do? Pee into the river? Maybe I'll just lock myself in one of those for the next hour and hide myself away. From Eve, at least.

'We're literally going in a straight line – up and down. Oh shit, why didn't you say?' she tells me.

'I shook my head...'

'That tells me nothing!'

'It's the universal language for no,' I tell her, feeling slightly desperate.

'Can I do anything to help? Have a glass of champagne? Maybe it'll take your mind off things? Maybe have a breadstick? They have ginger ale,' she says, walking up and down the buffet table looking for solutions. 'Or look into my eyes. Focus on something, right?'

I look into her eyes. I love her eyes, I always have, but at this present point in time, my main worry is that I will vom on her brand-new supermarket dress and that will ruin things forever.

She drags me out onto the deck of the boat where I see the choppy muddied waters beneath us.

'Look for the horizon,' she tells me, pointing out.

'We're on a river. There's no bloody horizon. All I can see are buildings,' I tell her, exasperated, half laughing.

'Well, what do you normally do when you're on a boat?'

'I don't go on boats! I stay on land. It's a healthy way of life. I don't need boats. I'm not a fisherman...'

She tries to stifle her amusement. 'I'm sorry? You do look a little...'

'Green? Look, just leave me. Go and watch the proposal. Probably best I'm out here so I don't spoil that and you can't see me make a royal fool of myself.'

'Don't be an idiot. I won't leave you. Do I need to Google anything?' she asks as the boat sets off, spluttering clouds of smoke into the river. We hear Gloria on the other side of the boat cheer loudly and Eve holds on to me tightly. Normally, this expression of not wanting to leave me and rubbing my shoulders to keep me warm would be a moment, it would be the moment given we're on open water, in black tie. God, Santa on the sax is even playing Dean Martin. But alas, it's not.

Eve gets her phone out. 'Please, no pictures,' I tell her.

'I'm Googling. It says here to distract yourself by singing,' she laughs.

'You're not funny,' I tell her, putting my hands to my thighs to steady myself.

'Excuse me, are you like James Bond? Are you here for photos?' I turn to see a couple of happy shiny Euro tourists with matching trapper hats and Spanish twangs.

I shake my head, quietly.

'Yes, he is,' Eve tells them politely.

I shift her a look. From what I can tell, Bond is generally better on boats when he's chasing people and killing bad guys. They nestle into me. What the hell am I doing? I pull a gun hand, trying to look debonair and not sick. This better make your social media, proper post, not story.

'Lovely. Everyone say Skyfall!' Eve says, giggling. She thinks this is funny. I need to get my own back here. The tourists say their thanks and then get distracted by St Paul's Cathedral.

'I hate you,' I mumble to Eve, leaning over the railings. I don't really. I'm almost enjoying the banter if I didn't think I was going to fill the Thames with spew.

'Are you all alright out here, sailors?' Frank asks from the door to the deck.

'Oh, Joe here hasn't got very good sea legs, that's all,' Eve explains on my behalf.

'Does he need a lifejacket?' Frank asks. Because that wouldn't be humiliating either.

'He just needs some fresh air. So, what's the plan?' Eve asks him.

'Oh, the crew are aware. I'm going with the ring in the champagne trick. She's just gone to the bathroom. And then I guess... I just hope my knees have it in them,' he says with a shake in his voice. I wish I could admit the emotion of the situation affects me but really all I heard there is that there is a bathroom. Eve leaves me for a moment and goes over to give Frank a huge embrace. It's unexpected so he laughs but hugs her back.

'Well, we are both rooting for you. You've got this. It'll be amazing.'

'I never know what the young people mean when they say that. You've got this. What is this?' he asks.

'I think it means you have this moment. Own it, make it yours.'

Frank pauses for a moment and then looks Eve in the eye. 'You are a very lovely young lady. Thank you. Could I ask a favour? It's a bit cheeky but could you film it? So I can show my grandkids. I mean, if green gills here needs your attention...'

That's me, isn't it? I shake my head. The less Eve sees of me being completely incapacitated the better. 'I'm fine, go,' I tell Eve.

She makes a face at me, partly amused, partly concerned, but follows Frank back into the boat, taking her place at a nearby table. I should be watching the proposal, shouldn't I? But instead, I watch her. I see her face fill with joy and emotion as the glasses are brought to the table and her eyes crease with laughter when Gloria shrieks as she sees the ring. She exhales softly to see Frank drop to his knee to propose, and then sheds tears that she wipes away with the tips of her fingers. And as Gloria accepts the proposal, pulling Frank to his feet, I hear her cheer along with the others in the soft light of that festive setting, I see her rooting for someone she met literally half an hour ago, I see someone rooting for love. I hold on to the side of that boat and look out as we approach Westminster. Focus on Big Ben as some sort of horizon. You can do this, Joe. You can't taste bacon in your mouth from this morning's breakfast. You can't.

'That's our third proposal this week,' I hear a person say next to me. I turn. It's Santa with the saxophone. I'd like to say he's an authentic Santa but he's possibly in his forties and the paunch isn't real as he swings it to the right of him so his saxophone has somewhere to rest. 'I wouldn't propose on the Thames.'

'Why not?' I say breathily, reticent to make conversation.

'All city rivers are a bit murky really, aren't they? Big rat swimming pools. Look at that, could be a bit of wood, could be a human turd... Who knows?'

It's like Santa has said everything in one complete sentence to try to make me barf.

'I hate boats,' I tell him, putting a hand out to steady myself.

'You hate boats? I'm a respected jazz musician, mate. I've played at Ronnie Scott's and I'm spending my Christmas on this barge, dressed as some fat jolly wanker, tooting on about Rudolph and his bastard red nose.'

I force a hollow laugh under my breath. I hadn't realised this was a competition to see who hated boats the most, but I still win.

'You keep looking at that girl,' he tells me. 'She your missus? Don't tell me you're proposing, too. In your dinner jacket.'

'Nah,' I say, putting a hand to my mouth, trying my damned best to strain every muscle in my being. Don't look at the waves, don't imagine that same scenario in your stomach. Breathe. 'I don't keep looking...'

'You do. I'm Santa, I've been around, I know these things... You keep looking at her because you like her...'

Or maybe she's my horizon.

Or not. Because this boat is on a river, there's a lot of swaying, too much swaying.

'What's her name?' Sax Santa asks me.

'Jesus...'

'That's seasonal.'

'No... I–I... I'm so sorry...'

'Why?' he asks.

Because it's happening. The boat lunges forward, catching a wave. I slip, trying to steady myself and grab on to Santa but just don't manage to spin quickly enough, throwing up and into his saxophone.

EIGHT

Eve

'Oh, Joe, I am so sorry...' I turn and put a hand to Joe who's taking a small moment in the back of his car to recalibrate and wipe down his face with baby wipes we picked up at a Tesco Metro. Is this how I thought I would spend my Christmas Eve? Maybe not. In some other universe, I'm spending the day with Chris, buying last minute gifts and getting ready for dinner with my brother. Yet instead, I'm here in this little car, having just experienced the magic of a cruise down the Thames and Joe almost getting beaten up by a Santa with a saxophone. I put my hands to his rattling car vents trying to warm my fingers. 'Here, have some more Coke. I also got you some sweets, gum and crackers,' I say, handing him goodies. 'And I also got you these elf ears that were at the till.'

He perks up, takes the ears and bag from my hands, and like a man after my own heart, heads for the fizzy sweets first. 'I'm mortified, Eve... That poor Santa. I think I ruined his saxophone. How do you clean a saxophone?' he wails in the back, covering his face in shame.

'Maybe he can soak it in Dettol,' I say, trying to hold in my laughter. 'I'm sorry, I shouldn't make fun here.'

'They had to get a mop,' he laments.

This makes me giggle a bit more. 'You don't do boats?' I ask him.

'I don't do boats. Something to know about me.'

'What about pedalos on a lake? Can you do them?'

'I've never wanted to tempt fate.'

He sits there for a moment and closes his eyes to rest and there is something about him, the loosened tie, the hair spritzed with river breeze, the peaceful expression of his face that catches my eye as I reapply my make-up in the rearview mirror. He didn't have to go on that boat, we didn't force him, but maybe this underlines his commitment to our mission today.

'So, fill me in... How did he propose?' Joe asks, his eyes still closed.

'He just told her how he felt. It was really lovely,' I say wistfully. Frank took his moment and he did make it his, parts of his little speech still lingering. *You've helped my heart beat loud again. It feels like it's glowing again with purpose, and I want you to know that you did that, you've given me life.* Gloria was a big ball of emotion, so I hope she heard what was said. I'm glad at least that she can watch it back with my amateur videographer skills.

'Here, watch the video,' I tell him. I take out my phone and prepare to show Joe but as I do, he can see that my phone screensaver is still a photo of myself and Chris, a selfie taken on a city break to Lisbon and we both take a moment to realise it shouldn't be there.

'I should probably change that, eh?' I admit quietly, staring at Chris' face.

'I mean, I would,' Joe replies. I think that's what's really warming about Joe at the moment. I think others would be angrier, they'd tell me how I should be feeling, what I should be doing, but he doesn't do that, he quietly just props me up and lets me work out things for myself. There are hundreds of photos on my camera roll, waiting to be deleted, hundreds of memories from early morning selfies to birthdays to weddings that I will need to erase. If only I could really do that in real life. There will be so much to do to remove all trace of that man from my life. Well, maybe it starts with a screensaver.

'Well then, smile...' I say, turning the camera on the both of us in that car, and taking an impromptu selfie. I look down at it and I seem to have captured a moment where we've both decided not to smile but pull some pretty awesome faces instead. I laugh as he arches his head around to look at the pic. I set it to screensaver.

'Seriously? I look like I'm both furious and mid-sneeze. I don't think I want that memory preserved on your phone,' Joe tells me.

'It's funny. I need funny right now. I can look at this picture and think about this moment we shared in a London NCP car park getting ready for a wedding.'

'In Olive, my ridiculously little car. It's a classy memory,' Joe adds.

'I don't know, the Christmas décor in here is growing on me...'

Joe chuckles under his breath. 'Here, pass me your phone. Let's see that proposal video...' he says. I hand him the phone and watch his reaction from the back seat, a broad grin, a quiet yes muttered under his breath as Frank proposes. 'The old dude did well. That's good stuff. Almost worth that hour of extreme seasickness,' he says, handing the phone back to me.

'Thank you. Again, for all of this. For tagging along. Are you having fun? I'm sorry if this morning didn't feel like fun...'

'I've had better hours, but it was worth it to...' he hesitates. 'To have you be my best gal pal and hold my hair back while I threw up over that boatside.'

'It's what us girls do for each other,' I say, in a fake Valley Girl accent and it's a relief to hear him laugh.

I put my phone down and finish off reapplying some blusher and powder, watching as he unbuttons his shirt and applies some more deodorant. He catches me looking.

'Do you need any?' he asks.

'I'm good. What else do you have in that bag?'

He rustles through his toiletry bag but looks a bit panicked. 'Mouthwash, plasters, baby talc?'

'For your... baby?' I ask.

'Well, no, but you've seen my jingly shorts and sometimes there is... chafing. But my sisters have also taught me a bit on the soles helps with new heels.' He throws me the container and I apply some to my feet, shrugging my shoulders but secretly thinking his concern for the welfare of my feet is a little bit adorable.

'So, this morning. I meant to say, Gabriel was so nice, he seems like a really cool bloke. How did you guys meet?'

'Oh, we were on a course together,' he says casually.

'Course?'

'In a previous life, I was a medical student. Gabriel's a junior doctor.'

I stop for a moment to take that in. It explains the big text-book I stubbed my toe on in his bedroom. There is so much to piece together about this man that I had no idea about. I think I always just knew him as Joe who I saw once or twice a week. The one in the shop who had about three different jobs, one of which sounded like he hung out with Magic Mike a lot. I applauded his industry, but I never questioned the whys or the very busy nature of his life.

'How did I not know this? Why are you still not a medical student?' I enquire.

He stops for a moment and shrugs his shoulders. 'Life just got in the way.'

'Oh.' I wonder whether to delve into that cryptic answer without sounding like I'm prying. Was it the money? The politics? Was it just not for him? But these are not questions to ask in a Mini when he's just hurled in and around the Thames. 'Can I also say I was very impressed by how clean your bathroom was for two men living together?' He looks strangely relieved by the compliment. Good swerve, Eve. I put my make-up brushes back in their bag and notice Joe filling his face with Pringles. I forgot we also stocked up on supplies last night – everything from tinned cocktails to Malteser reindeer. It would seem we will spend the majority of this day in Olive the green Mini, with snacks, having car picnics, laughing. Amidst the alternative realities out there, for the while, I don't mind this at all. 'You seem better now,' I mention.

'I am on land now. As long as this next wedding isn't on the river then I am good. 'Can I ask a weird question...? Can you smell me?' he asks me.

'Why?'

'I'm paranoid now. I can't go into this next event smelling of vom.'

'Come here,' I tell him. He sits forward in the back seat and I lean over, putting my cheek next to his chest. I inhale deeply. 'You smell great.' I flinch as I say that. I mean, he does. There's certainly no hint of river sick but there's a hint of scent and whatever shower gel he uses peeking through. He sits back in surprise and watches me curiously. I don't know if there was another way of saying that. You smell non-vomity? You smell like a normal man?

'And what about me? Has the river completely fucked my make-up and hair?' I say, trying to smooth down my hair.

'It's just missing' – Joe says, passing me my comedy ears – 'these.'

I giggle and put them on.

'Shall we?' he asks me. 'This next wedding should be far more straightforward.'

'Let's... Do you have the rings?'

He pats his tuxedo pocket and smiles at me. I'm glad he's here. I should tell him that. I should. But I don't.

Joe

'I will be back for Christmas, I promise.'

'Technically, Joe, it's Christmas already,' my eldest sister, Carrie, explains to me down the phone just in case I was unaware of the arrangements of the festive calendar.

'I've just got a lot to do today. I'll drive down some time on Christmas Day.'

'So vague. We've made a bed for you.'

'Meaning you've pumped up the air bed in the study... Who am I sharing with?'

'Holly's boys. It won't be the same if we all wake up and you're not here,' she pleads. 'What about gifts?'

'We can open them when I get there...'

'The kids will be feral by then. Mum made you a stocking.'

'Carrie, I'm twenty-seven. I think I'll be alright not waking up and racing down the stairs to see if Santa's been.'

'Stop being difficult,' she warns me. 'We never miss Christmas.'

'Shut up. You missed Christmas that year when you got drunk and fell asleep and ended up on the wrong train to Kent.'

'Don't be a tool. I will literally eat all the parsnips so you won't have any...'

'You wouldn't...'

'Watch me...'

There is a silence, and I can hear her cackling on the phone.

'Just cover for me. I will be there, but this is different, it's important,' I tell her, glancing over at Eve listening into the conversation. 'Look, I'll give you a ring this evening.'

'You better, Joe, or I'll come to London and find you and slap you myself.'

She hangs up and Eve side-eyes me as we walk alongside the Thames onwards to the next ring-delivering mission, the winter breeze still biting but the fresh air and walk doing my topsy-turvy guts the world of good.

'Apologies. That was an angry festive sister,' I explain.

'Does she have a name?' Eve enquires.

'Carrie. She's the eldest, the one who still thinks she can boss me about.'

'She sounds angry about you going home. Seriously, if you need to get away...'

I shake my head. 'Not at all. They're just angry they don't have a kitchen hand, there's no one to bully into peeling all the vegetables or getting the extra table out of the spooky shed at the end of the garden. I'll go when we're done. It's all good.'

Eve is quiet as I think she tries to work out why I'm here, why I'm enduring this marathon of ring bearing, but after seeing Frank's proposal, it's dawned on me that what we're doing is pretty special. We're making sure these special moments that they're trying to create go off without a hitch, and I'm fortified by that sense of purpose. I mean, I get to spend time with Eve, too – let's not forget that much.

However, if I was looking to make an impression on Eve, I don't think what happened on that boat helped one bit. Of course, to build a relationship, there are moments where you want someone to see you vulnerable, but I don't think she needed to see what came out of me or witness me clinging to a random pole on a boat telling her the world was spinning and that I thought I might be dying. And the aftermath probably didn't help either, lying there in my car telling her my elf shorts sometimes chafe, asking her if she wanted deodorant, i.e.

implying she might smell, and then getting her to smell me. Those are not classy moves that one puts on a girl, all that smell-based talk.

'Are you OK with walking?' I ask her. 'We can always jump in a taxi.'

She links her arm into mine. 'Oh no, parking the car again would have been a faff. It's only five minutes away plus, you know. London at Christmas, it's a bit special, isn't it?' she says, looking up at the fairy lights hanging over the lamp posts, red London buses whizzing past with festive messages, the smell of a street vendor roasting chestnuts across the road. 'Plus, I think that talc trick works, well done you.'

'Stick with me. I know lots of tit tape hacks, too,' I say. Did I just talk about tit tape? Did it make it sound like I use tit tape? 'I mean...' Please laugh.

But as I try to backtrack, I sense I may have been saved by Eve's attention being diverted elsewhere. She freezes as she looks out on to Somerset House and the ice rink that they set up in the grounds. She leaves me standing there on my own as she walks up to a gate, watching.

'Well, if you wanted to see London at Christmas, that is the place, isn't it?' It's always a splendid sight, the towering tree to the front, swathed in gold and lights and all those usual things in the surrounds that lend themselves to the season: hot chocolate, rosy joyful cheeks and comedy woolly hats. But when I look down at Eve, I start to see tears fall down her face and she looks upon all of this in some state of shock.

'Whoa, are you OK?' I ask her and she falls into me, into a hug, still sobbing.

'Sorry. I'm such an idiot,' she says, lifting her head and trying to wipe her tears with her hand. 'Ignore me.'

I try to work out what may be happening. Did she possibly have a traumatic moment ice skating as a child? I always think quite baffling we let members of the public engage in the sport without formal training where very sharp blades and ice are involved.

'Is this a Chris thing?' I ask, taking a wild guess.

She nods as more tears start to fall. I fumble in my pocket and hand her a tissue. 'I really am very sorry.'

'Please don't apologise. All of that only happened yesterday. Was ice-skating your thing then?'

She stops crying to snigger under her breath. 'Yes, every winter we came out dressed as Torvill and Dean, in purple chiffon and diamante.'

I try to return the laugh but show some sense of empathy in my eyes.

She takes a deep breath. 'Back at my flat, when I found Chris and... Allegra, the other woman, I found other things. There was a printout for an ice-skating session at Somerset House. They were going to have a date here yesterday morning... after their sex, before I came back that afternoon.'

To admit that much to me out loud must be gutting for her. 'Oh. Ouch.'

She continues to cry, wiping her eyes, trying to save her eye make-up, and attempts to shrug it off but I can see how her hurt penetrates so very deep. A passer-by walks past just as she blows her nose loudly and gives me a dirty look like I might be the cause of her tears. I scan around the streets.

'Look, let's grab a quick coffee before the next ring delivery. Come with me.' I pull her hand towards a pretty patisserie shop across the way, *Le Manger*, hoping it will provide a corner of privacy for her. A bell rings as I push against the dark wooden door and we join a queue as two girls behind the counter in berets wait to serve us, just in case we didn't think this place wasn't French enough.

'Bonjour, Monsieur, Madame... How can I help?' one of them asks. I look around the place with its café decor and classic French prints. It's a classy Noël in here, from the music to the cinnamon stick decorations adorning the place but the pièce de résistance is the glass counter where lines of cakes, tarts and confections sit in neat lines, waiting to be bought, consumed and savoured.

'Two cafés au lait, please,' I tell the girl.

'Un moment,' she replies, as she rolls her eyes at the old lady in front of us in the queue, taking her time. I glare back at her for her lack of patience. This lady wears a fur-lined trench coat and in her handbag sits a very small dog who stares back at me, as if he's looking into my soul. I smell, don't I? She tries to get some money out of her purse, but she drops some coins and her umbrella.

Eve drops to the floor quickly to help. 'It's OK. I've got it,' she tells her, putting a reassuring hand to her back.

'Merci,' she replies in withered tones and puts a hand to Eve's arm, giving her a kind and enquiring look, noticing she may have been crying. 'Je paierei aussi leurs cafés,' she tells the girl behind the till. The old lady then looks at me and scowls. I didn't make her cry, madame. That was the big ice-skating place across the way, the crappy ex. Eve looks at me, confused.

'The lady would like to pay for our coffees,' I tell her.

Eve shakes her head, but the lady insists. 'C'est Noël.'

'Nöel. I know what that word means, it's Christmas. Merci, madame,' Eve tells her and I watch as she helps her to a table, while I carry a tray of coffees and cake. The old lady pats the seat next to her and takes another look at me, still trying to work us out. Are we together? Why is she crying? Is this the beginning of a date or the end of a very long night?

'Parlez-vous francais?' she asks me, still not sure about me.

'Oui, Madame. Vous semblez être très en colère contre moi. Elle ne pleure pas à cause de moi, si c'est ce que vous pensez,' I tell her.

Eve swivels her head at me. 'You speak French?'

'Yeah, a bit. I think she thinks I made you cry,' I say,

watching out for this old lady in case she attacks me with her fork or sets her small dog on me.

Eve is quick to react. 'Oh no, he is mon ami.'

'Pas ton petit ami?' the old lady asks.

'Non,' I reply. 'Elle avait un petit ami, mais c'était un gros con...' I gesture this is why she may be tear-sodden and sad.

The old lady nods, taking a sip of her coffee and reaching out to Eve's hand.

'What is she asking?' Eve says.

'I'm explaining to her that you're crying because your boyfriend was an arsehole. *Un connard* or *un con.*'

Eve nods at the lady. 'Not him,' she tells the lady in slow tones. 'Not a connard.'

The old lady laughs and looks at Eve's face again. 'J'espère que ton ex se fasse attraper le pénis dans un piège d'ours.'

I choke on a sip of coffee as the lady guffaws heartily, Eve's eyes turning to me.

'She said she hopes Chris gets his dick stuck... in a bear trap.'

The old lady pretends to be a bear. Eve bursts out laughing and wipes the tears from her eyes. 'Je m'appelle Eve,' she says in her elementary French.

'Enchantée. Henriette et Jovie,' she tells us, pointing to her dog. She turns to me and looks at my face. 'Tu devrais remplacer l'idiot. Vous feriez un beau couple avec vos tenues chics. C'est Noël, après tout.' I can tell Eve has lost track, but I know exactly what this woman just said. She said we look cute together in our fancy clothes and should get together because it's Christmas. I shake my head at her.

'She said we both look very chic,' I tell Eve.

Henriette pushes her patisserie at Eve, steals a fork from another table and encourages her to take a bite.

'Chaque Noël, je viens ici. Je venais avec mon amant, mais'

– she puffs out her cheeks and turns her palms to the air – 'il n'est plus là.'

'She comes here every Christmas; she used to come here with her love, but he's now passed,' I repeat to Eve who instinctively grabs her hand.

'Ne soyez pas triste pour moi. Clément était un homme bon. Nous avons vécu une belle vie ensemble et nous avons baisés comme des lapins. Il était exceptionnellement doué.'

While I'm pleased to hear that her dead lover, Clément, was a good man, she's also told us that he was exceptional in bed and they shagged like rabbits. I don't dare translate that out of respect to him. I turn to Eve. 'Don't be sad, her love was a good man, and they had a good life.'

'Mais, je viens ici. Je me souviens. Dans la meilleure pâtisserie en dehors de Paris, et les noms rigolos des gâteaux me font rire.'

'She comes here to remember. Best patisserie outside of Paris and she likes their funny Christmas themed cakes.'

The lady seems to have warmed to me with my knowledge of French.

'Ne pleure jamais pour un homme. Mangez plutôt un excellent gâteau.'

'Never cry over a man, eat excellent cake instead.'

The old lady smiles at me. 'Ou baise un beau garçon comme toi.' I take a sharp inhalation of breath, my eyes wide. Eat cake or fuck a nice-looking boy like me.

'What did she say?' Eve asks, trying to join in with the joke.

'Cake is the answer.'

'Oui,' Eve replies. 'C'est delicieux.'

'Une Perdrix dans un Poirier.'

I smile as she says it. 'This one is called A Partridge in a Pear Tree.'

A magically perfect piece of cake. Eve smiles at me and that winter light streams through the window and catches her face perfectly as she tucks strands of hair behind her ear. The old lady watches both of us.

'Well, merci for the cake and the excellent life advice,' Eve says. 'I just need a moment to fix my face in the ladies. Excusez-moi.' She pushes her chair back, heading over to the bathrooms by the counter. I watch her walk away, Henriette observing the concern etched in my face.

'Your French is good...' she tells me, settling in her seat, taking out a cigarette that I'm sure she can't smoke in here. She gives her dog a treat from her pocket.

I turn to her smiling. 'Merci beaucoup.'

'You did not translate a lot of what I was saying,' she tells me, taking a sip of her coffee. 'My Clément would be sad.'

I shake my head at her. 'Madame, you used some exceptionally naughty words. This is Le Manger, it is not a Starbucks,' I say, mocking her. The old lady finds this hysterical and cackles, frightening her dog and making the coffee cups rattle. 'Plus, you were trying to force a romantic situation between the two of us.'

'So? I am French and an old romantic. And also quite old. It is allowed. I saw the way you look at her.'

I shrug my shoulders.

The old lady looks me up and down. 'Well, if you're not going to seduce her, do I have a chance?' she asks me.

I laugh, but then she winks at me. Oh shit, she's serious. I've heard about her husband. I don't think I can compete.

I think it may be time to leave.

NINE

Eve

Ring 2: Flat profile, 18k yellow gold wedding band. Engraved. For Mike.

I don't know French, not really. I mean, there are phrases etched into my memory. I am sure I could introduce you to everyone in my family, tell you all the months of the year and give you some solid directions to a post office, but it turns out Joe speaks French like a proper French person, and this is new information. Bilingualism is strangely hot. I really think that's how they should sell foreign language courses. Not that I've told him he's hot, but it's another detail about this man revealing itself to me. He walks with me into this hotel now, our arms still linked, and I pull him closer. Is it for the warmth, the security or the French? Either way, I appreciate the arm. At the end of the day, Joe knew what I needed when I broke down in front of that ice rink and he didn't shame me for expressing any of that. He's still here, propping me up.

'Merry Christmas, Eve,' a doorman says in tails and a posh

hat, waiting by the kerb. I giggle at the formality of it all, maybe because he said my name. 'Both of you look lovely today,' he comments.

'Why, thank you,' Joe replies, 'It's all her though, I know.'

The doorman winks and I blush, not quite knowing how to take the compliment. At least it tells me that I managed to fix my make-up in the patisserie before and don't look like a big sobbing mess.

'In my supermarket dress,' I whisper, trying to downplay the comment, pushing my way through a heavy brass revolving door, Joe right behind me.

'That's how well you pull it off,' he says, his hand to my shoulder. He's cute, if mistaken. I pause to take in his touch. Probably not the best place to do that, though, as the door keeps revolving and I trip slightly, both of us stumbling into the foyer of that hotel. It's a classy entrance.

'Gotcha,' Joe says, catching me. I like how he does that. How he holds my hand and keeps me upright. It's not going unnoticed. 'Wow,' he mutters under his breath.

I'm not sure if he's aiming that at me but then my gaze follows his, admiring the grandeur of this very posh hotel. Definitely wow. Our heads swing back like children in wonderment, trying to take it all in. 'Am I allowed to say this place is swish as fuck?' Joe says under his breath, just in case this establishment doesn't allow for such words.

I'm not even sure that term does this place justice. From the high ceilings and ornate décor, the tree laden in bows, lights and gifts, the animatronic Christmas scene, the counters selling truffles and high-end handbags, to the fancy luxurious leather sofas where people sit in sunglasses being charmed by the concierge, phones in hand waiting to hear news of the whereabouts of their private jets. I suspect the clientele of this place did not spend last night running around a giant supermarket filling their trolley with marked down mince pies.

'Yep. Fancy pants all round,' I say, not entirely convinced that I belong. We stand back as a man with a large luggage trolley stacked to the rafters with Louis Vuitton shopping bags swings past us. We both look around, silently acknowledging the grandeur but also to take in all the splendour, the man on the grand piano in the corner playing some classy Christmas songs. Hold up, is that a real reindeer? 'Can you imagine ever getting married in a place like this?' Joe continues, looking bemused by the excess of the place.

'Well, you know me... I'm all about the bling,' I reply. He laughs, as we walk past a counter where a box of truffles would cost you in the region of sixty pounds. 'This isn't me at all.'

'What is you then?' he enquires.

I'm silent for a moment. Is he talking about weddings or me? Because yes, I imagined marrying Chris. Three years into a relationship you do envisage the future, and I thought about our wedding, just not in a place like this. He'd have hated it for a start. He's the sort who would have let me plan the wedding, and his main preoccupation would have been the stag do and the free bar. The thought fills me strangely with relief.

'I've never thought about it really. I don't think it's this grand – it's smaller, simpler, more intimate, like the patisserie place we were just in...'

'With a slightly unhinged old French lady in the corner.'

'Who most certainly fancied you,' I joke.

'Yep, let's not talk about that or we might get more of what happened on that boat.'

I giggle but seriously, I never need to see that ever again. 'And what about you? Is this you?'

'Not in the slightest. I'm a beach wedding man.'

'In flowing white linen? But the sand!'

'This is why I always carry talc,' he jokes. 'So where is this ring going?'

'We need to head up to one of the suites to meet the groom

and best man and hand over the ring and then we are done,' I explain, leading us over to the lifts, pressing the buttons as the doors slide open. If we didn't know this hotel was ultra-fancy before, we know now as there's also an older man in there with little round spectacles, in a hat, his sole purpose it would seem to push buttons and make sure no one gets stuck in the doors.

'Which floor?' he asks us politely.

'The Fraser Suite, please.'

'Thanks, Melvin,' Joe says to him, glancing at his gold name badge.

He stops for a moment, grinning, for someone to have used his name and not barked orders at him. 'Certainly. You must be here for the wedding.'

'Kind of,' I explain. 'We're just here to deliver something.'

'Are you the people with the birds? I hear there are birds?'

'Uhh... no,' Joe says, laughing.

'It's quite an event downstairs. Giant candy canes, snow machines, five hundred red and white roses got delivered at 7 a.m., I believe they're serving turkey, too. I did have a peek. I love a wedding,' he explains. 'I think she's coming in on a sleigh.'

'That may explain the reindeer I saw downstairs then...' I say.

'We had someone come in on a horse once. Thing took a wee in the ballroom and we had to replace the floor.'

I look over at Joe and he bites his lip to hold in his laughter.

'Well, here we are... 28th floor – the Fraser Suite. Whatever you are delivering, have a lovely Christmas, you two.'

Joe stops to put a hand to his shoulder. 'Thank you... you t—'

But before he can finish, there is a shriek that rings through the corridor and something that looks like a giant candy cane streaks past us. Joe puts a protective arm in front of me as Melvin pops his head out of the elevator door. 'Good luck,' he says, escaping.

'You want to fight? Let's fight!' a balding man screams, half dressed in a morning suit, but with his sleeves rolled up. Oh, he looks ready to fight. Joe and I back into the wall as we see another gentleman stood at the other end of the corridor. He's wearing his suit, he even has a festive red and white buttonhole, but the man looks scared, petrified. He grabs a fire extinguisher from the wall. A room door opens and a woman stands there in a white silk dressing gown, her hair in rollers and her face damp with tears.

'Dad, please... NO! You can't... Just leave it!' she squeals. Another girl in a matching dressing gown comes out to placate her but this also does not go down well. 'How could you? I knew you would do this! It always has to be about you! I hate you. Just piss off!'

'But Abs, my stuff is all here... I can't just go out in the street like this...'

'SEE IF I CARE!'

The room door is slammed, and the girl turns slowly; if her anger could fume out of her nostrils then it would. 'You are so dead!' she says, pointing to the scared man at the end of the corridor. I don't know what to do but I feel I need to tell that man to run rather than just standing there trying to explain himself with his fire extinguisher. It's the two of them now and she has pretty fierce looking nails and, from the looks of it, some speed as she sprints down the corridor after him. The room door opens again and this time it's a couple of ladies carrying bags, cameras and hairbrushes, dressed head to toe in black, their eyes wide in shock.

'Excuse me, is that the Piper wedding?' I ask her as she heads to the lifts.

She sniggers, unimpressed. 'It was. She's just thrown us out. I don't think it's happening.'

'What happened?' Joe whispers.

'I thought I'd seen it all with weddings. Turns out the father of the bride has been sleeping with the maid of honour who she's known since school. Anyways, it gets better... The best man caught them shagging last night in the loos and put the video on a wedding group chat.'

Joe and I stand there, our mouths agape at the drama. That balding man must have been in his fifties, the maid of honour much, much younger. We hear raised voices in the distance and what sounds like a punch. I don't even want to know who that came from.

'Is the bride OK?' I ask.

'She's not great,' one of the ladies tells us. 'She's already made phone calls. They're turning away guests. The brides-maids are literally at war. Phones being smashed, someone's been taken to hospital because someone threw a champagne bucket at their head. It's not pretty...'

'Really? You're not hanging around then?' I enquire.

'One of them torpedoed my hairdryer across the room. It's fucked. A £500 hairdryer. If you do go in there, tell her she's getting the bill for that. I'm done here. I don't need this before Christmas,' she says, hurriedly pushing the buttons on the lift. 'I don't know who you guys are, but I'd go home.'

Both of them disappear into the lift as I lead Joe towards the bride's suite, staring at the door.

'Eve, maybe we should just...' Joe says, putting a hand to my arm. 'If this has gone to pot then I think the last thing she needs to see is a ring to remind her of the event.'

But I stand there quietly, the echo of a fight on a stairwell still happening and the sounds of some very loud crying coming from behind that door. This has very little to do with us, but I think back to myself this time yesterday, processing the same sort of emotional havoc. How I couldn't face telling anyone, not even my twin brother, and how isolating and overwhelming that felt. Just before Christmas, too. I knock softly on the door.

'Hello?'

Joe

'I TOLD YOU ALL TO PISS OFF!' a voice echoes out of that hotel suite and we step back in shock.

This is not a good idea. I don't know how to tell Eve this, but when a proper fist fight is happening and someone has grabbed for a fire extinguisher, then you know it's time to take your leave. Don't get involved. We can go downstairs to the foyer of this very fancy hotel, grab an overpriced Christmas cocktail and share a chocolate truffle.

'Eve...'

She looks at me, those big eyes wide with concern. 'But it's her wedding day,' she says, softly. 'And none of it is her fault. She must feel awful...'

And I sigh, deeply. That's Eve's kind, empathetic side coming to the fore, the sort of quality that made me fall for her, but it's that same emotion I saw on the boat. She wants today to mean something, she wants to root for love, she wants these ring deliveries to go well, without any problems. I watch as she tries the latch on the door and it opens. As we pop our heads around the door, the first thing I see is a wedding dress in the middle of the room; in fact, it takes up most of the room like some sort of ice cream bombe, covered in diamante and lace. However, around the dress, you see the signs of some sort of fight. Someone has thrown a bowl of crisps to the floor that line the carpet like confetti. I flinch a little at what I at first assume to be the bodies of small woodland animals strewn around the carpet that reveal themselves to be hair extensions. There's a champagne bottle on its side, bleeding bubbles onto the carpet. I rush over to rescue it before it can do any more damage. On the double bed lies a bride, sobbing. She sits up as soon as she sees us.

'Who are you? Are you from the hotel? God, you're not the bird people, are you?'

I shake my head.

'The wedding's off. I'm so sorry. I... I...' She falls to the bed again in tears and Eve slowly approaches her, grabbing at a box of tissues.

'We're actually from Caspar & Sons, the jewellers. We have your husband's wedding ring. It's been engraved. I am Eve and this is Joe.'

She eyes us curiously. 'Well, you can take the ring back. There is no wedding,' she sobs. I want to say sob, but it's more of a wail, the sort you hear from toddlers in supermarkets who've been denied treats. 'I can't... I don't...'

Eve goes to sit on the edge of the bed. I feel less inclined to do that so grab the fallen bowl and pick the crisps off the carpet, trying to be useful. Eve does very little but sits there, putting an arm around her back. She waits for a moment. 'Can I get you anything?' she whispers.

The bride is silent for a while. Then she sniffs, inhaling a fair amount of mucus through her nose. 'Do you have any chocolate?' she mumbles.

Eve rifles through her handbag. 'I have a Snickers?'

The bride nods, and Eve opens it, breaking off a bit for her and placing it in her palm. The bride shoves it in her mouth.

'I've been on a diet for three months. Do you know how much bone broth I've had to fucking endure for today?'

Eve shakes her head and hands her another piece of nutty chocolate.

'Do you want anything else? A cup of tea?' I ask, trying to be as helpful.

'I want to kill my maid of honour. Can you do that for me?' she bites.

There is a difference between boiling a kettle and murder, but I feel now is not the time to point that out to her. 'I mean, she headed for the stairs. I can make it look like an accident?'

She stops for a moment to try to laugh, scanning both of our faces again.

'Look, I can see what you're doing but you don't have to be here sorting out this mess. It's Christmas. Thank Mr Caspar for me for getting the ring here. Tell him I'll still pay him,' she says, taking some earrings off and tossing them on the floor.

I'm happy with that but Eve doesn't move from the bed. 'I just don't get it,' she mumbles.

The bride looks surprised. 'My dad was shagging my best mate. That's all you've got to get,' she tells us, pointedly.

'But can I ask... where is your groom?' It's an excellent question. We've seen a maid of honour, a father of the bride and a best man but someone's missing who's an important part of the puzzle.

'He's in his room. He had a massive row with the best man and one of his ushers is still drunk from the night before so about as useful as a bag of piss. I tell you, I'm having the worst Christmas ever.'

'I don't think so,' Eve tells her.

The bride's eyes are wide; half of her mascara is down her cheeks, making her look like she's just jumped out of a Japanese horror film well. 'What do you know?' she tells Eve in accusatory tones.

'What's your name?'

'Abby.'

'Abby, yesterday I caught my boyfriend of three years getting a blowie in the shower of my flat, so if you want to compare really crap Christmases then I am going to put my hand up in the air and say that I win. I win that all day long.'

I feel a rush of pride, because not so long ago, Eve was stood staring at an ice rink, hardly able to breathe. For her to say that out loud as some sort of comparative exercise and help this girl out is quite a thing.

Abby looks at Eve for a moment. 'That is shit,' she says quietly, taking her hand.

'So I've cried all the tears, I know that emotion you're feeling and I don't think you need to feel that way. What's your groom's name?' she asks her.

'Michael.'

'How long have you been together?'

'For the longest time, like years. I don't remember a time without him, you know?' There's a faint glow in her cheeks that reanimates her as she recounts that story. 'He's my Mikey.'

'So somewhere in this hotel, there's still a man who wants to marry you, right? A man who loves you?'

She nods, the tears still flowing. I worry about her dehydrating so hand her a lonely glass of champagne sat on a dressing table.

'Why Christmas? Why did you want to get married at Christmas?' Eve asks her, still feeding her chocolate.

'Because he proposed this time two years ago. In a Christmas market in Prague. It felt right,' she says, sighing.

'Then don't let other people shit all over your plans. Let's talk to the groom and see if we can save this day? Eh?' Eve suggests.

'I can't see Mike before the wedding...'

'Can we call him?' I suggest.

She goes over to her dressing table and retrieves her phone, putting the call on speaker.

'Babe,' he says. Wherever this man is, it also sounds like he's been crying.

'Babe,' she replies, sobbing in reply.

They both cry at each other for at least thirty seconds.

'Where are you? Are you still here? It's all a mess. Lisa caught up with Sean and she's taken out his tooth. The police have been called. There's an ambulance here. Your sister has taken your mum home with the flower girls because they were crying. I just...'

'I broke the hairdresser's hairdryer. I might need to replace it,' Abby explains.

'How the hell did this all happen? Seriously, how long has your dad been shagging Lisa? That's awful...'

Abby looks like she's going to retch from having to relive that memory, so I take her glass from her.

'It's just all a mess, babe. This wedding... This stupid wedding. I never wanted it, I never wanted any of this. The sleigh, the stupid flowers, live flocks of doves – you hate birds. You can't even sit on piers because you're scared of seagulls,' Abby cries down the phone.

'Do you know they put initials on the mince pies? Who needs personalised mince pies?' Mike adds, chuckling. 'This is all my mum, she went overboard.'

'It's not like my family was any better. Two hundred and fifty of our closest friends... I'm sorry, I'm so sorry...'

There's silence as we all sit there taking it in. I'm wondering how many doves constitute a flock. I picture them sat in a box, waiting for a wedding that will never be.

'If I may?' Eve pipes up.

'Who's that?' Mike asks.

'I'm Eve. I'm from Caspar & Sons, the jewellers. I believe we have your ring,' she says politely.

'Oh shit, I forgot you were delivering that. I'm sorry we wasted your time.'

'Don't be,' I intervene. 'I'm Joe. I'm with Eve.'

Eve puts her hand out to me, and I instinctively know to place the ring box in her hand. She opens it up to reveal a very stylish gold wedding band. You know the Caspars got the good polish out for that one. Abby starts crying as she looks at it, emotional to read the last-minute engraving to the centre.

'Is there any reason you two can't still get married? Today?' Eve continues.

There's a pause as they consider the proposal. I look over at Eve. I can see her eyes are lit up with hope. Even after all she's been through, she still wants other people to be happy and to fix things, for that ring to find its rightful owner.

'But our families...' Abby starts.

'From what I can see, your families have made this day more about them than you,' Eve says.

'This day should always have been about you two. What you want, right?' I preach. Eve looks up at me and smiles. 'Then get married. You still want to marry each other, right?'

'It's all I want to do,' Mike says, still talking through his tears.

'All I've ever wanted to do is marry you...'

'Then let's make this happen,' I say. Abby reaches over to grab hold of me and hug me whilst I look at Eve from over her shoulder, beaming. I guess we're doing this then. We're organising a wedding. I just hope Eve knows how to fix make-up because I don't know where to start with that.

TEN

Eve

'Hi, Santa? SANTA!' I ask, breathless, having chased this man down the road from the hotel. He may be dressed like Santa and carrying a substantial paunch on him, but he moves fast, and it's no mean feat catching up with him when you're in supermarket heels and it's the middle of winter.

He looks to check that there are no children around and looks at me from over the tops of his glasses. 'That's not really my name, but yes. Who are you?'

'That's not important. The Piper wedding. You were supposed to officiate it, yes?'

'I thought that the wedding was called off...'

I beam. 'It's on. The wedding is on. Can you come back?'

'It is? Really? Last thing I saw was an ambulance. Someone told me the father of the bride had died.'

'He didn't. He was chasing the best man and fell and broke an ankle.' Santa gives me a look like he doesn't quite know whether to believe me. 'We're trying to salvage something out of this shitshow of a day. Please. Help us save this wedding,' I plead, my hands in a prayer position.

'I'll still get a free meal, right?' he asks. I applaud the fact that Santa is in this for the free food.

'There's two hundred and fifty portions of turkey going spare. You could probably invite your whole family down.'

'And they will pay for my parking?'

'Yes,' I say hesitantly.

'Then let's get back in,' he says, still confused. 'Are you from the hotel?'

'No, I'm Eve. Nice to meet you, Santa. You're very convincing, by the way,' I tell him, as we U-turn back towards the hotel, the crisp night air making me rub my hands up and down over my arms. He has proper black boots for a start. I feel that too many Santas forget about the footwear needed for chimneys.

'Well, maybe I'm the real thing,' he jokes. I'd believe that more if he wasn't holding a Nike holdall instead of a sack. 'It's important to uphold the magic of the season. Too many little eyes are watching. I'm a professional...'

'I have no doubt. How's your ho-ho-ho?'

We walk into the hotel lobby, and he bellows into that space with both convincing volume and depth of tone, so much so that a group of kids turn around in wonder.

'That is impressive.'

'I try, my dear.'

I lead him over to the lifts where Melvin, the bellboy, waits there for us, beckoning us towards him.

'Thank you, Melvin. Melvin, this is Santa. I don't know if you know each other.' Both of the older gentlemen fist bump each other and I grin as he presses the buttons and the lift doors close. 'Oh, we're mates. How's it hanging, Santa?'

'Slightly to the left these days,' he jokes, and we all stand there laughing and trying not to think about Santa's penis.

'I see you've met the lovely Eve,' Melvin tells Santa. 'Make sure this one is on your good list. She's done a good thing today.'

'Really? That's lovely to hear. Is there anything in particular you want for Christmas?' Santa asks me. I sigh inwardly, not really knowing how to answer. I'm not sure I know anymore. I wouldn't say no to a car. But in all seriousness, eighteen hours ago, I thought I had everything I wanted, a man I thought I was going to be with forever, at least. My life was mapped out on a very different course, one I had faith in, that I thought was for me, but how life can change in a finger snap. Now, I'm in a posh London hotel, I've run around this place for the last hour trying to save something that isn't even my own to make me believe in hope again, in magic. What do I want? The doors suddenly open and Joe stands there. He grins.

'YOU FOUND SANTA!' he says, a little too excitedly, and jumps up and down, hugging the big man in red.

'You're not the groom,' Santa says, confused.

'No, I'm the new best man apparently,' Joe says. 'But the groom is waiting for you when you're ready.'

We step out of the lift and I look around at this rooftop garden, grinning from ear to ear. 'Joe, what have you done?' I gasp. It seems while I was beautifying the bride, helping her get in her dress and chasing Santa down the street, Joe and Mike became best mates and found an alternative venue for their wedding celebration, all in the same hotel on a rooftop terrace overlooking the London skyline but without the tinsel, giant candy canes and not a Christmas bird in sight.

Joe looks very proud of his work as he leads me round and points out the décor. 'The fairy lights were here but I went downstairs and got the trellis arch, some storm vases and flowers and candles and jazzed the place up. Check this out...'

He brings me over to stand under the trellis and then presses a button on a remote control. Snow suddenly appears, out of nowhere, falling on us gently and resting on his hair. I pick it out with my fingers, looking up to the sky in wonder.

'You did all of this?' I ask him.

'I felt invested in the project. Like some sort of supermarket sweep game show running around the hotel, getting it sorted. But I think you forget, I have three older sisters... I also know how a wedding should look.'

'Well, you nailed it,' I say, high-fiving him.

'Here, help me with my buttonhole?' he asks me, handing me a red rose. 'I've never been a best man before. I feel guilty, I didn't even throw him a proper stag do,' he jokes.

I poke the pin through the flowers on his lapel and straighten it for him. 'Well, I'm chief bridesmaid and I don't even know her last name...' Both my hands on his jacket collar, I smooth it out with my fingers and catch his glance for one small moment. Blue eyes. I've not noticed them before, not in this way and surrounded by the glow of all these lights. Why have I not noticed you before? Santa joins us under the trellis for a moment, settling in to officiate.

'I prefer this set-up,' he says, looking around approvingly. 'Downstairs, there was going to be some sort of Christmas dancing flash mob coming down the aisle with children dressed up as penguins,' he mutters, flicking through some notes. 'Well done, you two. Now, kiss,' he tells us.

Both of us look at Santa, confused. 'We're not the ones who should be kissing,' I explain, hoping he's not had a senior moment and forgotten who he's marrying today. He points to the top of the trellis under which we stand, where a sprig of mistletoe hangs from the top.

'I believe it's both Christmas and a tradition,' he tells us. 'And bad luck if you don't. And this couple don't need any more bad juju on a day like today.'

'Did you just make that up, Santa?' Joe asks him.

He looks affronted. 'You forget, I am Santa. I make the

rules. It's what I do. Now please, kiss. I have a wedding to officiate...'

Joe turns to face me and puts his palms up in the air to suggest we may as well just make the big man happy. But what's the deal? Are we going for the cheek? A quick peck on the lips? While I'm still dithering, he leans in, and kisses me gently. I close my eyes, feeling his lips on mine, parted gently, the warmth of his breath, our bodies pulled into each other. I inhale sharply and then relax, my whole body relenting.

'There you go, Santa,' Joe says, stepping back from me and I see his face blazing with emotion, embarrassment maybe? I can't talk so I exhale softly, pausing as he edges away from me. What on earth just happened there? I hear Santa chortling and then he winks at me. I don't quite know why.

'Eve...' I snap back into the room at the sound of Joe's voice. 'Places?' he jokes.

'Oh, yeah,' I say, still in some high state of happy shock, heading to the lobby to find the bride in her massive domed dress, pitched around her waist like a gazebo.

'Bouquet, young lady,' I tell her, handing her a bunch of red and white roses.

'Thanks, Eve.' She beams, shimmying her shoulders around. 'Let's get married!'

And as we turn out into that rooftop garden to the sound of John Legend, me the ever-faithful lone bridesmaid, I can't quite breathe. It's a crisp December day, the sky blue and misty and the hum of London sings to us from below.

I look up. At Joe. We kissed. We don't do that sort of thing. I tell myself not to stare at him. At the end of that aisle. With his blue eyes. In that tux. This is not what we do.

Joe

SHITTING HELL. WE KISSED. I MIGHT DIE.

> You won't die. Tell me everything. Where is she? Is she next to you?

>> No, because I'm in the toilet, texting you and having a mild panic attack.

> Which toilet?

>> The toilet of some 5* swish hotel. I'm best man at someone's reception.

> This is news. I'll find out more later. Look, just stay cool.

>> I AM NOT COOL.

> Stop using caps.

>> I CAN'T.

> Do I need to come there and sedate you?

So, I am not quite sure what happened there. We were stood on that rooftop garden, under the lights, and I was showing Eve the newfound excitement of the snow machine and suddenly a man dressed as Santa was haranguing us into kissing because, well, mistletoe. And it was a blur. I blame Santa. For all of it.

As I return to the table of the hotel restaurant, where we are having the world's smallest wedding reception, I think about the best approach moving forward. I need to downplay the kiss completely and not look like it affected me in any way at all. I just got to kiss you, Eve. No biggie. Be cool, Gabriel said. Don't do some strange happy dance in the middle of this very upper-class establishment with their fabric napkins and tiny forks.

'JOE!' Abby squeals as she sees me coming back to the table. Abby is married now and immensely drunk as she and Mike feel it essential to make a large dent in the champagne that was supposed to serve two hundred and fifty people. She throws her hands around me and kisses me on the cheek. I like how love

saved the day, how they realised its importance above everything else. Teary but genuine vows were traded on that rooftop
and I, for the first time in my life, was best man, wedding plan-
ner, ring bearer and official witness. I hope they name a child
after me.

'Santa's got the shots in,' she tells us. 'You joining?' Santa is
not in a good way. He, too, has had champagne and at least two
turkey dinners and I worry given it's one of his busiest work
nights.

'Unfortunately, I am the designated driver for the evening
so no, but you crack on. I'm sure Eve...'

I look over at Eve, who is already partaking in the shots and
holds one aloft before downing it and beaming at me. She pats
the banquette space next to her, the way someone would
beckon a puppy over and I gravitate towards her. As soon as I sit
down, she puts a head on my shoulder. Breathe, Joe.

'Fuck. I'm pissed,' she mumbles.

'What's in the shots?' I ask.

'I am guessing cranberry and some very potent vodka.
Look at this place, it's so festive, isn't it?' she says, cradling one
of the crackers on the table. 'Oooh. I've got a joke. You love
jokes. Why do reindeer like Beyoncé so much?' she asks
excitedly.

'I have no idea.'

'Because SHE SLEIGHS!' she spurts out in exaggerated
tones, her nostrils flared with glee, and I bite my lip to stop
myself from laughing. She's so merry. I count the shot glasses in
front of me. That would be three, on top of the champagne she's
had today, and our day isn't over. Maybe I need to tell her to eat
more roast potatoes to soak it all up. These are good roast potatoes, too. You know these aren't out of a packet. Don't mention
the kiss. Treat it like it never happened.

'You guys...' Mike says, throwing his arm around Eve's
shoulder. His wife joins in the group cuddle, and I watch a lady

on the table opposite stare at us for possibly ruining her swanky festive dinner in a nice hotel.

'Have we said thank you yet?' Abby tells us. 'I swear you guys were sent down from the Christmas spirits to look after us today.'

'I love you both,' Eve tells them, hugging them tightly.

'We love you, too. I really think we were brought together for a reason. We should be mates, like new besties. We should all go out together. In the summer, we can go to Ibiza!' Mike suggests.

Eve is drunk so claps her hands excitedly. I'm not sure how to say I don't want to go on holiday with people I've just met but smile and nod, amused by the joyful celebration around the table. There is still a lot to do today. People from the hotel keep filtering in to talk to Mike and Abby about the ballroom, the band who showed up and have no one to play to, the man with the birds who needs paying but they are too far gone, too excited. And from the way they are especially handsy with each other in full view of all of us, I suspect they want to also get into one of the suites upstairs to celebrate their wedding night in the traditional way.

'Well, as much as it pains me to do this, Eve and I have to make a move. We have another ring to deliver,' I say, looking at my watch.

Mike and Abby protest loudly to the shock of all the other paying customers, except Santa who I think has passed out on the seats next to us.

'I want to stay.' Eve pouts at me. 'You are the best man. This is a poor show from you.'

I look at Eve's eyes looking in about four different directions and think about how much alcohol she consumed yesterday. I am doing this for her health more than anything else.

'We can celebrate with them again another time,' I say, soberly.

'But you haven't even given a speech,' Abby remarks. They all look over at me, leaning into each other in drunkenness, almost like dominoes waiting to topple. If that gives this reception the conclusion it needs, then so be it. I stand and clink a glass with a teaspoon quietly.

'QUIET, EVERYONE! THE BEST MAN IS SPEAKING!' Abby shrieks. Loud enough for the rest of the restaurant to stop what they're doing. An audience. Great. The lady on the table opposite puts her fork down over her gravadlax, glaring at me.

'When Mike asked me to be his best man, I thought... hell, why not? I've known him and his lovely wife for forty-five minutes. How could I refuse?'

The diners look confused but everyone at this table laughs louder than that joke really deserves.

'But you can be around someone for forty-five minutes and you can get an idea of what they might be like. When we were trying to get the trellis arch in the service lift, Mike was practical and didn't take the mick when I got my end wedged in and fell on my arse.'

'No, I was busy taking pictures instead, mate,' he jokes.

'And as a couple, I see how well you know each other, how you genuinely care about each other and other people. I've seen the generosity in how you've offered all this leftover drink and food to staff and nearby homeless shelters. I see joy. Real joy in how much you love each other, how excited you are to be in each other's company, how both of you were smiling like loons through that whole ceremony.'

The tears are back now as Mike holds Abby tight, kissing her messily on the forehead.

'I like that I've only spent a fleeting moment with you, and I know this. I know with some certainty that this is what love looks like.'

Eve looks at me for a moment when I say this and I swear,

the room stops moving. This is what love could look like. If, only if, you felt the same way about me.

'You soppy bastard... Come here!' Mike shouts, leaning over, grabbing my cheeks and giving me a massive kiss on the lips. If that woman across the way wasn't fond of us before, I'm not sure how she feels now she's seen the groom drool down the best man's chin.

'So,' I say, grabbing my glass of sparkling water. 'A toast to the bloody beautiful Mr and Mrs Piper...'

Abby squeals with delight. 'I'M A WIFE!' she tells the restaurant, not that they couldn't tell from the giant white dress (we had to put her in her own corner), but I laugh. Speech done. People clap, still confused.

'Come on, you,' I tell Eve, touching her arm. 'Time to go.'

'I love you, Joe,' she mutters drunkenly.

She doesn't. I pat her on the head. 'I'll go and get your coat.'

The coats are stored on some pegs leading out to the toilets and I head there to obtain Eve's faux-fur jacket. Once I get there, I stop for a moment and lean into where it's hanging. Given we only paid thirty-five pounds for this thing, it's surprisingly soft. Maybe I should tell her while she's drunk. I love you, too. It might not even be love, it could be mere infatuation, but I think we could make love look like that, too. We wouldn't be so loud and handsy per se, but I think I could make you that happy. I take the coat off the peg and head back to retrieve Eve. I hope she can walk because I tried carrying her last night and that didn't quite work.

'So, the bloke you caught in the shower, I hope you chopped his balls off,' I hear as I approach the table and immediately duck behind a curtain.

'I threw his phone out of the window,' Eve replies, in drunken loud tones.

'Yes, girl,' Abby shouts, high-fiving her.

'Wait, you're not with Joe?' Mike asks. Some best mate he is to at least not know.

'Nah, babes. They're just mates. She caught her fella in the shower yesterday with another bird,' Abby adds. 'Is Joe single? Get with him them. No offence, babes, cos we're married now but he's fit as fuck.'

I hear Mike laughing. 'You don't have to tell me. My boy is easy on eye, that's for sure. I saw the little kissy kissy under the mistletoe,' he jokes.

'Oh, it was just a kiss. He's a work mate. He's lovely, one of the nicest blokes I know but I don't want to go there.' My heart lurches.

'Eve, the best way to get over someone is get under someone else,' Abby says. 'And you should be all over and under that like a rash.'

Mike seems unfazed at how his new wife is chatting about the best man. 'She's not wrong. Just have some fun. It's Christmas. Go pull his cracker... Tell him Santa's not the only person coming tonight.'

Drunken cackling ensues at all the innuendo.

'Maybe,' Eve replies. 'But... not Joe...'

I stand there behind this bloody curtain, clutching on to Eve's coat. What? My chest suddenly feels heavy. I look up at the ceiling of this room, decorated in fairy lights, like stars, randomly scattered about the place, not aligned, not falling into place at all. Oh. Really? OK then. *Not Joe.*

ELEVEN

Eve

I'm drunk. I was probably drunk yesterday but today I'm that sort of drunk where I feel in the right conditions, I could probably run a marathon as long as I got to stop for a kebab on the way home. I know why I'm drinking. I'm basically confused as hell. Yesterday, I caught a man I thought I loved in the worse circumstances possible. That image still makes my eyes twitch like they're on fire and my heart still feels fractured, raw with hurt. The alcohol numbs for a moment.

However, let's pour some more feelings on to the shitshow batter that is my life and give them a good old shake because I'm currently lying on the back seat of a green Mini, listening to Elton John as he steps into Christmas and all I can do is watch the back of Joe's head as he drives us to the next ring delivery, wondering... After that kiss under the mistletoe, my brain seems to have rewired itself. This is Joe. You can see him in a new light now. You're allowed. He can be someone you kiss. But then, he's also Joe. Lovely Joe who seeks out people's names, carries you to bed and has a kind and pure heart – who you shouldn't drag into your relationship drama because it's too soon, it's too cruel to use him as some sort of rebound person. But look at how he's revealing himself to you. He was always a handsome man, that was never in doubt, but on a day such as today, he's made things better, he's made you feel exhilarated, happy – he's done his absolute best to help distract you, despite everything that's happened in the last twenty-four hours.

Through my drunken fuzziness I'm aware I'm downplaying the kiss to remove the awkwardness. We were just getting into the spirit of things. It wasn't romantic in the slightest. He's acting all cool, too, and hasn't brought it up so I shouldn't either. We have many more hours to spend together so why make it an issue? He is an awesome wing man, and that he should stay. I am far too messed up in heart and mind to do anything else. I look at him in the front, and I can see his eyes in the rearview mirror, a slight frown on his brow. He's quiet. He's stopped lip-syncing his songs and he looks mildly serious. Maybe he's tired? Tired of me? He wouldn't be the first man to think that. I am drunk, though, and it's not fun babysitting a drunk. Maybe I'll sing to him to cheer him up.

'I'm sending you a Christmas car to say it's nice to have you neeee-arrrr...' I sing along, out of tune, not really knowing the words.

'Why would Elton send a Christmas car?' Joe asks from the driver's seat.

'Because he's rich as fuck,' I blurt out. 'You've stopped singing? Why?'

'I don't think I started...' There's a shift in tone from him, like he may be angry with me.

'Are you OK?' I mumble from the backseat.

'Yeah, just... It's been a day, eh?'

'And you weren't even drinking...'

'Well then, who would drive? Plus I don't really drink,' he tells me, grumbling at the gears sticking.

'Why not?' I ask.

'I've just seen the damage it can do when done irresponsibly.'

'Are you calling me irresponsible?' I say, giggling.

Joe doesn't reply straight away but his head remains still, looking out on to the road. 'No, but you're definitely drunk.'

'We should stop for chips,' I suggest. 'This is when a motorway services would come in handy, eh?'

I see him smiling from the front seat. I've broken him down with my services talk.

'I'll see if I can find somewhere. I'd rather just get the next ring delivered,' he replies, his mood shifting again. 'It's getting late. Rings four and five might have to wait until tomorrow now. We'll still get them there in time. I'll let Mr and Mrs Caspar know.'

'On Christmas Day?'

'I guess.'

'I'm sorry.'

He doesn't reply. He's mad at me, isn't he? I guess he didn't anticipate this bleeding into Christmas Day itself.

'Do you know how they met? Mike and Abby?' I tell Joe, kicking my shoes off and resting my feet on the perforated ceiling of his car.

'I do not. Please don't kick in my roof, this is a fragile car...'

'They met at school. They were in the same science class. They've been together for nearly ten years.'

Joe doesn't reply to this.

'What's been your longest relationship?' I ask him, realising my drunkenness is turning into philosophical, chattering nonsense. I move my head around. Crikey, my neck is bendy.

'Two years. Her name was Amandine...'

'FRENCH!' I shriek, so loudly that the radio vibrates. 'That's why you can speak French?'

'Yes. I learned a lot of French by being with her. *J'aimerais mieux foutre un âne que toi.*'

'So romantic,' I mumble.

'I would rather fuck a donkey than you,' he says, plainly. 'I think that was my favourite.' I think I see his shoulders shaking with laughter and I'm relieved I've changed the mood of the car for a moment.

'Was she pretty? I bet she was pretty,' I grumble. 'Was she gammmmiiinnne?' I don't know why I say that word like that.

'She was but she was cruel. I stayed for too long. What was your longest relationship then?' he asks me.

'Chris,' I whisper. Naturally, just to have to say that out loud in my inebriated state does not sit well in my muddled old head so I feel tears run out of me, down my temples as I lie there, not knowing how to be comfortable or how to digest that I am in some strange limbo of feelings and emotions. It is, however, drunken crying so I whimper sadly as I weep, getting progressively louder. The tears are pouring out of my eyes now, making their way into rivulets that drip down my chin.

'Are you OK back there?' Joe asks quietly.

'Maybe I did something wrong in all of this? You know? I was thinking about this. In the greater scheme of things, I wasn't enough...'

'You are enough,' he says, quietly, in the way you talk to a highly drunk person, in tones that you hope can coax them down off that precipice of high emotion. 'You are more than enough.'

'But it wasn't enough for him,' I sob.

'Or you know, maybe he was a king dick?' he says sharply.

'He wasn't always a dick,' I say, not sure why I'm defending him. 'Maybe I just have a real knack of falling in love with the wrong people. Before Chris, I dated a man who used to eat his own toenails. While they were still on his feet...'

That was supposed to be me relating a funny anecdote. Joe doesn't reply, some steely look in the corner of his eye. Just endure the drunk, keep her safe, hope she passes out soon.

'Was that what it was like with Almondy?' I say, tears forming snot bubbles that dribble all over my face.

'She didn't eat her own toenails,' he tells me.

I half laugh, still sobbing. 'You know what I mean... Why did that end?'

He grips on to the steering wheel tightly. 'Because she didn't love me back.'

I cry when he says this. Comedy tears that you see coming out of cartoon babies, like garden sprinklers. I can't think straight but my emotion is peaking, the alcohol has opened some sort of floodgate and the back of Joe's car is bearing witness to it all. Why is this car spinning? It's like I'm in a Tardis. Maybe this love story is different. Maybe I'm travelling back in time to change it all, everything. Or maybe. I grab my phone and scroll through to find Chris's contact, putting it on speaker and ringing his phone. I'm surprised when it starts ringing. I obviously didn't throw it out of that window hard enough.

'Who are you calling?' Joe asks, shifting his head around to see.

'Santa?' I say, unconvincingly.

Hi, this is Christopher Lay. You know the drill, leave me a message and I'll get back to you as soon as I can.

The car stops at a traffic light, and Joe reaches around trying to get the phone from me. 'Don't do it, Eve. Give me the phone.'

It's a strange play-fight, with him trying to grab my phone and me having the skills of a drunken ninja dodging him. I open my window and extend my hand and phone out, sticking my tongue out at Joe who gasps in disbelief. There's a beeping noise encouraging me to leave my message. A cyclist whizzes past. I drop my phone.

'My phone!' I yell, unbuckling myself messily, opening the car door and hanging out of the car to rescue it off the tarmac.

'EVE!' Joe roars. 'What the hell!' He turns on his hazard warning lights and jumps out of the car to the pavement side, looking aghast when he finally sees me. Don't look at me, Joe. Not like this, like some drunk seal hanging out the side of his car, trying to steady herself on the pavement.

'You can't park there, mate,' I hear a voice project out to him, the sound of car horns and Elton John. I can still hear him singing to me about Christmas forever and ever.

'I'm so sorry, Chris,' I whisper into the phone. 'I'm sorry you didn't love me back. I hate you. You've broken me.'

And those are the last words he hears me say, as I hang up my phone, slink back into the car and very casually and instantly pass out.

Joe

Amandine. If you really want to know about Amandine, I dated her for two years thinking I was young and hip, dating a Parisian with a blunt fringe who used to smoke in the bath, but the truth was she was cruel. She once threw a pineapple at me in rage, was strangely rude and judgemental about my viewing habits (*What is this snooker? It is boring. Like you...*) and then toy with my emotions, usually making me believe I'd done something wrong and trying to win back her approval. It took two years of her doing that to realise that wasn't love.

I never thought Eve was like Amandine. I always thought her kinder, more compassionate, but maybe they do have one thing in common. Maybe they both don't love me back, not in the way I loved them. Ever since I heard Eve's admission to Mike and Abby, I can't get those words out of my consciousness.

Not Joe. I guess that was that then. I don't know when I fell out of contention for her affections, but the words are gutting, all the same, to hear that someone you care about doesn't return the feeling.

I'm still not sure what to do with that feeling of rejection. In any other scenario, I'd flee and run home to the comfort of my family at Christmas, but part of me knows Eve is still hurting, still vulnerable and I've made a promise to deliver some rings. I have to follow through on that much, despite the sting of knowing Eve and I will never quite be. That said, she's making it a little easier for me to de-crush given that she's stopped my car slap bang in the middle of Earl's Court and made me have to come out and rescue her phone that she's dropped out of the window.

I look at her now as she's passed out in my back seat and I try to arrange her into the car so she's at least safe, grabbing an old hoodie she can use as a pillow and chucking her shoes in the boot. Cars behind me honk their horns, glaring at me for holding up the traffic. I better not get a ticket for this. I like you so much, Eve, but please don't throw up in my car either. My upholstery won't survive. I look down at her phone which has survived falling onto the street and see a familiar screensaver of the both of us in this very motor. That is what we'll never be and my heart fractures, just a little bit. I should probably confiscate this from her so she doesn't get the chance to phone Chris again. He's still on her mind, but that's only natural, and it's stupid of me to think I'd just slide in there and replace him.

'You broken down, bud?' a van says, slowing down next to me, looking me up and down in my dinner jacket. Yes. The girl I like doesn't like me back. I am very broken down.

'All good,' I tell him, putting a thumb in the air. 'Cheers though.'

I get back into my car, putting her phone on the seat next to me. Just deliver the next ring, Joe. That is the most important thing in all of this. Christmas music still blares out of my car and I turn it down, not really knowing how to connect with my jolly. Maybe I could just do these last three rings quickly with her in the backseat. Drop them off, job done. Then this will be over and far less torturous of an experience. I can deliver her to a family member who'll take care of her, and I won't have to think about how she doesn't want me.

Eve's phone suddenly rings next to me. For a horrible moment I think it's Chris. But when I glance over, the name 'Noel' is on the screen. Her brother.

'Ummm, Eve...?' But I hear her snore lightly, and look round to see her drooling into my hoodie.

The phone doesn't stop ringing. One missed call after another and Eve not even flinching. I pull into a petrol station and stop the car, answering it immediately.

'Hello?' I say, starting to sound exasperated.

'Who is this and why do you have my sister's phone?' Noel says sternly. 'If you've kidnapped her, I have a locator thing on my phone and I will find you. Put my sister on the phone now!' He is shouting, reminiscent of Liam Neeson looking for his daughter with his very special set of skills.

'I haven't kidnapped your sister. She's here but she's asleep,' I say plainly.

'Why is she asleep?'

'She's been at a wedding. She was drinking.'

'It's 5 p.m.'

'On Christmas Eve?'

Noel pauses. 'Hold up, have you just had sex with her? Are you a hook-up?'

'NO!' This may very well be the most random phone conversation of my life. 'Not at all.'

'Then who are you?' he asks rudely.

'Joe, a friend. You're her twin brother.'

'I am,' he says, still suspicious that I know this. 'Is she staying with you?'

'She has been, yes.'

'Can you tell me if she's alright, is she safe? I'm going out of my mind here.'

'She's OK. She's drunk but she's safe.' I glance at her in my backseat. She nearly fell out of my car a moment ago, but I picked her up. Despite everything, I'd always pick her up.

'How drunk?'

'Pretty smashed.'

'The sort of drunk you'd be if you'd just broken up with someone?' he asks.

My car shakes as a lorry goes past us a little speedily. I glance back at Eve. Nothing's going to wake her from that nap, is it? I'm not sure whether to break that confidence as I know she's not told her brother anything yet.

'How did you find out?' I ask.

'I went round to her flat to drop off gifts. Chris was there, the flat was a tip, he told me everything.'

'What did he tell you?' I ask, curious why Chris is still alive in this case.

'That she broke up with him. It wasn't working... I literally spoke to her yesterday so I'm not sure why she's not told me any of this?' As soon as the words leave Noel's mouth, I scowl because Chris obviously lied again to save his own skin. He's changed the narrative and made her the bad guy. But why was he in that flat? To get his belongings? Confront her? 'You're very quiet, whoever you are. Please tell me my sister is alright, that she's safe. I'm seriously worried,' he tells me with a tremble in his voice that immediately evokes some emotion in me because I think about my sisters in the same situation, how they'd have my back for an eternity.

'Noel, I don't know how to tell you this...' I say, glancing back at Eve. 'She found Chris with someone else. In their flat. Only yesterday. The fact they've broken up is all him.'

'What? But Chris said...' His voice is trembling.

'I wouldn't believe anything that shitbox tells you.'

His anger seems to shift towards the correct person now. 'I knew it. I had a feeling but he just... I will hunt that bastard down.'

We take a moment to process how awful this must be for her.

'How is she?' he asks.

'She's a bit of a mess,' I tell him.

'Then that will be a change. I'm normally the hot mess in this partnership... You said you were at a wedding? Whose?'

'She's found some distraction with work – she's doing a favour for the jewellers' where she works and delivering some rings. I'm helping out, too.'

'Well, that's good of you both. I know I don't know you but let her sleep and get her to call me. Tell her...' He pauses. 'I bloody love her and just look after her, yeah?'

'I'll try.'

'One last thing. Do you know why she didn't tell me? Our dad?' he asks.

'Because it's Eve,' I say. 'She didn't want to—'

'—ruin Christmas?'

'Pretty much.'

He laughs under his breath. 'Well, it sounds like you know my sister. Tell her I'm here and to call me as soon as she can.'

'Will do. And I guess, Merry Christmas, Noel.'

'I believe it's Merry Christmas Eve,' he replies.

I glance back at Eve again in my back seat as Noel hangs up. This was supposed to be her day. I watch as her breath shudders in her sleep. What the hell am I doing? The sky has faded to dark now. And it is Christmas Eve, I keep forgetting. This would be the time I'd be hanging up my stocking. Making sure

we had enough carrots for the reindeer, fizzing with anticipation about the next day. I'm not sure that excitable feeling sits in
my bones at the moment, though. Not after what I heard in that
hotel. I rest my head against the steering wheel. If I can't be
with her then maybe I just need to deliver some rings and look
after her. I reach over to my glove compartment and get out the
gift I'd wrapped for her, placing it inside my jacket pocket,
ready for when all of this is done.

TWELVE

Eve

'Is it Christmas yet?' I say, sitting up as Joe's car lurches to a halt. I look out the windows at unfamiliar cobbled streets, multi-coloured houses all lit up with lights and festive décor. How long have I been napping? I feel my current state is fuelled by cumulative drinking, my body telling me it can't cope anymore with all this emotion and alcohol, and the only way it can stop me from abusing it anymore is to shut it down with sleep. I look down at a puddle of drool I've left on Joe's hoodie and wipe down the damp side of my face.

'It's all good. You just sleep. I'm just going to drop off this ring,' Joe tells me, adjusting his bowtie in the rearview mirror. I catch a glimpse of myself as he moves away. It's giving me zombie festive chic. I try to flatten out my frizz.

'Where are we?' I ask, looking out of the window.

'Notting Hill.'

I suddenly remember dropping my phone out of a car window. 'My phone?'

'In your bag, safe. Don't ring Chris again,' he tells me.

'I did do that, didn't I?' I say, mortified.

'You left him a voicemail,' he tells me. 'But chances are he'll never get it because you threw his phone out of a window, yes?'

'Yes.'

'Phones and windows seem to be a running theme. I'm leaving mine here to charge so don't go near it, OK?' he tells me, bemused at how I seem to be perfectly still but swaying. 'There's a bottle of water there if you need it, and some Coke. Stay hydrated.' His tone is a little flatter, pedantic. He's annoyed with me, I can tell.

'I will. You're lucky I've got a big bladder so I can retain all this fluid,' I tell him. That's a winning sexy factoid about yourself, Eve. He doesn't reply. 'You don't need me to come?' I ask him.

He forces a smile, shaking his head, and leaves the car. This either means I look such a state he doesn't want to be seen with me or he doesn't think me presentable enough to be representing Caspar & Sons' bespoke ring delivery service. I open the Coke, spilling a little on my dress and downing it furiously, then burping quite loudly. I really hope he didn't hear that from across the road. Oh, Joe. What is going on here? I don't even know what I feel anymore. I think I might be falling for him. I kissed Joe. Why can't I stop thinking about that kiss on the rooftop?

This isn't right, though, and doesn't feel fair to Joe at all. I need to behave. I'm just drunk. Needy. Stop watching him walk towards the house and studying his arse. That's terrible behaviour. He approaches the yellow house that is wrapped in ivy, a twiggy wreath as large as a lifebuoy hanging on the modern wooden door. He straightens out his jacket and turns to the car to smile. He's just a very excellent friend. I put a hand in the air. I don't think I should hold my breath like this when a friend smiles at me.

I catch my reflection again and stare with pity at the girl

looking back. Not that it matters anyway. Whereas Joe is revealing the true loveliness of his character, I may very well be doing the reverse. It's like he is seeing the very worst of me. Some poor emotionally sodden, drunk, rejected version of myself. He's seen me sob cry. He's watched me drool in my sleep. I may as well fart in front of him now, tell him I can't do simple addition and that I like watching snooker on the television.

My phone ringing grabs my attention and I reach around in my bag to find it, happy to see the number.

'Mrs Caspar! We're on our third ring. It's all...'

'Where are you?' she says hurriedly.

'We're at Mr Tolv's house in Notting Hill.'

'ABORT! ABORT! ABORT!' she shrieks.

'What? Abort what?'

'The ring. To the address in Notting Hill. It needs to go somewhere else,' she squeals. 'Don't bring it into the house.'

But as I look up to the house, I see a man inviting Joe in and the door shutting behind him.

Oh my life, oh my days, oh my shit. I don't know what to do. Mostly because I'm really quite drunk but also because I seem to have misplaced my shoes. How have I lost my shoes? We have a ring emergency. It turns out the giver of the ring is not in that house where Joe has just entered. Mrs Caspar missed a voicemail. If Joe hands over that ring to the person in there then he'll spoil their surprise proposal or worse, they will think Joe is proposing to them. The ring needs to be somewhere else, the person in there needs to be somewhere else. I have all the info, but my head is swirling, working out what to do. We can't ruin this. Joe's not got his phone so I try to find my shoes. Sod shoes. I get out of my car with bare feet on the super icy cold cobbles and creep towards the house. This is cold and undignified and not a solid plan but hell, this may sober me up quicker than that Coke will. The door is closed. Do I knock on the door? How do I fix this? Maybe I should set off a car alarm. I jog on the spot when I reach the house, pulling my fur wrap around me. The curtains are slightly open revealing a wonderfully on-theme Christmas tree in red and white with wooden decorations and I see Joe standing there, chatting with someone. No, I think they may be arguing. I run back to the car and scan the back seat, grabbing a lipstick, then head to someone's recycling bin where an old cardboard box is propped up against it. I rip off one side and write a scrappy message on it and return to the window, jumping on the spot, hoping Joe may see me. DON'T GIVE IT TO HIM. I look in again and see the man is sat down now, crying. Oh my, what have we done? And all at once, I think about the same emotion I felt when I saw a ring I was given only yesterday. My eyes well up. Or maybe that's from the fact I can't feel my feet anymore.

'Excuse me, miss... Are you OK?' I hear a man's voice say.

I look up for a moment. 'Santa?' I say, widening my eyes. I'm really very drunk. Santa's come for me. To tell me off? To save me?

'Well, not officially. I've just been at a party. I dress like this for the grandchildren.'

I readjust my eyes. Oh yes, that's a stick-on beard and there's no glass in his spectacles. He gives me a kind enquiring look while I keep jogging. He's holding a pair of house slippers in his hands and puts them on the floor. 'I'm also a podiatrist, the other eleven months of the year. Look after your feet. It's very cold.'

I slide my feet into the slippers, sighing out loud to feel the sheepskin lining around my toes, then turning to see his whole family looking at me through the window of their house, waving curiously. I wave back.

'Is there a problem here?' he asks. 'You're not one of those protestor people, are you?'

I shake my head. I care about the environment, but I don't quite know how I'd be making any sort of statement standing here in an empty street.

'I just need to tell a man in that house something,' I say. Except I'm not pointing at the house. I seem to be drunkenly pointing at a skip outside someone else's house.

The man smiles. 'Is it like that film *Love Actually*?' he says hopefully, glancing down at the cardboard sign in my hands, looking confused at the very red and manic nature of my writing that I'm smudging with one of my hands. There's two possibilities here: she's either in love or demanding a ransom.

'Oh no. It's just he's got a ring... He can't give it to him...' I explain, my teeth chattering. 'It'll ruin everything.'

'Because you love him?' he asks, smiling, a hopeful, warm look in his eyes.

'Oh no,' I reply. I've been crying which must make me look even more lost and lovelorn than usual. 'I mean...'

'Maybe just go in there and tell him how you feel?'

'I... I can't. It's not...'

'It is Christmas after all.'

But I don't feel that way about him. I can't feel that way about him.

Santa offers me a sympathetic hand as I stumble over the cobbles. Cobbles are the enemy when you're drunk, they really are. No wonder so many medieval people died young. 'Well, however this ends, young lady, please take care. It's cold out here. And Merry Christmas. I hope you get what you want. When you're done with the slippers, just leave them outside the green door,' he says, pointing towards his own home. I turn to wave at all his family.

'Thank you. Merry Christmas to you, too... Santa,' I mumble, looking down at his black dress moccasins. Now I know you aren't real. However, I'm still confused. Because I'm drunk but because it's not like that. With Joe. This isn't love. I want to say it, but I can't quite get the words out. I turn again to the window. Joe and the gentleman in there are chatting. I don't think they're arguing anymore. The other man is in a pinny. Now they're hugging? Please just look at me. Catch my eye, Joe. Notice me. Please tell me we've not fucked up here – I don't think my emotions could take that.

And suddenly, he looks up from that embrace and sees me. He raises his eyebrows, squinting his eyes, completely perplexed. It's the sign, right? Or the house slippers? Either way, he laughs and looks at me through that window and gives me a thumbs up. We're good. This isn't over. But the comfort and intensity of that look floors me, and the warmth of my breath fogs the air with relief.

Joe

'Evening.'

'Evening?' The man at the door is in Christmas jumper, apron, jeans, Timberland boots and thick-rimmed tortoiseshell glasses. It's that trendy baristo look that lets you know he has a sourdough starter in the kitchen and only uses Himalayan sea salt. He stands there for a moment studying my face and I can't read that look. Is it anger? Confusion? 'Who are you?' he asks, looking down at the dinner jacket. I really feel we're overegging the well-dressed look with these ring deliveries.

'I'm Joe,' I say, glad drunk Eve is safely in the car as I don't think he'd be too impressed by her drunken tomfoolery.

'Oh dear, are you one of those singing telegrams? This feels like something my mother would do,' he says in strong suspicious tones.

'Definitely not. Umm, I have a delivery for you.'

'You're well-dressed for Amazon,' he mumbles coolly, his expression changing.

'Oh, I'm not from Amazon,' I mutter hesitantly. I study the number on the house again, just in case it's the wrong one.

'I take it you are looking for Lukas,' he tells me.

'Yes...?'

He takes a deep breath. 'You better come in then.'

Oh. He's not the groom then. That explains why he's a bit off with me. I'm not sure I want to step over the threshold given this less than warm reception, but I guess the sooner I hand this ring over, the better. The hallway to the house is warm and low lit with fairy lights and Nordic garlands, two pairs of matching felt clogs by the base of the stairs, the smell of roasted meat wafting through the house. It feels like a Christmas house for grown-ups. The man who isn't Lukas closes the door behind me then stands there with his arms folded.

'Lukas isn't here,' he tells me, a scowl on his face, pointing a carving fork in my direction. Why has this suddenly taken a menacing turn? This feels like the start of a Christmas crime thriller. He's going to lure me in with wine and cookies and then keep me in the basement, making me listen to Cliff Richard on loop until the end of my days.

'Now tell me who you really are.'

I hold my hands up in the air. Do I run? Do I try to kick the carving fork out of his hand? I'm too young to die. 'I wasn't lying. My name is Joe. Who are you?'

'Theo. Lukas' boyfriend.'

Oh. OH. Mr and Mrs Caspar should really have run through these ring deliveries with better indications over who they were actually for.

'Your surprise tells me you didn't know I existed,' he says, angry but tears starting to well up in his eyes.

I flap my hands, trying to calm down this misunderstanding. 'No. I mean, this is a surprise but...' I can't seem to quite get my words out because it's obvious the ring I have in my pocket is for this man, right here. I can't tell him that, though, because that would ruin the surprise, surely. I can't give him the ring. He's also still pointing the carving fork at me.

'How long have you been sleeping with him?' he asks me, the tears starting to roll down his cheeks. He takes off his glasses to wipe them away. Do I yell? Is this a moment to yell or run?

'I'm not sleeping with him,' I say, panicked.

'Please. Don't lie to my face! Tell me the truth.'

'I can't... I'm so sorry... Lukas needs to tell you... I mean...'

'Please do NOT take me for some sort of idiot. Look at you. You're just his type... God, you look like a bloody model.' The carving fork falls to the floor, and he storms into their living room. I don't know where that carving fork has been, but I kick it under a shoe rack hoping he won't go on the attack again. I tentatively follow him into his living room and look around to see the perfect real tree, the impeccable concrete and white décor, the pictures of them lined up on the mantelpiece. Inside, he finds a tissue box and blows his nose loudly. 'I knew it. The last month he's been so nervous around me, on the phone, taking phone calls in secret... I knew something was up, but I didn't think it was this.' He continues blubbing.

'This really isn't what you think it is,' I tell him.

'Then what is it? You're in a dinner jacket, for fuck's sake. Five years, we've been together. We're down to adopt. I can't believe... I guess he's been lying to you, too, about me?'

'Just take a seat. Please?' I ask him. I have no idea what to do or say. He does what I tell him then looks me in the eyes.

'Theo. There has been a very big mix-up here. Please. I'm not sleeping with your boyfriend. I'm not gay. I'm not from Amazon. I really think you've jumped to the wrong conclusion.'

He seems to gauge a sincerity in my tone that relaxes his shoulders.

'But then why all the secrets? We've always been very open

with each other,' he tells me. 'He must be hiding something from me. None of this makes sense.'

I see the look in his eyes that veers between all these different emotions but the primary one being love. He loves this man so much, he's trying to work him out, to know whether his trust has been broken.

'Sometimes secrets aren't bad,' I tell him, trying to level him out.

'Secrets are always bad,' Theo tells me.

'But it's the season of secrets, isn't it? The gifts we hide at the back of wardrobes, the way we pretend to like our relatives, the white lies we tell about jolly men filling our stockings?' Was that the right turn of phrase?

'I don't get you,' he mutters, looking as if he's trying to track my train of thought. 'You have secrets?'

I shrug. 'We all have secrets. I've been in love with the same girl for two years but have never told her and don't think she's that interested but hey...'

I've divulged something to a complete stranger I didn't really need to and again he furrows his thick brows in confusion.

'Why doesn't she like you?'

'She said so.'

'Then change her mind?' he says.

I stare back at him. But how? I realise we've changed the subject. 'I just think you've immediately thought the worst of Lukas here. Maybe the truth is not as bad as you think it is.'

His expression calms for a moment as he looks at me, trying to work me out. 'So you're telling me there's a secret he is keeping from me and you know the secret?'

'Perhaps?'

'If I pay you, will you tell me what it is?'

'No.'

'But he's not cheating on me?'

I shake my head. If the little band of gold in the box in my pocket tells me anything, it's that I can be sure of this at least. 'I'd say that he loves you very much.'

He closes his eyes to gather his emotions, the tears starting to flow again and he leans towards me searching for an embrace. I don't deny him the comfort and hug him, but not before glancing out the window into the cobbled streets and seeing Eve, holding what seems to be a homemade sign up into the air. What on earth have you been doing? That looks like it was written in blood. DON'T GIVE IT TO HIM. Yeah, I got that much. I half laugh, giving her a thumbs up. Theo breaks away from me to follow my gaze as Eve drops her sign quickly and waves, stumbling over her own feet.

'I hope and assume she's with you?' Theo asks me.

'She is,' I say, curious as to where she's found slippers. I hope she didn't get them out of the bin where she found that cardboard. She turns the card and hastily writes another note with what I now believe to be the brand-new lipstick we only bought yesterday.

GET READY. WE'RE GOING OUT.

'I am intrigued now,' Theo tells me. 'Like out-out? It's Christmas Eve.'

'I will admit to having no idea where but, hey, it can't hurt to put on a coat and see what happens?'

'And you're not some spy/assassin who's going to drive me to an industrial estate and kill me?' he asks.

'I know the outfit is a bit over the top but no. Surely I would have killed you already because this is a terrible ambush otherwise...'

His laughter in response is more relaxed, more inclined to trust me. I'm just glad he didn't see Eve's first sign. 'And you are sure I won't have to get changed?'

'I think you look great as you are.'

He smiles at the compliment. 'I have pork ribs in the oven. I need to take them out first.'

I don't know if that's a euphemism, but I nod.

As he heads to the kitchen, he turns to me though. 'I was a bit dramatic before, thinking the worst. He's a good man, he is. I just love him so much. Can I ask that we keep that between ourselves?' he asks me, still unsure about me and my mission here.

'Season of secrets,' I say, shrugging my shoulders.

THIRTEEN

Eve

Ring 3: A 22k gold vintage band (circa 1927). For Theo.

'Your travel sweets are even Christmas themed,' Theo tells Joe as he sits in the front seat, looking around his very small but festive Mini. 'It's giving me vintage kitsch. You're a man of many surprises, eh?'

Joe laughs. Tell me about it, Theo. It was supposed to be a simple ring drop off and I was supposed to just continue napping in the back of the car, but it's now become a whole other mission. It would seem we have not ruined this proposal, not one bit. I took Joe aside and told him we just need to deliver Theo (and the ring) to Trafalgar Square. And Theo is going along with this. I'm not sure what words were exchanged but somehow Joe has kept the secret and persuaded him this is a good idea. It even looks like the two of them might have bonded.

'So you're also in on this, Eve?' he asks me, reaching around to look at me in the back seat.

'Yes,' I say, trying my best to keep schtum but failing as the excitement and residual drunkenness makes me grin broadly. Instead, I giggle. And I continue to drink because I found a stash of classy cocktails in a tin I bought last night. I put a finger to my mouth and pass one to Theo in the front seat.

'Any clues?' he asks me cheekily, clinking my tin.

'I'm afraid not. Oooooh... TURN THIS ONE UP, JOE!'

I'm lucky that Theo finds me vaguely amusing and turns up the music as I sway in the back seat to a bit of Chris Rea. 'This is Joe's favourite Christmas song,' I say, hoping Joe doesn't find me too strange for remembering that. I don't think he does but he does give me a look that tells me it was easier to drive when I was laid out sparko in the back seat.

'So, tell me more about your Lukas,' I enquire as I sway, mimicking playing a piano.

'So you know Lukas, too? Interesting... We've been together for five years. We met in a bakery in Shoreditch. There was only one sourdough loaf left and we were being polite trying to offer it to each other, so we split it in half and traded numbers.'

'A yeast-cute,' I say drunkenly, chuckling at my own joke. No one else laughs.

'He works in theatre, I'm in graphic design. We have a cat called Olaf. He's my best friend,' he says, a happiness coming over him to talk about his little family. 'Not the cat. Lukas. I'm sorry if I made you think he was anything but a good man,' he tells Joe.

Joe shrugs as he drives. 'Don't worry. You care about him deeply, that much I knew.'

'He's always been very open and honest with me so the last month it's been weird to see him so different.'

I frown; I can't help comparing his words to my present situation, thinking about the openness and honesty that was lacking in what I had with Chris. Maybe I was a fool for not having seen what was happening before my very eyes. But I don't react.

I just keep playing my imaginary piano, impressing myself with my ad libs.

'Are you guys going to give me any other hints? Is it a good surprise?' Theo asks.

'Yes,' I say, Joe pulling the car past the bright lights of Piccadilly, The Ritz and weaving into the streets of St James' Square. It's a detour through parts of this city that know exactly how to do Christmas. There are more Christmas lights than bricks.

'Are we going to a restaurant?' he asks.

'No.'

'We're not going on a boat, are we?'

I see Joe's body stiffen and I roar hysterically. 'Definitely not. Park up here, Joe. We can walk up.'

As the car stops, we organise ourselves and Joe comes round to my side of the car, offering me a hand as I step out. His touch feels different to me at the moment – there's something there that makes me not want to let go. I stand and stumble slightly on my heels as he catches me.

'Steady on there, Bambi. Are we still a bit pished?' he jokes.

I can't reply because I know that's only part of why I stumbled. Breathe, Eve. Park that feeling for a moment. You must. 'Let's go find Lukas,' I tell them in a sprightly manner.

'Trafalgar Square?' Theo asks us, staring curiously down the streets. We both nod as we edge closer and it reveals itself to us. Naturally, it's teeming with people, but it's always been one of my favourite parts of this city. I think it's how people mill and congregate here. They stand still for a moment to take in Nelson, his lions, they swan in and out of the National Gallery, they lie on the stately stone stairs and take many pictures. An excellent decision from Lukas to propose here. I shrug my shoulders as Theo wanders over the street to find his love, leaving Joe and I watching.

'What's the deal here?' Joe asks me.

'I have no idea.'

I turn and see that Joe is shivering from the cold. I link my arm through his and I feel his body lean and mould into mine. It feels right. I just can't tell him that. We then watch as a tall man stood at the top of the stairs waves to Theo, and his expression changes. It relaxes. That sort of moment when you see someone with whom you can be yourself, an attraction towards someone you know and have the greatest of feelings for. We catch up with him, trying to dodge the crowds, the street artists and a couple of men in reindeer onesies on a charity collection.

'Well, good evening,' Theo says, greeting Lukas, kissing him on the cheek. 'I don't get it. This does not feel like a surprise.'

'So damn hard to please,' Lukas tells him, grinning, strong Nordic tones in his voice. They embrace and he sees us walking behind. 'Eve and Joe?' he asks.

'Yes, we are so sorry, Mr Tolv,' I tell him.

'It's fine. Do you have it?'

Joe nods.

'Have what?' Theo asks.

Lukas then puts a thumbs up to one of the street artists and, well, I can't quite believe what comes next because a Santa barges past me and starts... well, dancing like he's Fred Astaire. That's impressive with that extra padding he's obviously carrying. And music. Out of nowhere, there's a band. The most carefully hidden band I've ever seen. And it's not just them, it's a chorus of women in red dresses, men dressed up as toy soldiers, who appear in some amazingly choreographed routine that encircles us. I'm talking dozens of people flash mobbing in costume but with style, not like they've learnt this routine in their bedrooms. Theo's jaw has dropped, he's half laughing, half embarrassed at the attention and being lit up by a thousand lights of other people's camera phones. Everyone around me is dancing. I feel like I'm on stage with *The Nutcracker* and have forgotten my part.

'What are we supposed to do?' I whisper to Joe, panicked.

I look up at him and he grins then offers me a hand. I still have alcohol flowing through me, so I'll take that dance. I grab his hand and he pulls me in to him, so that my body presses against his, engaging in a less well choreographed sidestep. He mouths the words, fake crooning, and I drop my head back with laughter. Why does this feel like it makes sense? I don't know what to do. Why can't I breathe? Kiss him. Kiss him again just to be sure.

But then the dancers stop, the music pauses and someone hands Lukas a microphone. He clears his throat and I hear a tremble in his voice as he says, 'Theodore Dove. You are the best man I know, and I want to tell everyone that, today. Everyone. You all should know this man, right here. I am so lucky to call you mine, that you have chosen me to be yours and I want us to be together forever. I want us to walk down the same path, I want to be by your side, I want to just be here, with you. So...'

Joe seamlessly hands him the box in his pocket and Theo points at Joe, laughing. Now he gets it; *that* was the secret.

'Will you do me the honour, this Christmas, of being my husband?'

Theo stops for a moment and the whole of Trafalgar Square takes a breath, a pigeon stops mid-flight, a bus stops moving.

He grabs the microphone. 'YES! A million times yes!'

And the crowd roar, people cry, I think someone throws a baby into the air. Theo and Lukas embrace tightly and kiss, their foreheads touching after to take the moment in. I cheer loudly and applaud. I am happy, I am. I'm smiling a smile so large it hurts my face, but at the same time, tears sting my face. I would be completely heartless to not feel the joy in this moment, but I also feel the fractures in my heart start to throb. I reach out trying to find Joe's hand to hold so I can feel something else. His palm meets mine and our fingers intertwine tightly.

'You idiot,' Theo says to Lukas. 'So this was what all the secrecy was about...'

'I thought go big or go home... no?' Lukas replies.

'So all those times you were in the larder whispering...'

'I was trying to negotiate rates with a choreographer.'

'And why here?' Theo asks him, amused.

'Because there's a man with a big column and a sturdy Norwegian,' he says, pointing to the famous Christmas tree at the centre. 'I know you're a fan of both...'

Theo cackles in reply. 'And YOU!' he says, pointing at both Joe and I, laughing and coming over to embrace me. 'I tell you, these two did an excellent job escorting me here.'

Joe and I look at each other, grinning. 'It was our pleasure,' I tell them. 'Mr and Mrs Caspar send on their congratulations. We're actually from the jewellers'.'

Theo looks down at the ring and back at us, understanding that maybe we've gone above and beyond our actual duties today.

'We are so sorry, Mr Tolv, that we nearly spoilt this,' Joe tells him.

The famous Lukas looks Joe up and down. 'Well, I should be glad he didn't go off and elope with you. Mr Caspar had you hidden away, didn't he? It all came good. Thank you, both, I appreciate you going the extra mile.'

Theo embraces Joe again, saying something into his ear and they trade words I can't quite hear before parting. Our job here is done, I guess. Other people start to gather around the happy couple to offer their congrats and the jazz band starts up again. And why the hell not? This feels real, like what the season and love should feel like, and I adore how that feeling is contagious. Maybe it will help me heal a little. Tourists in sensible shoes and outdoor coats couple up to dance, kids sway on the stone steps, and a policeman nearby sashays with an old lady with a trolley bag. I dance there on my own, alcohol still swimming through my veins. In my mind, it's a whole scene from *La La Land*, the romance of it infusing me.

'Shall we?' And then there's Joe. He stands next to me, one hand in his pocket, the other looking at his watch.

'Shall we what?' I say, giggling. I grab at his arm, persuading him that more dancing is what's needed. It's fucking Christmas Eve. Let's dance into the night like Emma Stone and Ryan Gosling, like we're in a film. There's even a band. I can't deny, this is helping me get my Christmas on in the most magical way.

'Let's get you to bed.'

I stop for a moment. He wants to take me to bed? I swallow hard. And something overtakes me for a second. I want to say it's the Christmas spirit, but it's more likely the spirit that was part of that Christmas cocktail in a tin that I downed twenty minutes ago. I step closer to him, our cheeks touching, his body pressed against mine. And there's something about the touch of him, the warmth of his body, that intoxicates, that draws me in, and I kiss him, the whole of that square just happening around us, the air standing still, his lips brushing against mine, his hands moving to the small of my back. Kiss me like this forever please, until Christmas Day at least. Take me to bed. Be...

But he suddenly steps away from me. 'No,' he whispers. 'We can't...'

I stand there trying not to look like the moment was jarring in any way. 'Oh,' I gasp. 'I just thought...' That grand romantic feeling is suddenly replaced by complete shame, worry, disappointment.

He looks at me, shell-shocked. 'You're really drunk. And you don't want me. This isn't the right thing to do, not when you're like this.'

My bottom lip starts to quiver. 'I'm so sorry. I just... I get it. I'm a big fat mess, I wouldn't go near me either.'

'It's not that at all. I just don't want to be that person,' he tells me, still holding me close.

I swallow hard. *That person.* I was stupid to think I was even a viable prospect, embarrassed that I would take advantage of our friendship and put it in such an awkward position. Ceremoniously dumped by Chris and now rejected by the lovely Joe. They need a new word for feeling completely and utterly crushed. The feeling turns to tears and Joe looks completely horrified, pulling me into a hug in the middle of that square, his embrace tempering out my mood, giving me a chance to at least hide my face from him.

'I just want to do the right thing here. You're amazing, you know that, right?' he whispers into my ear. I try to take in the compliment, still tearing up. 'Please don't be upset. It's Christmas Eve, Eve.'

I drunkenly wipe my face down on his shoulder. 'You said that already, this morning,' I mumble.

'I did. Shall we get you back to mine? Get some stockings up?' he jokes.

'Stop talking in innuendo,' I say, still emotional, still delirious.

'Or maybe we can put some cookies and milk out for Santa?' he asks.

But I don't reply. I hide inside him. Forget we ever kissed. Please, Joe. Just look after me. Stay with me. I'm sorry. The hug is so warm, such a comfort, that I close my eyes, holding him close.

Joe

Christmas Day

Merry Christmas.

I remember, one Christmas I was adamant that I was going to stay awake the whole night so I could catch Santa in the act. He was not going to fool me again. I set up camp in the living room with a torch and had it all planned out. He'd come down the chimney, I'd take a picture and then I'd have a casual chat with him, play it cool, explain why I'd cut off my sister's doll's hair because she stole my football stickers. Of course, it never happened. Like some sort of magic, my mum and dad managed to orchestrate Christmas around me when I passed out around midnight. I woke up tired, grumpy that I'd missed it all *but* with a brand new Scalextric that compensated for all that disappointment.

I wish I was that ten-year-old boy now, sat in that living room full of life, wrapping paper and colour. Because I didn't sleep last night. I didn't get to meet Santa. I'm not sure that I got what I wanted at all. Trafalgar Square was magical but confusing. It usually is, there are far too many exits and people. But it started with Theo mumbling into my ear, pulling me in for a hug to say goodbye.

'Eve's the girl, isn't she? The one you've been in love with for two years.'

I smiled, hoping the sound of the crowds and Christmas swing music had drowned him out so Eve didn't hear that.

'Please tell her... She's kind of adorable. 'Tis the season,' he pleaded quietly.

'Season of secrets,' I said back to him. I was in love with her. *Was.* It's important for me to start putting that in the past tense now that it's clear it's not happening. But then the kiss... Less a kiss, more of a drunken mis-aimed smooch. One that felt so incredibly right for the briefest of moments, one I allowed myself to get caught up in because it was Eve. But it was also wrong. Emotionally and rationally, it didn't feel like a kiss because she wanted me. She didn't back in that swish hotel, when she was marginally more sober, so what she wanted was a drunken snog, to replace her sad feelings about Chris, and any follow up would have taken advantage of her drunkenness and made both of us feel like shit.

No one wants to wake up on Christmas Day like that, full of regret. It's times like that when it sucks to be both sober and practical. You are many things, Joe, but you're not a dick. Your sisters would be very proud of you. So, I kissed her and I brought her home. Just not like that and I really don't know how I feel about any of it. All I know is that I've woken up on Christmas Day feeling a tad hollow.

I hear the keys turn in the door and the familiar footsteps of Gabriel walking through into our living space, jumping out of his skin when he clocks me sitting there without the lights on.

'JESUS! What on earth are you doing?' he squeals. 'I nearly shat myself.'

'I'm having a coffee. There's some in the pot if you want it,' I explain, pushing some of my reduced-price mince pies in his direction, 'Merry Christmas.'

'Merry Christmas,' he says, dancing towards me, full of the joys of the day that I can't seem to find. He gives me a big hug, looking at the sofa, unslept on. I remember the last time I messaged Gabriel was when I was freaking out after Eve and I kissed in the hotel.

'YOU SLEPT IN THE SAME BED!' he squeals, realising he's being quite loud. 'On Christmas Eve! The universe has spoken.'

'I didn't sleep with her,' I say.

'Oh,' he says, his face immediately registering his disappointment. 'Why? What happened after the kiss?'

'She got more drunk, there was another kiss but then I realised I'm also a gentleman, so I didn't take it any further. I slept on the floor next to her.' I say slept. More like I lay there, overthinking, making sure she didn't choke on her own vomit.

'Such a gentleman,' he tells me, sitting down at the table. 'So why so sullen this Christmas morning?'

'I am not.'

'Yes, you are. You're normally a morning person and you

LOVE Christmas. Anyway...' he says, reaching into his ruck-sack. 'I will see your mince pies and raise you some of them good cinnamon pastries from that Swedish bakery near the hospital. They were giving them away last night,' he tells me, placing them all on the table.

'Maybe later we can braid each other's hair and sing Christmas carols together,' I tell him.

Gabriel stops. Sarcasm is not my usual remit, so he knows this is something more. 'But you kissed... that's a good thing,' Gabriel reminds me, confused.

'And nothing. I got the impression last night that it will lead to nothing. I think I've been friend-zoned and the last thing I wanted to be is some drunken rebound shag. That's just not the way to do things. It's all a bit messy, mate.'

Gabriel sighs and pouts to hear me say it out loud, and I puff my cheeks out hoping it may contain some of my emotion. 'Oh mate, I'm sorry. I know how much you liked her.'

'It is what it is. It was a stupid crush and I just need to move on.'

'But you did the decent thing, I guess. Her loss. Complete-ly,' he says, offering me a pastry. I bite into it and for a moment all that sugar and cinnamon soothes my soul. 'So you've been up for how long?'

'Long enough to know Santa didn't come.'

'Bastard. I shall write a letter of complaint. We're the best people I know. And long enough to have washed her dress?' Gabriel tells me, pointing to her green dress hanging off our kitchen doorframe.

'Yeah, she stripped out of that at the front door. It has seen things it shouldn't have, that dress.'

So have I. Eve was drunker than she thought last night. After the kiss, she fell asleep standing up, so I had to stumble-carry her to my car. When she got through my front door, she then dropped her dress to the floor. In any other scene, a removal of garments in this fashion would be a precursor to high romance. But no, instead she stood there in her bra and knickers, told me she was boiling but then crawled up the stairs, like a cat. She may have even miaowed. And because I'm some mug who still pined after her but had some modicum of practicality and respectability about his person, I took her upstairs. I tried to protect her modesty, I made sure she was safe, tucked up in my bed and I washed her dress before the drink stains had a chance to ruin it completely. On a wool cycle as it says on the label because my mother and sisters trained me well.

'Here, maybe this will cheer you up,' he tells me, getting a gift from the sideboard in the living room and placing it in front of me. For a person who spends his life sewing, stitching and bandaging humans, his wrapping looks like he had a physical fight with the Sellotape. 'Merry Christmas, matey.'

'Gabe,' I say, patting his back firmly. I slide my finger under the brown reindeer paper, grateful for a friend who still loves me, who's trying to save this day for me. The gift reveals itself. It's a hoodie. On the front, a cup of coffee and the words HOT CUP OF JOE. I hold it up, shaking my head and smiling.

'Well, it made me laugh. There's also a Nando's card in there and I expect you to share...'

'Well, if we're doing this now...' I say, heading to a kitchen cupboard and then back to the living room. 'Here,' I say, handing over my holly-patterned wrapped box.

Gabriel's eyes light up because he knows how much I love him and that he loves a kitchen appliance. He slips his fingers under the wrapping paper until the gift reveals itself.

'YOU GOT ME AN AIR FRYER!' he squeaks, clapping his hands.

'Yes.' I wonder when Gabriel got to this point in his life. He pulls it out of the box, thumbing through the manual, bouncing with joy. It's a pick-me-up at least to see him so happy.

'So did you get all your rings delivered?' he asks.

'Only three. Two more to go then we can part ways.'

'And then you can go and enjoy your Christmas. Get all your stuff in the car today and head off when you're done with your rings. Be with family. Before you know it, it'll be the New Year and you can have a fresh start.'

'I was thinking that. Maybe I'll quit Caspar & Sons and just look for something new.'

Gabriel heads into the kitchen, pouring himself a cup of coffee. 'Or, you know, just maybe you could come back to medicine?' He pops his head around the door to check if I've heard that, hoping he hasn't overstepped especially as it's Christmas Day.

'Maybe,' I say reluctantly.

'I don't want to push it. I know you had a hard time with your dad, but it's been a while now...'

I am silent and suspect Gabriel knows that maybe he's drawn out this conversation a little too long. He does this every so often to test the waters, to the point where I wonder if my sisters have had a hand. But the fact is, I had to stop medical school. My dad got diagnosed with cancer and I had to put family first and help look after him. I saw medicine and the frailty of life in all its glory, close-up, and the reality was sobering, tiring. It made me put my life on hold for a small moment to take that in.

'And hey, I just miss a work buddy who had my back and would buy me coffee and hug me in the lift,' Gabriel tells me, trying to pick me up.

'We did hug a lot in that lift. More than men should...'

'No such thing. Your hugs would get me through the night shifts and make up for all the nurses who shouted at me. I love you, man.'

'I love you, too. Your buns are exceptional.'

'I know.'

I laugh and watch as he pushes another one in my direction.

'Merry Christmas.' A voice suddenly comes from the living room doorway, and Eve appears wearing her Christmas pyjamas we bought two nights ago. She looks up at me sheepishly and we share a moment to quietly relive what happened last night. 'You're not wearing your pyjamas.'

'Oh, I prefer a robe for Christmas Day itself,' I explain. The truth is, I wasn't sure if we should match anymore. 'Merry Christmas,' I say, getting up from my chair and going to hug her. There is some awkwardness there but mostly because she looks so fragile, which is a kinder way of saying she looks part drowned cat and part possessed doll.

'I don't want to ask but how did I get into these?' she says, pulling at the fabric of her pyjama top.

'Upstairs. You started undressing and I may have helped you so you wouldn't wake up naked and think the worst.'

'Oh,' she says, blushing.

Again, it wasn't the stuff of high romance. More like dressing a small child who isn't fond of the outfit you've picked out for them. There was a point when she kicked me and flashed me a boob. I'm pretty sure Austen never wrote a scene like that.

'Well, from where I'm sitting it looks like someone had an excellent night,' Gabriel comments, trying to lighten the mood, gesturing at both of us to sit down with him. 'Merry Christmas,' he says, raising his mug to her.

'Merry Christmas. I think I did,' she says, glancing at her dress hanging up. 'You washed it?'

'I did.'

'Joe, I can't remember much of the car ride home. Was I a nightmare? I'm so sorry,' she tells me, tucking her hair behind her ear.

I look at her as she sits there forlornly, her bare feet curled up on the seat to avoid the cold of the laminate flooring. I want to dissect everything from yesterday. The flat rejection, the drunken kiss. But my better side tells me no one needs that sort of discussion when they're hungover, in somebody else's house on Christmas Day. I'm not a Grinch.

'We got you home safely, that's all that matters,' I say shrugging. 'Look, I don't have much of a Christmas spread but we have coffee, juice... We need to rehydrate you. You resemble a very sad raisin,' I tell her, a little too truthfully. She doesn't argue with that. Gabriel heads to the kitchen as Eve leans over the table, whispering.

'I didn't yack on anything, did I?'

I shake my head.

'I also...' She holds up one of her hands where there's a plaster on her palm.

'That was from when you got bitten by that reindeer.'

'You what now?' she says, eyes widening.

I grin. 'You scraped your hand on the pavement when you got out of my car. It was a very graceful move, like a cartwheel but not.'

'Oh. So you did this?' she enquires, looking at my handiwork.

'I didn't want it to get infected,' I explain. 'It was bleeding a fair bit.'

Gabriel returns with coffee, juice and paracetamol, looking a little smug. It's a bandage and antiseptic, I didn't sew her hand back on, but I know what that smile also means. It means he knows I still care about her. Well, I'm not a monster. I used to hug him in the hospital lift, he knows that much. But it's also Eve. You don't turn off feelings like that so quickly.

'Well, that was very kind – thank you,' she says, still trying to catch my eye.

'He's good like that,' Gabriel adds, watching the both of us. I see him trying to salvage this. He's a mate for trying. 'So, where to today?' he asks.

'Dropping in on a wedding in Kilburn and then another

ring in Hammersmith,' I explain, watching Eve's face grimace as she downs her juice. 'I can do this solo if you're suffering?' I tell her.

She shakes her head meekly. 'No, I should see this through... I must... I might do this one dry, though,' she says, holding her hand to her mouth to burp lightly.

'That would be my medical recommendation,' Gabriel says.

She takes one of the pastries from the table and puts it to her mouth, sugar sticking to the side of her mouth and chin. I throw her a napkin.

'I see Santa's been?' she says, looking at the ripped pieces of wrapping paper on the table.

'Oh yes. I needed to show my man some love,' Gabriel explains.

'Who got the air fryer?' she asks.

'Me!' Gabriel tells her, hugging it. 'It might be the best thing I've ever received, and I got a lightsaber when I was ten. Shall we try it?'

Eve giggles, sipping at her coffee. 'If you like. It's made me realise, though... All I got you were those stupid Xmas pyjamas, I should have got you something else,' she says to me.

I pause. 'Well, I haven't got you anything either, so it's cool,' I say, pulling a face. Gabriel examines my face closely. He knows I have a gift. He saw me wrap the gift when we were watching *Bondi Rescue* on the television, and I was helping him wrap a sit-on toy car for his nephew. He's widening his eyes at me, confused, just give her the gift, no?

'Permission to buy you something crap from a petrol station today?' she jokes.

'Well, all I ever wanted was a Christmas-scented Magic Tree.'

She narrows her eyes at me cheekily and I watch that expression closely, still with pangs in my heart. All I ever wanted was you.

'Or maybe drop me to mine? Do you like olive oil? I have a set there that would be perfect. It was meant for someone else but I'd rather you have it...'

I try to appear grateful. 'I do love olive oil. I'll just ignore what you said about it being for someone else.'

She laughs again and I see Gabriel's eyes shift between the both of us.

'It was for meant for Chris's uncle,' she says but her mood suddenly drops at the mention of his name, on today, of all days.

A thought suddenly comes to mind that I've forgotten to tell her something in the drunken chaos of yesterday.

'Oh. Yesterday,' I interject. 'I forgot to tell you your brother rang when you were asleep in my car.'

'He rang?' she asks, confused.

'I answered your phone, he was persistent but also worried about you. He kind of knew about Chris, so I filled him in on some of the other details. I'm sorry if that was the wrong thing to do.'

Her expression suddenly changes, looking confused. 'He knew?'

'He'd been at your flat and Chris was there and...'

'Chris was there?'

Gabriel's eyes move between the two of us, sensing the jovial mood from before has shifted.

'I'm just passing on the message here.'

'Was Noel really angry?'

'I've never met the man before. I'd put his anger at a healthy eight.'

I sit there thinking how much information she needs to hear this Christmas morning. I don't think she needs to hear how Chris changed the narrative about their break-up. But it's Christmas, she should at least give her brother a call. She sits there contemplating what I've just told her then she looks up at the clock on the wall.

'Why was Chris at our flat?' she asks.

I shrug my shoulders.

'Well, if we set off early, let's head to mine before delivering our rings today. To get your olive oil, at least. One of them is chilli infused.'

'Yay!' Gabriel says, trying to inject some joy back into the room. He does love chilli.

We all laugh but I see Eve's expression telling me Chris still lingers in her thoughts. I saw her eyes cloud over again at the mention of his name. Whether bringing him up was the wrong or right thing to do, it's probably why the two of us are not quite meant to be.

FOURTEEN

Eve

It's Christmas Day. It was a strange feeling to open my eyes and a) not know where I was and b) wonder how and why I got into my Christmas pyjamas. But all those feelings that should have been fizzing about in my veins were replaced with some very empty feelings of disappointment. Reminiscent of the time I was ten and I camped out in our front room on Christmas Eve to try and catch Santa in the act, only to fall asleep and miss the whole event.

My first thought was, it's Christmas and I'm alone. It was only then that flashes of the night before came into view. Joe. I looked around the room. It was definitely his room, but he wasn't there. I shouldn't have kissed him. There was me trying to capitalise on a big romantic, cinematic moment in Trafalgar Square to see if there was a spark, but I must have looked like a drunken desperate lech. I did a lot of solo dancing and I may have shown him my boobs. Why on earth was I miaowing? But then I think about the words he used to try to let me down gently. *I don't want to be that person. This isn't the right thing to do.* Maybe I should be grateful that he didn't take advantage of me in a vulnerable position. Thanks to him we avoided an even more awkward moment where we would have been lying on his bed together, naked and trying to make small talk on Christmas morning. It's completely understandable. I'm not a catch at the moment, I'm the opposite of a catch. I'm a throw – someone you should throw far, far away. We're friends. I know that now. And friends we will stay. These last few days have taught me that he's too precious to lose. I hope he still thinks me worthy of being a friend at least.

'So, this is where you live?' Joe asks, back in the tuxedo as we head up the stone stairs to my flat in Brixton. My flat. I've brokered in a quick pit stop before our last ring deliveries today. I had to come here. For olive oil, obviously, but after what Joe told me, it is intriguing to me why Chris came back here – to chat, to make amends, to put this right? As I go through the main foyer of the building, a door to a first-floor flat opens and the occupant stands there and beams at me.

'EVE!'

'Mrs Milkov, Merry Christmas.'

She comes over and hugs me warmly, wearing her big signature trench coat and headscarf. We love Mrs Milkov because she shouts at delivery men and people trying to sell us Gousto boxes. When she goes away, I help water her window boxes and houseplants and like to meander through her house and admire all her embroidered cushions.

'Merry Christmas, lovely girl. Look at you! So pretty!' she exclaims, eyeing me cautiously. 'Are you off to a party?'

'Kind of. Are you off to your son's house?'

'Yes,' she says, her arm pointing in the direction of bags of gifts. 'I am just waiting on my taxi. Come, come, come...' she says, urging us to follow her. We go through the door, lingering in the hallway until she appears with a foil-wrapped box. 'These are for you. You're always such an angel with my plants.'

'You shouldn't have.'

'Nonsense, thank you for your lovely card,' she says, looking at me again, confused but scanning across to Joe. 'You're not the boy who lives with her. Who are you?'

'I'm Joe. Merry Christmas, madam.'

'Joe is a friend, just a friend.' I don't know why I grimace when I say that.

'And the other boy?'

She holds my gaze for a moment. She knows, doesn't she? She knows everything that happens in this building. She tells me when there are parties, when people come to read the meters and when cats come in the foyer and she has to chase them out with a mop. It's likely that she saw Allegra coming and going. I'm not quite sure what to say and can understand why she felt it not her place to say anything.

'I'm not with Chris anymore.'

She nods but her lips are pursed together trying to contain her emotion. I look beyond where we stand, and I reckon she must have seen a lot of what occurred here two days ago. Mainly because I can see some hardback books on her coffee table that were meant for Chris's dad and a lovely basket that was once part of a hamper. I like seeing everything repurposed.

'Can I show you something?' she asks me. She heads to a drawer in a table and pulls out a ring. I know that ring, unfortunately. 'I found this in one of my window boxes.'

I smile thinking about Mrs Milkov standing outside our flats, possibly with a large net catching what came flying out of those windows. I hope she got an iPhone 14 out of this. She holds the ring between her fingers. It doesn't catch the light in this dull hallway, it doesn't shine, not at all. She holds it aloft like I might want to take it, but I don't move, Joe studying my face.

'Finders keepers,' I whisper to her.

'Really?' she says, her eyes lighting up.

'Really. In the New Year, I'll give you the address of a lovely shop that will buy it from you. Or you can wear it, up to you.'

'I should have got you more than some crappy chocolates then,' she jokes, her face creased up with warmth as she puts the ring on one of her fingers. 'I'll shock the family today and tell them I got remarried to a twenty-five-year-old flamenco dancer.'

I laugh, watching the gold band slide over her wrinkled skin.

She looks up, concern in her eyes. 'Are you sure, Eve?'

I take a deep breath to see that ring for one last time, on someone else's finger. Sadness tinged with regret but acceptance that that ring was just not meant for me.

'Very sure. Merry Christmas, Mrs Milkov.'

Mrs Milkov safely in her taxi, we climb the stairs to my flat and I think about the first time I put my key in this door. Chris and I had been going out for eight months and under my arm was a potted plant that my dad had gifted us. It's funny how you recall moments like that. It was the summer. I remember I had denim cut-offs on and the first thing we did was get in the flat and have a shag on the wooden floors. I often wonder if the neighbours heard us. I remember the parking ticket we got as the van we hired was parked in the wrong place; I remember eating a Chinese takeaway on the floor, him throwing a prawn cracker at me; a moment when I was putting mugs on a shelf and thinking this was all I ever wanted, a space for my mugs and a feeling of security, love, growing old with someone in a third-floor flat forever. But now that flat is empty, cold, grey and the front room, unfortunately, is filled with a lot of opened presents that are half eaten, the Christmas tree dark and switched off, a strong stench of alcohol simmering off the upholstery.

'Welcome to Chez Eve. I'm sorry about the mess,' I mumble as I try to kick some of the debris out of the way. Joe looks around, a bit lost for words. The sadness just sits heavy in the room like gloom, like no one lives here anymore. I go over and turn on the Christmas lights to at least add some warmth to the room. Joe starts to sift through the place whilst I head for the bedroom trying to look for clues about why Chris was here. I spoke to Noel briefly before and he filled me in. He told me he found the knob end stood here, faking real glassy-eyed grief that I had dumped him, weaving Noel a whole catalogue of lies. He was so convincing that Noel even hugged him. I guess he'd had months of practice in lying. What was Chris looking for in here? Did he come for his passport to leave the country? Did he come to make amends before Christmas and have a reasonable conversation about everything? Did he come for me? However, everything is as I left it, parts of my bed stacked like they're ready for a bonfire. I sit cross-legged in the room, staring blankly at the walls for an age, listening to Joe next door, sweeping shards of glass off the floor.

'Are you OK?' he asks me, resting against my doorframe, and I see him looking at all the parts of my bed, peeking in at the relics of my shame. He comes and sits down on a floor space right next to me. Why does he look so well? His eyes shine with such kindness. My eyes feel different – raw, so very tired.

'Say something, Eve. Please,' he mutters.

'It was a shit ring, wasn't it?' I say.

'Extraordinarily shit. I hope Mrs Milkov cashes it in for a weekend break somewhere.'

We both sit in that cold room absorbing the silence.

'I am sorry, this is not how you should be spending Christmas. Just give me a moment?' I ask him. He nods softly. 'Did you find your olive oils out there?'

'I may have glanced at the set in question. You didn't tell me it had a holder and dipping bowls.'

'I'm fancy like that.'

He laughs under his breath, and I rest my head on his shoulder. He doesn't flinch, not like last night. It's soothing to know that he's here, to feel the reassuring warmth of his body next to mine.

'I truly am sorry about yesterday, too. The drunken kissing, crossing that line. I appreciate you so much as a friend, the fact I put all of that in jeopardy is selfish and wrong of me. I hope you can forgive me.'

He pauses. 'There was drunken kissing? Don't remember it. You must have kissed someone else.'

I'm flooded with relief to know I didn't ruin anything. He kisses the top of my head to reassure me further. I don't know how this feels but it feels nice not to have lost him, to still have an ally.

'I can't imagine having someone do what Lukas did for Theo,' I mumble, looking at the ground.

'Hire out dancers and a brass band to take on Trafalgar Square? I'm pretty sure that's some extra behaviour for a couple,' he replies.

'I mean, the grand gesture of it. You know? I always thought moments like that were cheesy, extreme – people should just know you love them without shouting it out into the world. Relationships should just be full of smaller, more private moments of magic. I think I'm just struggling to remember when I ever had that with Chris... Not even a small gift, anything from him that proved to me that he knew me or wanted me to feel special. Even the ring felt like a token.'

I hate to radiate such sadness on Christmas Day but it's like all these conclusions are landing at once. All the love I've witnessed over the last few days has made me realise mine didn't compare.

'Nothing? Not even a well-written card?' Joe asks.

'We didn't even have a song. I'm trying to think how he would have proposed. Probably in our kitchen. He'd never have opted for a grand gesture, and maybe that's because he didn't think I was special enough for that.'

My lip wobbles as I say that, and Joe puts an around me.

'Grand gestures can go wrong, too. With my side hustle at the entertainment company, I've had to show up at people's work before and deliver messages of love. Often with gifts...'

'Really?'

'I once had to deliver a puppy for someone's birthday. The recipient was allergic, the pup peed everywhere. It was a big corporate building in Canary Wharf. I got thrown out.'

I try to summon up a laugh.

'My mum used to tell me it's the sum of all those moments – the big, the small. I'm sorry you felt Chris never offered you any of that. Was he not a gift giver then?'

'No. He never really put much thought into his gifts. He was a big giver of random things. Candles. He gave me a lot of candles.'

'Because you like ambience?'

'Because he didn't know what to get me. That and a box of Ferrero Rocher...'

'For all those low-lit ambassador events where you want to spoil your guests.'

I cackle a little too hard at his joke, then I get up and head to the wardrobe to fetch a box, right at the back. 'Do you have a sandwich toaster?' I ask him. 'It's brand new. Never used. It also does waffles. I think Gabriel might like it...' I get out the box, placing it by his feet.

'A sandwich toaster AND an air fryer? He may very well explode with joy.'

I grin broadly, coming to sit back next to him again. 'I gave this to Chris when we first moved into this house. I remember the note I wrote with it. *I can't think of anything I want to do more with you than make toasties and grow old.* He never even got it out of the box. It's been in the back of the wardrobe. I fucking love toasties. Do you know how much I love toasties?'

'I'm going to guess quite a bit,' Joe says.

'Do you know what he said? He thought toasties were a bit basic. Basic. Who says that?'

'Pretentious wankers, that's who. Panini snobs.'

'Toastie sandwiches are things you eat together, on a winter's day, when you're hungover. Cheese toasties dipped in tomato soup. Those are the things that make a home.'

I think back to my mum who used to overload our toasties so the cheese went everywhere and stuck to the machine in yellow sticky cobwebs.

'Well, I will use it wisely. I'm a huge fan of cheese,' Joe says, still looking around this room.

'Don't ask about the bed,' I plead.

'I thought it was some sort of trendy art installation myself. Should I ask about all the open gifts? Were you looking for something? I did that once. I thought I wrapped up the scissors,' he tells me.

'I was hungry,' I reply.

'So was I. I may have eaten some of your Aunt Bea's short-bread. I apologise.'

'Aunt Bea will be fine without,' I say blankly.

'Who was the olive oil set for? Just so I can think about them when I use them?' Joe asks, a pained expression on his face as he tries to dig me out of my heartbreak hole.

'Uncle Arthur.'

'And what do we know about Uncle Arthur?'

'He grabs my arse when I hug him.'

Joe flares his nostrils. 'Fuck him then.' He sits there for a moment, thoughtful, but then puts his hand into his pocket, pulling out a piece of paper. He rubs his thumb along the paper.

'What's that then?' I signal.

'I... I didn't know if you wanted to read it. It was a note I found stuck on the fridge. It has your name on it.'

I don't recognise the note but flinch to see Chris's hand-writing on the front as he holds it up to me. 'Have you read it?'

He shakes his head.

'Can you read it out for me?' I say, frozen, with tears in my eyes.

Joe nods silently and opens it up.

Joe

'She seems nice?' I tell Eve as we walk up the stairs to her flat, having met Mrs Milkov from downstairs. Eve clutches onto the brightly coloured foil box present she gifted her, expressionless, silent, like she's walking towards the place of a former haunting, waiting for ghosts to jump out at her again. She's been like this all morning since I told her about her brother's call, and so when she asked to come here for a moment, I agreed mainly out of guilt. I'm not that desperate for an olive oil set but, before I extricate myself fully from my crush, I still need to be her friend through all of this. To let her know that even if this isn't love, I still care.

'I water her plants when she goes away.'

'That's a nice thing to do.'

'She makes me talk to them, too.'

'What do you say to them?' I ask, as she fumbles around in her bag for her keys.

'I compliment them. Don't you look green today?'

I smile but follow close behind her on those stairs. 'Do you think she woke up and wished them all Merry Christmas, too?'

Eve doesn't reply but stares at the red front door in front of her, a wicker heart hanging on it, placing her fingers on the gingham ribbon to straighten it. Oh, Eve. She's so quiet. Too quiet. She was silent in the car, too, deep in thought, and not even my Christmas playlist could help. And then Mrs Milkov showed her that ring. That really quite awful ring.

'Welcome to Chez Eve. I'm sorry about the mess,' she mumbles as she places Mrs Milkov's gift under the tree, switching on the Christmas tree lights.

I've never imagined where Eve lived but I guess if pushed I'd picture somewhere homely with a sense of calm and order. Maybe a cute simple Scandi style lamp – she looked like the sort who would read with big woolly socks on, totally Hygge style. What lies before me, though, resembles a really graphic crime scene. Somebody mugged this room off properly. It's filled with a lot of opened presents that look like a wild dog has had a go at them. I can't quite imagine how hard it is to come back here.

Eve doesn't say much but heads to the bedroom. I leave her be, digesting her silence, wishing there was a more useful, funnier, constructive way to help her. I try my best to tidy things into piles but notice shards of glass under my feet so head to the kitchen to look for a dustpan and brush. It's a small galley-style kitchen but there are hints of Eve all over it. Rows of novelty mugs on display on a shelf, Kilner jars of oats, couscous and pasta, labelled with her writing, a little ceramic bowl full of hairbands and bracelets. My phone suddenly buzzes in my pocket.

It is fucking Christmas Day and you are not here. You've made Mum cry.

Merry Christmas to you, too. I explained everything to Mum this morning. She was not crying. I will be home by tonight.

You didn't call me. I got a text and that is unacceptable.

I rang all the other sisters. I just like you less, Carrie.

> Eating all the parsnips now, loser. I hope Santa brought you COAL.

> I'll see you all this evening.

> Loser x Love you x

I stand there in the kitchen staring blankly at Eve's fridge. I'm not sure how you're supposed to hurry along someone's analysis of heartbreak but now I'm preoccupied by the vision of my sister scoffing a platter of parsnips, all for the sake of a sisterly grudge. I need to hurry this along. On the fridge is a Christmas postcard of a very grumpy cat in a Santa hat. You're funny, grumpy cat – I feel you but while I'm looking at it something else catches my eye. A note, a piece of paper folded in half with Eve's name on. I reach for it and put it in my pocket.

In the living room, I try to be helpful and sweep the floor but, hey, there's shortbread there, too, so I help myself. In fact, there are so many gifts (olive oil sets included) and I think about how she must have bought them all, wrapped them, for people who she thought were family. Gift tags are strewn on the floor in her handwriting, with hand drawn holly sprigs, and it pains me to see all that love, all that care wasted.

I look through to the bedroom where she sits on the floor, cross-legged, staring into space. I edge towards the door, leaning against the doorframe.

'Are you OK?' I ask. 'Say something, Eve. Please.'

She turns to me gaunt, pale, so very sad. And I go and sit next to her. I let her rest her weary head on my shoulder. And I listen. Because that's what friends do. I listen to all that heartbreak, all those times that shithead took her for granted, realisations about love coming to the fore. I'm happy she's coming to these conclusions on her own but, God, that must sting.

'I truly am sorry about yesterday, too. The drunken kissing, crossing that line. I appreciate you so much as a friend, the fact I put all of that in jeopardy is selfish and wrong of me. I hope you can forgive me.'

As a friend. Does that feel like a big fat arrow through my heart? Yes. But she's drawn that line in the sand now. At least she's said that much out loud so I can move on. 'There was drunken kissing? Don't remember it. You must have kissed someone else.'

She continues, skittish, emotionally all over the place, giving me a sandwich toaster from the back of the wardrobe and going on about toasties. But we sit there together on that floor, and I try to make this right for her by letting her talk, by offering small nuggets of wisdom, by taking that sandwich toaster. It also makes waffles. Gabriel will lose his shit. It will take time to heal from all of this and get closure. I pause for a moment. Closure. Is that what the note on the fridge was about? I think for a moment about the best course of action and reach into my pocket. She notices the piece of paper in my hand immediately.

'What's that then?' she asks.

'I... I didn't know if you wanted to read it. It was a note I found stuck on the fridge. It may be nothing, but it had your name on it.'

Her eyes widen at the sight of Chris's handwriting on the front which makes me think she's not seen this note before. 'Have you read it?'

I shake my head. The note wasn't for me.

'Can you read it out for me?' she says, emotionally.

I nod silently and open it up, scanning the words.

Seriously?

No.

I can't read this out to her. Can I? I take a deep breath. I am sorry you have to feel any of this, lovely Eve. And yet she does. And even if she can't ever be mine, it does pain me to see someone I care about so much be hurt in this way.

'My dearest Eve... I have no words to explain what you saw this morning. I am so sorry I've done this. You are the most wonderful person I know. You are kind, selfless, you care about people. I see it in how you ask people about their days, in how you cry when people tell you about their pets, how you'll make a cup of tea for everyone in the damn room. You ask for nothing in return. I love how you stand at countertops and sway to music that no one can hear, that you bite at your thumbnail when you're thinking really hard and always have an umbrella. I will forever be sorry for what I've done to you. Chris.'

She sits there to take in the words.

'Are there kisses at the end?' she asks, confused.

'Two,' I reply.

'I do always have an umbrella. My mum taught me that. It's to protect my hair. It goes frizzy when it's wet.'

My heart hurts to see her so sad. 'I'm sorry... I—'

'Please don't apologise to me,' she cries, tears streaming down her beautiful face. 'If I'm so kind and caring, then why did he do something so awful like this?'

'Because he's a knob?' I suggest as she blows a huge snot bubble out of one nostril that I wish I hadn't seen. 'You spoke to Noel this morning, right?' I ask her.

She nods, weeping gently.

'So did he tell you how Chris fed him a bunch of lies about how your relationship ended?'

Again, she nods, sadly, tears trailing down her cheeks.

'That was a coward's move. That's not how someone behaves towards someone they care about.' I grab her into a massive hug, trying to infuse some security and love into her. I care. Please don't be so sad. I'm here.

'I just don't get why he came back then? Just to leave me that note?' she sobs. 'If you found that note on the fridge then why was in here? Noel said he was in our bedroom, looking for something. I just can't...'

It's only then that Eve catches sight of something at the back of the wardrobe. A cream and forest green Fair Isle jumper. She pauses for a moment before scrambling over, grabbing it and then burrowing through the rest of the clothes there like an angry mole.

'The absolute fucker....'

'This is true,' I confirm.

'No, it's why he came back here,' she says, staring at handfuls of clothes, shaking her head. 'He came back here to get his jumper for his family Christmas party. We were going to match. There was me thinking maybe he came back to see me, but he came back to leave me his note and for his bloody jumper... The bastard...'

I'm half following her line of thought, half trying to placate her, but I see her tracing her finger across the patterns of the jumper and something is simmering, fizzing under her skin.

'AAAAAAARGHHH!' she screams, picking up a piece of the dismantled bed and throwing it at the wall opposite, leaving quite an impressive dent. She covers her mouth with her hands. 'Oh my god, I'm so sorry.'

'Did you just apologise to a wall?' I ask.

She cry-laughs maniacally. 'I did. Why am I apologising to a wall?'

'Because you're nice. He's less nice...'

'HE'S A SHIT!' she squeals.

'Let it out...'

'He's a cowardly, horrible, piece of piss.'

I'm not sure you can quantify urine in that way, but I like this process, this catharsis.

'And I want to say this to his face. NOW! I want to see him in his jumper that I bought for him and end this... properly,' she says, angrily waving a finger in the air, her face contorted with rage.

'Now?' I question.

'Now.' And with that she storms into the next room. The note lies there on the floor, and I pick it up, glancing over the words. She's angry now? I can only imagine her reaction if I'd read out what it really said. I scrunch the note up and throw it on to a pile of scrap wrapping paper. Were there any kisses? No, there weren't. Not at all.

Eve, I don't know what you think you did this morning but the management company has called me and fined us for littering and damage to the gardens outside. I'll send you the bill because that was all you. You can buy me a new phone, too, and that ring cost me £1K so think about how you'd like to pay me that back. We could have had a reasonable conversation about all of this. If you want to know why we finished, it's because we got boring. I don't want a life like that. I'm only twenty-nine and I just want more out of my life. I'll get a solicitor to chat about how we split the contents of the flat. That rug in the bedroom is mine.

FIFTEEN

Eve

'Do you want a shot?' I ask Joe, still here, like some loyal faithful chauffeur, as he stops the engine of his car. I pass him the bottle of vodka that was a Christmas gift for someone else that now belongs to me as I sit in the passenger seat, my knees jittering with nerves. I told him to drive to Chris's family home. I reeled the postcode off by memory and even gave him directions and now we're here. Fuck.

'I thought you were going dry today?' Joe asks me, raising an eyebrow.

'Just one shot for Dutch courage.'

He looks over at the bay window of the house across the road, filled with a giant Christmas tree, the buzz of a festive gathering in the background, then back to me, slightly apprehensive. 'So, what's the plan here?' he asks curiously. 'Chris is in that house?' He looks down at his watch. There is no plan as such, but we have about an hour to exact our revenge and I haven't a clue what that might entail.

I'm not sure what I expected when I went home to the flat.

Maybe Chris had come round and cleaned the place, perhaps he'd be sitting there on the sofa, contrite, wanting to apologise. We could have ended things properly with some sense of decency. But it was nothing like that at all.

And as soon as I walked in, I knew it was no longer a home, just a third-floor flat where I once lived, all good memories now replaced by the image of him standing with his wang out in the shower, nonchalantly. Like it wasn't even a thing. I should have thrown something at the wang. This may be my biggest regret in all of this. And he came back to this space, our space, not to apologise or close this chapter of our lives but just to leave me a note and pick up a Christmas jumper. Sadness is now replaced by pure incandescent rage. That thought alone makes me want to burn the place down. But I won't. Because my name is on the lease and other people live in that building.

I nod, biting at my thumbnail. 'Do you think I could scale that roof? I could pee down the chimney.'

'And I would veto that plan,' Joe says, laughing. 'Tell me about this party.'

'It's his mum and dad's house. They have all the extended family around for Christmas Day – grandparents and all. Chris is certainly there.'

'You want to talk to him?' he asks.

'I want to hurt him.'

'Physically?'

'I should have brought parts of the old bed to throw at him. Maybe we could put some dog poo through the letterbox?' I suggest.

'Look, as much as I'm in this, my limit is going to a park to look for dog shit on Christmas Day,' he says, amused, putting a hand in the air.

The sound of laughter that fills the car for a moment is welcome. What exactly am I doing? Will I just charge on in there? Embarrass him? Throw a drink in his face? This has the potential to just hurt me more, to shame me and not even give me any sort of upper hand.

'How do I look? Is my eye make-up halfway down my face?'

'Your eyes look... fine. Look, they know you, but they don't know me. Maybe we do what we did at that anniversary party? We wing it. We get into that party, and we just make it up as we go along?'

'But what if it goes wrong?'

'Then I'm there...'

I like that his words already make me feel more confident, more powerful, like I can go in there and do anything. We exit the car and walk up to the big blue door of the house. Breathe, Eve. You can do this. I press the doorbell, listening to the voices behind, conscious that Joe has put a calming hand to my lower back.

'Oh, my goodness! EVE! You made it! So lovely, Christopher told us you were poorly. You look gorgeous. And you've brought a... friend?'

Chris's mum, Miriam. For her, Christmas is about big earrings, crushed velvet skirts and a berry lip. I've always been the person she turns to when she needs information about her son – less a daughter-in-law, more her son's social secretary. Every year she gives me a foodie gift that involves chutney and an M&S voucher for exactly ten pounds. Heads suddenly pop up at that door like meerkats and the air sticks in my throat because for years, I've got to know them and made them my family, I have anecdotes and intimate knowledge about each of them. What am I doing here? Because for a start, I'm not in a Fair Isle jumper but I'm glad I'm not because all these graphics are not kind on the eyes. And then, at the back of the crowd, a face I recognise that drains of colour to see me standing there. I need to say something, anything, but I can't.

'Hello, everyone!' Joe says with a hand in the air, saving the moment. 'My name is Olaf. Lovely to meet you all. Chris, didn't you tell them we were coming?' Joe turns to me, his eyes sparkling, both of us trying to keep a straight face. We may as well have fun whilst we're doing this. I don't know what accent that is, but it sounds like he's going to play us all his hurdy gurdy.

The crowd of people turn to stare at Chris, still looking lost for words.

'Yes, Christopher – Eve looks perfectly well. Come in out of the cold,' Aunt Bea mentions. We both step into the house and the door closes behind us.

'Yes, everyone, this is Olaf. He is a visiting student from Sweden, and he's been staying with us,' I say, trying to play along.

'Hello, Christopher's family! How are you all? Hey, Christopher!' Joe says, waving at him at the back of that hallway.

'Marvellous. What part of Sweden?' quizzes one of Chris's aunts.

'Stock... holm?' he says slowly, and I giggle quietly.

'Well, you are most welcome today. Always room for two more!' Miriam says. 'Chris, do go and fix something for our guests.'

'Why don't I help?' Joe says, going up to Chris to shake his hand. He reaches for it firmly. Oh dear. This is not the time, Joe. 'Good to see you, my friend! Your family are adorable.'

Chris leads the way into the kitchen, and I follow them worriedly. Please don't fight. Kitchens are not sensible places to have these sorts of confrontations anyway. Too much hot gravy and knives in the vicinity.

As soon as the kitchen door closes on the three of us, Chris turns to me. 'What are you doing here? How dare you. And you're not Swedish... you're that bloke she works with, John or something. Why have you come here? What are you playing at?'

'Could ask you the same,' I tell him. 'Nice jumper, by the way.'

He narrows his eyes at me, and I instantly want to knee him in the baubles. Now? Shall I do it now?

'Both of you need to leave. I've not squared this up with my family yet. You're going to ruin everyone's Christmas out there if you do this now,' he loud-whispers, anger in his eyes.

'Did you square it up with Eve before you had an affair? What about her Christmas?' Joe asks, calmly.

'I don't care about Eve.'

'This is quite clear,' Joe replies.

This is not just sad, it's shameful that I thought this person felt some sort of love for me or that I loved him. He stands there glaring at me when suddenly the kitchen door flies open and his mother enters, headed to the fridge.

'Christopher, enough chat. Get these two a mulled wine.'

'I'll just have a sparkling water, maybe a juice. I don't drink,' Joe replies in his Scandi accent.

'At Christmas? How does one cope?' she shrieks.

'I don't drink all year round.'

'Whyever not?' she replies haughtily.

'Because my father suffered from liver cancer,' he says coolly.

He did? I glance over at him, moved by him confessing something so profound in this moment, but no one else seems to respond. I look at him and he catches my eye. You never said? He smiles back at me, reassuringly. Chris looks ready to either run out the back door or smash up a kitchen drawer.

'I am so thankful you're here actually, Eve. You know how terrible everyone is in there with helping so it's good to have my little catering assistant on board,' Miriam says with heavy hints of condescension.

'Did the turkey have its bath?' I ask as she pushes a mug of mulled wine in my direction. I take massive gulps from it to help me survive the moment.

'It did,' she replies.

'I hope it lit candles, and played a bit of Norah Jones, too,' Joe replies, still sticking with his accent.

'They bathe the turkey in brine, in a bin,' I tell him.

'It's how Nigella does it, Olaf,' Miriam adds.

Olaf. I giggle when she says his name. Maybe it's the mulled wine or it's because this situation is so bloody ridiculous. However, for once, I'll admit that it's nice to have the upper hand, to reclaim some power, to make Chris sweat.

'Come and look at my bird!' Miriam announces.

'But we've only just met,' Joe tells her and everyone laughs. Except Chris, of course.

In the corner of the kitchen, she unveils her splendid golden turkey. 'I like to dress him in foil and keep him juicy. Moist breasts are so important.'

'Indeed,' Joe says, trying to be Swedish and not burst into hysterics at the same time.

'So, tell me, Olaf, are you enjoying London? What's it like living with these two?' Miriam says as she checks in on some potatoes in the oven. 'They're a lovely couple, aren't they? Eve is practically family.' Chris's eyes glance to the floor to hear her say that. 'And are you attached, Olaf?' she asks Joe as I watch her ferry dishes around the kitchen.

'Yes, my girlfriend's name is Allegra.'

My eyes widen at this, and I hold my mug near my face to hide my reaction. Chris coughs and chokes slightly on his beer.

'And what is she doing for Christmas?' Miriam continues.

'Oh, she's tied up with work. She's on her knees with the stress.'

He takes a sip of his water and winks at me. I turn to the window to try to hide my amusement.

'How awful. Well, I hope she's as lovely as Eve.'

'Oh, that's impossible.'

I wink back at him. Charmer.

'Eve, your friend is delightful,' Miriam tells me, as she locks her arm around him. I pick up a sausage roll on the counter. Oh, Miriam, the same every year. You under-season the sausagemeat. 'You must come on through and meet everyone,' she says, picking up the platter, Chris following, panicked.

We all take a walk through to the dining room, already laid with amaryllis centrepieces and festive place cards and tables full of family photos, many of which feature my face. I am quiet when I see them, wondering how they will be replaced and stop at one of them, last Christmas. I'm sitting on Chris's lap, happy. Don't freeze, don't cry.

'You can do this,' a voice whispers into my ear, a reassuring hand on my shoulder. I can.

'Oh, it's Eve and her Swedish friend. How lovely...' It's Chris's grandmother, Clara. God, I used to crochet with you and listen to the problems you had with your knees and bowel movements.

'Nanny Clara, this is Olaf,' I say, introducing them.

'How great!' Joe exclaims, throwing his hands into the air. 'Merry Christmas!'

'Aren't you a handsome thing? Come here and give Nanny Clara a kiss,' she says, pulling him close and giving him the sort of kiss usually reserved for over-friendly giraffes. Oh, Joe. I owe you many gifts for enduring this.

'Come sit by me. Hello, Eve, darling,' she says, patting the sofa. We take our seats, Chris hovering over us worriedly.

'And this is Crackers,' I tell Joe as the family cat complete in his tartan seasonal waistcoat winds his way around our legs.

'Hello, Crackers,' he says with Chris in close proximity. 'Is he your cat, Chris? I hear you're partial to a bit of festive pussy.' I choke on my drink as Chris's face stiffens in reply.

'Don't you dare,' Chris warns him in a hissed whisper. 'My grandmother is ninety-five. This will end her.'

'What's that, Christopher? Is it the end of the party? That was quick. Is it time for bed?' she says.

'No, Nanny. It's just Olaf is going soon,' Chris says. I can't stand the tension. Are they going to face off? I don't think Joe would do that. Chris might. How long do I sit here for? Until I've had a few more Christmas canapés? Until the end of this instrumental Christmas album? Until Nanny Clara tries to snog Joe again? Or until I end this properly? I need to do this, don't I? We have a wedding to get to. Even if I'm enjoying Joe's torture of Chris and backhanded comments, I need to end this. Take a breath, Eve. You have done nothing wrong. You just loved him.

I stand up. 'So, I just wanted to say a little something. As it's Christmas...' I announce to the room, holding a cup of mulled wine to the air. My hand trembles and I look at Joe to help me steady it. 'I met Chris when my lovely mum passed away, about three years ago now and I remember I loved being a part of this family. You took me in, you had these big family gatherings that were always full of love and togetherness, and I remember clinging on to it so tightly. I held on to Chris so tightly because I loved being a part of your family. So, it pains me to have to do this because I will miss you all very much but... no.'

'No... to what?' Miriam asks.

'Chris bought me a ring for Christmas. I think it was an engagement ring.'

There is an audible gasp from everyone in the room, aunts put their hands to their mouths. 'Well, where is it?' cries his Uncle Bob.

'I don't have it anymore,' I whisper. 'I don't want to marry Chris.'

'But Eve...' Miriam exclaims, visibly moved. 'Whyever not?'

Don't say it, Eve. That is not your job. Ever. Don't say those words. Chris remains quiet. If he says nothing and puts this all on me then I will punch him. I will punch him hard. Say something, find your gonads from deep inside of you and do the right thing.

'Because I...' Chris whispers.

'What a cruel thing to do, Eve, especially at Christmas,' an aunt mutters.

'Was the ring not to your liking? We didn't have you down as that sort of girl,' says another.

I look down to the floor so they can't see me crying.

'IT'S BECAUSE I FUCKED UP, OK? Are you happy? I messed it all up,' Chris spurts out.

The whole room goes silent, someone cupping their hands over a young niece's ears. I stand up in front of him and lean into him. It's amazing how the scent and touch of someone you knew so well for so long can suddenly feel alien, can feel like the last thing you'll ever need. I reach in and kiss him on the cheek.

'We're done here, Chris. We're done,' I whisper.

He looks me in the eye for one last time. He seems sorry, sad even, but maybe I don't trust those eyes anymore. The room continues to silently witness everything when suddenly, a voice pipes up loudly.

'But how... What did he say?' Nanny Clara asks in loud tones.

'He messed up,' Joe says, in equally loud tones so her ninety-five-year-old ears can hear. 'HE HAD AN AFFAIR.'

Chris glares at him from across the room. Joe realises he may have said that in his terrible Swedish accent, a little too loudly.

'I should go,' he says, slinking off in the direction of the kitchen.

'HE HAD WHAT?' an aunt screams. 'WITH WHO?'

'BUT IT WAS EEEEEVE!' another thunders. And well, I

don't need to deck anyone because ninety-five-year-old granny rises from her wingback armchair and she goes for her grandson herself. Except she swings. And misses. Chris falls back. A tree starts to tilt. I hear a yelp. I think that was Crackers the cat. Baubles fly. A child sobs. Someone cries out about mulled wine and a cream carpet. 'YOU HAD AN AFFAIR?!' I hear as I back out of that room, ever so quietly, into the hallway and out of the front door.

Outside, I search for Joe but see him inside the car, the engine on to make a quick getaway. I take a deep breath. I exhale. All of it. I wasn't sure how that was all supposed to go. I'd imagined that to be wronged so badly meant I would rage, all my emotion would unleash on him, but instead I feel something else. I feel free. I feel calm. I look up into the bright winter sky and exhale, my breath misting the air in a huge cloud of what I think people call closure. I walk over to the car and open the door.

'Why, hello,' a Swedish voice says from the driver's seat. He smiles, his tie undone slightly. Talk about something which is starting to bring me calm. I smile back.

'I'm sorry I left you in there. Were they awful?' he says. 'I should have waited.'

'It's fine. You half snogged his grandmother for me,' I tell him laughing, getting in. 'You were amazing in there. Thank you.'

'I've learnt that my Scandinavian accent needs work though...'

I'm hit by fits of hysterics again, both of us peering over to a frosted massive bay window, hearing raised voices, watching Crackers the cat squashed against the glass. I can't quite understand the emotion, but I think it's me just processing the grief of the situation. From intense sadness to rage to a giggling mania, complete with tears.

'Are you OK?' Joe asks me, confused.

'Yes, Olaf.' I titter even harder to say that name aloud.

He laughs back, grateful that I seem lighter, less aggrieved, that I owned that moment and made it mine. This was all Chris. Never me.

'Well, since you're in a good mood, I have something to tell you, a secret...'

'Yes?' I ask, curiously.

'Well,' he says, hesitantly. 'I was really angry to see him. To see his smug face. To think how much he hurt you so... I stole their turkey...' He points to a large foil-wrapped package in the back seat.

'You stole the... what now? The turkey-turkey?' I say, staring at him in disbelief.

'The very one.'

'You're amazing. That's the best thing anyone's ever done for me.'

And I laugh. I laugh so very, very hard.

Joe

Ring 4: 18k white gold, floating round diamond semi eternity band. For Faith.

Yes, I stole the turkey. I'm not sure why but we've had three days of bedlam, so this felt like something else to add to the chaos. I escaped the melée happening in the front room while Eve shamed Chris in front of his whole family, I went straight into the kitchen, and I carried that moist bird to my car. I was angry – furious to see him but even more so because of that note. The venom in that note pushed me over the edge and stealing that twat's turkey felt like the next best thing to punching his lights out. I'm a proper hard nut, me.

'La-la-la-la-la,' Eve sings to herself in my car seat and I won't lie, it's a nice feeling to see her transformed from the girl who was sat in my passenger seat earlier this morning. She simmers with excitement over what just happened, seeming free of all that emotion that weighed her down. Balance in the universe has been restored and she can at least enjoy the rest of the day ahead.

'So on to the next wedding, Batman,' I tell her, reminding her of the task at hand as I negotiate the streets around the North Circular.

'I'm Batman? Surely I'm Robin in this situation?' she jokes. She looks over at me, positively glowing, and it's hard not to grin right back at her.

'No, you were the hero back there. I'm but a sidekick in all of this.'

'Hero?'

'You fought back. You found a way to draw a line, some people never do that. They just get haunted by relationships forever. It was a classy move.'

'And completely improvised,' she tells me, trying to play it down. 'I'm not normally that level-headed. I normally get dumped and drink myself into oblivion, not that I've been drunk at all over the last few days,' she jokes, not before looking at me and pausing for a moment. 'By the way, your dad – his cancer. I didn't realise. I'm very sorry about that,' she says, facing me, her eyes softening to let me know she cares.

'You weren't to know,' I reassure her.

'How is he?' she asks.

'In remission but it took a while – some ops, some chemo. I moved back home for a bit to help.' She's quiet, watching me thoughtfully. 'But it's why I gave up drinking. Why I normally just tell everyone I'm the designated driver. I spent enough time around chemo suites with people who'd drunk their livers away, so I had a revelation that maybe it wasn't worth it.'

'I'm sorry if I made you feel uncomfortable – I've hit the

bottle quite hard in the past few days. I'm not normally like that,' she admits.

'I know... You had your reasons...'

She puts a hand to my arm and I feel it all, all that sincerity, that kindness and it kills me.

'Thank you though, really. For all of it. For coming to my flat, for going in Chris's house with me. You didn't have to do that. On today of all days.'

I did. I had to make sure she was OK. I still care. She looks into my eyes for a moment, and I exhale softly trying to contain that emotion. 'Well, it'll be a Christmas morning I won't forget. They all tend to blur into one otherwise. I'll always remember that time I faked being Swedish, snogged someone's gran and then stole a turkey.'

She laughs, getting a mirror out of her clutch to fix her eye make-up.

I'd only do it for you. I'd only snog someone's gran for you.

'So,' I say, trying to snap myself out of it. 'Rings. Let's get this done. Nearly there.'

'Agreed, just two more rings,' she mutters, looking a little sad for a moment. 'And then after that?'

'Christmas. I'll probably drive straight home. I've packed my car up already. I could probably drop you in to see your brother? Your dad?' I suggest.

'Yeah. If that's not too much trouble?'

Nothing will ever be too much trouble. I need to stop this. 'No trouble at all.'

She cocks her head to thank me and then studies the map on her phone. 'Here, take a right here.'

I do as I'm told, navigating the half-empty streets. 'So, what's the bet on this wedding having some element of drama?' I joke.

'Who knows?' she grins. 'I sold this ring actually.'

'Tell me more?' I ask.

'His name was Emmanuel, and her name was Faith. They'd known each other forever. They were mildly hilarious as a couple because they wanted to try everything on and take comedy photos and they were just so excitable. It was nice to see.'

'And the Christmas Day wedding...?'

'They're making a day of it apparently. Just take a left here and park up somewhere.'

'Are you sure?' I ask, scanning for spaces.

'Yep, BUT LOOK OUT FOR THAT—'

'—SHEEEEEEEEP!' I scream. The Mini screeches to a halt and we both sit there, rattled but also confused. This is North London, this guy is not common around these parts. He stands there in the street, illuminated by the glow of the winter sun and bleats softly at us. I wave at him. A man suddenly runs into the road, holding a crook and what looks like a tea towel to his head, though he has Jordans on his feet.

'COME HERE, YOU ABSOLUTE TOSSER!' he bellows, bundling it up, putting a hand up to apologise to us.

'Are you seeing this?' I ask. 'Or are Miriam's sausage rolls making me hallucinate?'

'Nah, I see it.'

It's not just a man with a sheep. It's a line of children wearing white smocks, tinsel halos and wings, another man with an afro and a crown wearing purple satin pyjamas, a life-sized star in gold leggings and someone who has the unfortunate honour of being a palm tree.

'I think we follow that star then it'll take us to the church?' I joke.

Eve smiles and we park up and follow the throng of people to a red brick building and church, unassuming in stature but buzzing with light, music and farmyard animals. As we walk through the doors, we are greeted by a huge crowd of people in school nativity mode, and I have flashbacks of being an angel, wearing a re-purposed pillowcase as a costume. Kids run about in this simple church hall, with its shiny parquet floors, folding tables and paper tablecloths, a dubious looking fake Christmas tree in the corner that certainly hasn't been updated since the eighties. But the people, the calypso music, the wonderful chorus of smells of food and alcohol float through the air, putting a great big grin on my face. To see all the families around adds some earthy antidote to the normal excess of Christmas.

'Eve? From the jewellers'?' a voice says, and a man comes up to us in the sharpest of suits, a red tie and buttonhole completing the look. He embraces Eve tightly and looks over to me.

Eve gestures towards me and does the introductions. 'Mr Day. Yes, it is. This is Joe, also from the shop.'

'Please, I am Emmanuel. I bloody hope you've got a ring for me?' he asks.

'I do,' Eve replies.

'I believe that's Faith's line,' he jokes and Eve hands him the box. He opens it and beams – no nerves, no worry etched on his face. Just a look like a kid waiting for his Christmas Day.

'You are both amazing to get this here today.'

'We're just sorry we couldn't get it to you earlier,' I say.

'It's cool, the Caspars kept me in the loop. Are you going somewhere?' he says, looking at our outfits. 'Please stay. My family like a party so there's a pre-show, an after party – there's a lot of food.'

'Oh no, we...' I try to say, but he shakes his head and interrupts.

'Nah, I insist. Mama, come here,' he calls to a lady standing nearby. 'Remember I said we went to that amazing ring shop? They got Faith's ring engraved and look at this bling.'

A woman in a brightly coloured festive kaftan of sorts

comes over. 'You're joking,' she says in a lilting West Indian accent. 'That is some ring.'

'And these lovely people are from the jewellers' and hand delivered it here. This is my mum, Joy.'

Emmanuel's mother glances over at me and I can't quite tell if it's a look of disdain or misguided lust or judgement of the fact that I'm completely overdressed for a church hall wedding.

'It's nice to meet you both,' she says warmly. 'Emmanuel, have you seen your cousin?'

'Felix? No.'

'We've had an absolute nightmare. We were supposed to have a nativity scene and the boy showed up stoned. At Christmas. Can you believe the disrespect? Now I've got to find someone to be Joseph.'

Eve laughs and Joy looks at her strangely, wondering what part of that conversation is funny. 'Oh,' Eve says, backtracking. 'It's just... His name is Joe. You're a Joseph, right?'

I put a hand in the air. Joseph is the name on my formal documents. Joy checks me out again, her eyes narrowing.

'Mum, don't you dare... I'm so sorry about her...' He turns back to his mother. 'They're here to deliver a ring, not be part of your circus.'

She casts him a look. 'We are here to celebrate the coming of the baby Jesus...'

'And here's me thinking we were here to see me get wed,' he complains.

'Hush now,' she says, putting a finger to her lips to silence her son.

'How are you with babies, Joseph?' she asks me. Eve bites her lip, looking at me. We know what this lady is asking. I have to do this, don't I? We're in a church.

'I'm OK? I have nieces and nephews?'

'Then maybe you've been sent to me from God Himself,' she asks, putting her hands to the air in praise.

'I guess the only problem is my costume doesn't really speak lowly-carpenter-Jesus'- dad, you know?' I say, looking down at my suit.

'Well, my niece is Mary and she's not exactly a virgin, you know? We can get you changed. All you got to do is stand still and look nice. You both come with me.'

Eve puts a hand to my arm and looks at me. 'We got time for this?' she asks.

I pretend to look at my watch. I guess the longer we draw this out, the longer we can be together. I better go and get my Joseph on then.

SIXTEEN

Eve

I'm starting to think that it's some sort of conspiracy that none of these ring deliveries have been simple drop-offs. Because it's Christmas Day, and I'm stood in a vestry of a church trying to work out how to get Joe into an old curtain panel with arm and head holes cut out. Joe undoes his shirt and a row of children dressed as stars look up at him as he gets stuck. This does not feel simple.

'This isn't unnerving,' he tells me. 'Shall I leave the shirt on or off?' he asks, draping it around his shoulders.

I pause, my eyebrows raised. I need to stop doing this, the staring, the general lusting – but he's not making it easy. I focus on his face. I kissed you and made an absolute fool of myself yet still you stick around like the wonderful person you are. You bring me to my flat, watch me break down then come with me into my ex's family Christmas to be the ultimate wing man. I understand that we are just friends but he's making it hard for me to un-notice him. Even in the car ride over, everything he did had an effect, his hands on the steering wheel, the colour of his eyes, the way he was very polite and considerate at junctions. I need to de-crush from this man immediately. Now he's standing in front of me, top off, and I want to lick him. That is not right, at all. Not at least in a church.

'Ummm, maybe on? This is basically a fabric sample, you'd be flashing abs like a stripper. We don't want to excite the old aunties, I don't think that's how the nativity works.'

'Yeah, but on and it does look like Joseph has come straight from the office and thrown on a kaftan. Off it is.'

He takes it off and I avert my eyes for a second. I may be doing this too obviously because he sniggers under his breath.

'You literally saw my jingle bells two days ago. I believe you also flashed me drunken boobs.'

'It's different when it's in a church,' I explain, aware that my cheeks are flushing. I gather the smock so he can pull it down properly, but carefully as I can see that someone's handstitched this quite precariously. I smooth down the material with my hands and bite my lip.

'Don't laugh at me,' Joe says.

'I'm not laughing, I'm...' I hesitate.

'There's a business idea though, eh? A nativity with strippers.'

'The Three Wise Men with their "gifts",' I add.

'A shepherd with his big staff...'

I guffaw and immediately stop myself as those star children are still looking at us both closely. 'Shouldn't Joseph have a beard?' I ask.

'I have a five o'clock shadow? Maybe Joe had a go on the Gillette a few days before. Or do you have a kohl pencil, I could draw one on?' he jokes. I slip my fingers under the elastic on his headdress and tuck strands of his hair around to make him look less seventies tennis player and more New Testament.

'It's Monty Python meets Aladdin,' I say, stepping back to take the costume in fully.

'You are hilarious.'

'It's why you love me,' I reply.

And then silence. You don't love me. This isn't where this is going. I understand that. He looks me in the eye for a second. Or maybe. 'Look, when this is all finished, when we've done the last ring... maybe after Christmas...' I say.

But before I have time to finish my sentence, someone comes bounding over in a dressing gown, her hair in rollers. 'Hold up, you're the ring girl, Eve,' she says to me. I recognise her instantly from the shop.

'Faith!' I say, embracing her. 'This is Joe.'

She looks at Joe curiously. 'Mama J, did you seriously ask the jeweller to step in for the nativity?' Her eyes widen as she takes in how his smock gapes at the arms to reveal a fair bit.

'Why not? He was willing. He's my new saviour now. We can pay them in pepperpot and rum,' Emmanuel's mum says frankly.

'I'm so sorry,' she says to Eve. 'I can't believe you're here. Did Emmanuel invite you?' she jokes.

'No, just he wanted some engraving done on the ring last minute, so we dropped it in ourselves.'

'On Christmas Day?' she says, horrified.

'It's a long story. It's a very bespoke delivery service. Plus, we love a wedding,' Joe adds, in his curtain smock.

She laughs to herself. 'Then that is very cool. I appreciate that. But this? This is not a wedding. This is chaos. There's a bloody sheep. There's three men dressed like a camel.'

There's something about Faith that I like. I sensed that positive energy straight away when she came into the shop. Even now she just exudes cool calm, she's letting it all happen around here: the animals, the masses of children running around, the nativity and wedding happening all at the same time.

'And you don't feature in the nativity?' I ask her.

'Nah, I'm just taking it all in before I marry my man.'

'But you're so very chilled,' I tell her, in admiration.

'Oh, babe, I won't lie – I've been at the rum punch but what is there to stress about when you're about to marry your soul mate, am I right?' Her happiness shines out of her and lights up the room. This is a girl who is so content, the world could crumble around her, the sheep could eat her veil, but she'd still have her love. 'Plus, I've known Aunty J since I was a baby. I know what she's about.'

'Oh, so this is a proper childhood sweethearts thing then?' Joe asks her.

'Mate, born in the same month and two streets apart for most of our lives. Aunty J likely has pictures of us naked in her garden running through the sprinklers.'

'It's the wedding programme cover,' she cackles from the other side of the room.

'Don't get me wrong. We haven't been joined at the hip our whole lives but there's something there, I can't describe it. Some would call it destiny.'

'Or stupidity,' a pregnant woman says from next to us, giggling and waddling over. 'Love leads to this sort of situation if you're not careful,' she tells us, pointing to her belly. 'You must be my hubs then,' she adds, putting her hand out to Joe.

I jolt before I realise what she means.

'Yes, I am Joseph. Nice to meet you, Mary,' he says, shaking her hand.

Faith looks him up and down. 'Well, it's good to have you here. Eve told us in the shop she had a boyfriend...'

I blush instantly. 'No, I did have a boyfriend.'

'You did...?' Faith asks, her eyebrows arching.

'It's a long story. This is... We both work for the jewellers'. This is my Joe. I mean, we're mates...'

I'm not sure why I fumble my words. He's not my own personal Joe. To make myself look more like a dick, I play punch his arm a little too hard and laugh.

'Well, I like me a long story especially if it distracts me from this madness,' Faith tells her. 'Tell me everything. Joseph, be a good hubs, stay with your woman,' she orders us.

She links an arm into mine and leads me away as I watch Joe converse with his fake pregnant wife. I'm not quite sure how my messy love life tales can distract everyone, but she leads me over to a corner of that space, where a literal herd of women in matching dresses are doing each other's hair and make-up, pulling at corsets and downing shots.

'Everyone, this is Eve, she brought the ring,' she says, sitting down to adjust her eyelashes. 'So, tell me everything...'

'The short version is that I caught my ex cheating two days ago,' I say, plainly.

That corner of the room suddenly goes deathly quiet.

'Excuuuuuse me?' a bridesmaid squeals. 'At Christmas? Who is this man?'

All her assorted bridesmaids stand there aghast at what they're hearing. It is a good story, I guess, and I will admit to liking their collective shock and immediate hatred for Chris. I also like how much easier it is for those words to fall out of me now without me breaking down into a ball of blubbering emotion.

'Was with him for three years, caught him in the shower with a work mate. Found out he was going to propose over Christmas and yeah, we're not together anymore.'

The women around me all respond with a mixture of anger, cheering and shock. Faith comes over to hug me tightly. 'Babe, that's bloody awful,' she mutters. I shrug my shoulders, not knowing how to respond. It was awful. But it's happened, it's just a shame you have to live through these things first before they become stories you tell to a bridal party, none of whom you really know. 'How the hell are you still standing?' she says, looking into my eyes. I shrug, not sure how to respond.

'Where is he now? What about the bitch he was with? You

want us to track her down on social media? We can go for her,' one of the other bridesmaids tells me, her hand forming a full claw. I don't doubt her.

'Or we can hook you up!' one of them says, pointing to me. 'We can find someone to replace this dick. Someone better. We can show him that you've moved on quick and with someone who's much better than this... what's his name?'

'Chris.'

'HATE HIM!' one girl shrieks, pretending to spit on the floor. Everyone cheers and I can't help but laugh. I think what a situation it would have been had this spirited entourage of girl energy been at my flat that morning when I found out. But hearing them talk about replacing Chris and moving on makes me think I've found that replacement. He's been beside me the whole time.

'One of the ushers today is single. His name is Donnie.'

'He played on the same football team as my brother.'

'And he's my second cousin through marriage.'

'And basically, the boy is *hung*. He's got to gaffer it to his thigh it's so big.'

The crowd of girls are keeled over in laughter, one of them hyperventilating. I can't help but be pulled in by the joke.

'What are you girls talking about?' Joy suddenly asks, appearing to calm down the furore and ensure these girls continue to get ready for this wedding.

'Giblets, Aunty J,' someone pipes up and we all descend into giggles again.

'So then, who's the man you came with?' one bridesmaid asks, and I see a group of them looking over at Joe, still chatting to his fake wife. They all tilt their heads as he bends down to do up her shoelace.

'Oh no, that's Joe, Joseph.'

'Obviously. Boy's got assets.'

Joy nearby hears this and sucks her teeth. 'Wash your mouth out, girl. That there is Jesus' father. Have some respect.'

The ladies all cackle in reply.

'But he's not really though, is he, Aunty J? Unless he's a priest? Is he some hot priest?' the girl asks, giggling. 'I've got some things I'd like to confess to him.'

Joy throws a hairbrush in her direction. They all keep staring when all of a sudden, someone gives Joe a baby. A real baby that I assume is playing Jesus himself. The baby whimpers a little at being handed over but Joe sways on the spot and he quickly settles. The group of girls looking over stop in their tracks.

'I think I just came,' one of them mumbles. Aunty Joy may indeed have an aneurysm. He notices all of us looking and stops to wave, finding me at the back of that crowd and lifting the baby to show me, pulling a face to show me he's not really sure what's happening. I beam to see it. I don't really know either but amidst everything that's happened, despite everything I know, he might be the reason I'm still here, still standing.

Joe

Is it terrible that all my time through school, given I even shared a name with the man, I was never chosen to be Joseph in the school nativities? I was an awkwardly tall child so I was always given minor roles where they could hide me near a wall – innkeeper or townsperson – so to be told by Emmanuel's mother that I can finally fulfil a lifelong ambition to be Joseph in a church hall nativity makes me strangely excited, even if I am in this very cold church wearing a brown smock and sandals when it's easily three degrees outside.

'Joseph, be a good hubs, look after your woman.'

I look over at the very pregnant lady before me and realise that's me. I am the hubs. I've done roleplay before. Not like that, like a buff butler in fancy dress, so maybe that was all preparation. I am an attentive nativity husband so do as I'm told as Faith locks her arm into Eve's and leads her away, towards the bride's corner to hear her relationship gossip. My Mary keeps looking me up and down, wondering if I'm up to the job. That sheep runs past us again. I have a feeling this sheep is not feeling these nativity vibes.

'So, I know we've just met and this is a terrible question, but are you really pregnant?' I ask Mary, just to be sure. The sure way would be to prod her stomach but naturally, I don't do that.

'Probably not the first time Mary heard that but yes. Eight months. I'm all about the method acting,' she jokes.

'Come, walk with me for a bit,' she commands.

'To practise our scene?' I ask.

'You're funny. It's not Shakespeare, mate. Our script is literally ten minutes long. I need to walk to move the baby or I'll piss myself.'

I don't want that happening. 'Then we will walk. So, tell me about this baby. Your first?'

'My third. My actual husband is outside looking after the other two. Don't tell God I had other babies before Jesus, please.'

'We're in church, I think he might have heard that,' I tell her.

She giggles. 'Don't make me laugh either because then I will piss myself proper and I'm dressed in light blue. There's no hiding that in pastels.'

'I promise, wifey. Just get you away from Herod and entertain our guests.'

'Not my uncle with the myrrh? I never know what to do with myrrh,' she jests.

'Straight to the charity shop, no?'

She looks me up and down, still trying to work me out. 'Well, Joseph. I appreciate you loaning out your services today. Could you do up my shoelace?' she asks me, and I bend down to see that she's in Reeboks. I don't know you, fake wife, but I like how practical you are, since we have a long night of walking ahead. I do up the lace and stand up straight again.

'It will be my honour to be that baby's fake father for fifteen minutes.'

I put a protective hand to my unborn child but lo and behold, a person suddenly appears next to us with a real-life baby. No pushing, no blood, not even crying, possibly wearing Pampers. Mary didn't even break a sweat. It really is a Christmas miracle.

'Oh no, you're this baby's father, too,' she says, handing me a real-life child, swaddled in white flannel sheets.

'Yours?' I ask Mary.

'Nope.'

I don't know this baby and look around for its parent. I'm not your daddy, mate, but you are a cute baby. You have big cartoon eyes. I cradle him and he looks up at me. Hey, Son of God. He pulls a face and whimpers, but I start to sway and reassure him until he looks back at me and laughs. I know. We don't look alike one bit. I'd question the parentage, too.

'Someone's got a fan club,' Mary mumbles under her breath.

I look up and see a row of bridesmaids stood, looking over at me. Oh. Hi. I haven't stolen this baby if that's what they're thinking but I also see Eve watching and hold the baby into the air. Look, I'm a proper dad now. And I have a... donkey?

'Whatcha.' A grown man in a donkey onesie comes over and shakes my hand, a roll of gaffer tape in his other hand.

'Joseph.'

'Obviously. I'm Donnie,' he tells me. 'Mary,' he says, nodding to my wife. 'You hopping on?' he asks her.

Mary shakes her head, blushing and slapping his arm. 'You're the donkey? Is this some sort of joke?'

'Aunty J obviously thought I had the right credentials for the part,' he says, flexing his arms.

'What would they be then?' I ask.

Donnie smirks.

Mary shakes her head at him. 'Yeah, he's a king ass. Come on, you two, Bethlehem is calling.'

'I have brought you frankfurters,' a mini King says, laying a gold box next to the crib on this church stage and the crowd murmur with laughter. I hope he bought buns, too. 'I bring myrrh,' another king says to me, and my Mary looks at me sniggering. Yep, we will put that to one side for the New Year.

I can't lie. I've done some ridiculous things over the last two days, but this may be one of my favourite things I've subjected myself to so far this Christmas. I feel powerful playing Joseph. I think we overlook his role as guardian and protector far too much. And I'll admit there is some sort of magic to be had in this church, too. From the majestic tree to the candles to the red and white wedding flowers that line the pews and altar. I have to admit, too, that I'm enjoying bringing the amateur drama to this wedding. It's a homely inclusive put-together nativity: pet-shop hay strewn across the altar, the hand-cut stars stuck to the curtains, the kids sat cross-legged to the front, dressed as lambs, picking their noses. There have been gaps throughout to belt out some Christmas carols, sung at such volume it would possibly take the windows off this place. I don't sing obviously, I mime with boyband feeling which makes Eve, seven pews back, giggle. Christmas is here. Eve is still here, too. As we all take our final tableau positions for *Away in a Manger*, I see her singing along, watching, smiling. I try not to stare. How do you turn off feelings for someone? I really wish I knew.

'Joseph, be a babe and grab Jesus for me,' Mary tells me. I feel like she would have said that a lot to her man. Oh, we're done. I do as I'm told as people clap and cheer loudly and I hold my fake son to my chest, swaddled in his white flannelette smock and robes. We filter off the stage and I make a beeline for Eve, looking around to see if anyone wants to claim this baby. I only agreed to do this father thing temporarily.

'It's OK, buddy. I got you.' Jesus doesn't seem too bothered and places his palms face down on my chest, finding warmth and shutting his eyes. I scooch over next to Eve, who is looking curiously at me.

'You have a baby...'

'I do. Such is the nature of the nativity,' I say wisely.

'Does he have a name?' she asks, pulling the blanket over to cover one of his chubby legs.

'He's not told me. I'm going with Jesus,' I say, leaning my head back to examine his face. 'I'll know for sure if he starts turning the water into wine later on in the reception.'

She giggles quietly. 'Well, he looks immensely peaceful. Well done.' She then looks down and blushes and I peer down to see my robes have opened up to reveal way too much thigh. 'Cover yourself up. That is not appropriate in the House of God,' she tells me. 'The holy water will start to boil.'

'Thank you,' I say, laughing but pulling a face. 'How did Joseph cope? There was no underwear in that time. Do you think he flashed wang a lot in public?'

'No doubt,' she says, giggling.

More nativity crew come into our pew and Eve and I move up so she's sitting next to me, close to me, our legs touching. I glance at her and see she continues to blush, like she's embarrassed, flustered. This is crossing that friend line, isn't it?

'Can I say that since Chris's house, you look a bit more relaxed?' I say to try and chill her out. 'A bit more like you might enjoy your Christmas?'

She takes a deep cleansing breath. 'I was enjoying it regardless, I think. You know, weirdly, the last few days have been fun. All of it really.'

'I think I've had fun, too,' I tell her.

Oh, Eve. What is this that we've developed over the last few days? I can't quite read what we are anymore, but I think I helped you and that feels important. After we deliver the last ring, it's time to get her back to her family and then after the new year, it'll be time for us both to move on, in whatever direction that might be. It breaks my heart but at least we had these three days.

I squeeze her hand and there's a moment where she looks at me and all these people, the music, the lights, the sound – it all stops. I exhale gently as she smiles at me again, a magical warming feeling from the contact. What is this? Did she feel that, too?

'Joe,' she whispers.

'I...' But we both suddenly jump out of our skins as an organ fires up, doors open and the bride appears in a doorway, ethereal, beaming, flanked by many bridesmaids. I count twenty, from little kids dressed as angels to older teens who've gone strong on the cleavage and fake lashes. But a radiance and joy from that bride tells me everything is alright with the world. I look over at Eve, silently watching this train of people, her face lit up to see this whole wedding unfold with such happiness.

'Merry Christmas, Eve,' I tell her.

'Merry Christmas, Joe.'

She turns to me. This is a moment. I can feel it. It feels warm. But maybe too warm. Hold up. That's not a feeling. I know that because it comes with a sound. Not just any sound, a sound like a drain has just emptied its contents, echoing through that church. People turn to each other in horror. Eve covers her mouth with her hands to stop her laughter.

'What the hell was that?'

It's my turn to try and restrain my giggles. Does she think

that sound came from me? 'Holy shit,' I whisper. Quite literally. I don't think there's a nappy in the world that can contain that.

She faffs, trying to cover the baby but also looking horrified at what's coming out of his nappy. 'It won't stop coming. It's like a mudslide,' Eve says, aghast. She whips off my headdress and tries to use it as an extra layer of protection on that little baby's butt.

How is he still sleeping through all of this? A lady down the pew gives us some serious side-eye. Hey lady, this is the Son of God. I'm quite happy to hand this kid back now. Any takers? Eve can't stop giggling and I shake my head at her, chuckling back as she gets a pack of tissues out of her handbag. That'll work. And for a moment, it's just nice to see tears in her eyes for the right reason, to see her laughing, healing, knowing that any crap Christmas memories from this year may be replaced by this crappy one instead.

SEVENTEEN

Eve

Can you fancy someone more after seeing them in a nativity? I feel that's slightly sacrilegious but there were little things Joe did at the front of that church that made my whole body sigh. The way he high-fived a very tiny angel, the way he kept putting a reassuring hand to Mary's back, the way he handled the baby Jesus himself sweetly, even when he crapped his pants in the most dramatic and explosive of ways. But now I can't quite handle being around him. Every time he's close, flashing thigh or cracking jokes, I giggle. The thigh is firm. I knew that already because I've seen him in the little jingly shorts, you could see there was definition, but that feels like a different time. B.C. Before Crush. Jesus knows.

Given he's spurned my advances already, there's just no clear way to say this out loud either. We could extend these Christmas adventures. How about it? I know we have one more ring to deliver but I wish it were ten more. We could drive around in your little car forever. Until the New Year at least. Is it weird that this is the fantasy I want to live out? Driving around London, living off fast food and meal deals and delivering happiness to other people, whilst we keep listening to his Christmas playlist on loop, just the two of us in our little festive bubble.

'I may need you to smell me again,' Joe asks me, back in his tuxedo now, in the back seat again, using our baby wipes to try and de-poop himself. I laugh watching him trying to sanitise his chest, thinking about how someone suggested he have a quick wash in the baptismal font. I politely decline the opportunity of smelling him, just because it feels dangerous to get that close to him again. I need to keep a reasonable distance and just see the rest of the day out.

We sit there in his car as the sky starts to change colour and the sound of Faith and Emmanuel's reception echoes down the street. The wedding is done. Except it's not. I've never seen such a loud wedding – from the heckling cheers, to the big gospel singing, to a relative two rows down who was sobbing with joy. For all the pretty, serene and dignified weddings I'd been to, this felt brilliant, like how every wedding should be, a huge exclamation of joy and love. For now, the church still simmers in that emotion. It's Christmas and it's time for people to party in the hall next door. If the wedding was loud then I anticipate the reception will be heard in the next borough.

'Despite the poo-nami, can I just say you were an excellent Joseph?' I tell him as he tries to get himself cleaned up.

'I thought so. Did you take any photos I could show my mum? She'll be made up,' he asks.

'Unfortunately not,' I say, grinning. He was also so good with Jesus. The way he let him grip on to one of his fingers, the way when he handed him over to his real mother, Jesus smiled back at him as if he knew of his innate goodness. Stop it, Eve. My phone ringing gets my attention and I answer it.

'WHERE ARE YOU?' a voice hollers out, making the windows of the car rattle. Noel.

'Noel...' I did give Noel a call this morning, sitting on the end of Joe's bed. We exchanged Christmas greetings, but I mostly sobbed to have to recount all that Chris drama. He sobbed back. But even that feels like a lifetime ago, where I was and felt like another person.

'YOU SAID YOU'D BE HERE BY 3 P.M. AND IT'S 3.05 P.M.!' He's not even on speaker but I am sure Joe can hear all of this. It's not even alcohol doing this. He's just loud, dramatic and welcomes the opportunity to embarrass me at every given turn. I did tell him this morning about the rings, but I also reassured him that he would have the pleasure of seeing my face today. It's nice that he's been clock-watching, waiting until we were reunited.

'We just have one more ring to deliver and then I'll be there, I promise.' I put the call on speaker to save my ear drums.

'EEEEEEVVVVVEEEEE!' I hear the hum of Christmas and plates rattling behind him and someone telling a joke. I know that laugh.

'Tell Dad I'll be there. I'll definitely be there. Where is he?'

'Dad is busy cooking chicken. We ran out of turkey.'

'How did you run out of turkey?'

'We didn't anticipate the rush. Is that reggaeton music I can hear? Where are you? You told me you've been delivering rings, you're such a liar. You're at a gig.'

I'm still aghast that they've run out of turkey, a Christmas staple. I look at the rearview mirror where Joe sits earwigging but also pointing downwards. Is he pointing to his crotch? I hope not. I may pass out. Oh, he's pointing to the seat next to him. Our stolen turkey, still chilling in the back of his Mini. I forgot that was even there.

'Hold up, Noel.' I cover the mouthpiece, turning in my seat. 'Did you not want that?' I ask Joe.

'No? I can't take it all the way to Brighton with me. It's too big for my fridge as well. If Noel needs a turkey, he should have it,' he explains. 'We can drop it off before the last ring.'

'Really?' I reply, surprised but also excited that I may see my family sooner rather than later.

'Yeah. As long as they won't mind me dropping in, though? I feel very overdressed.'

'Oh, where we're going, you'll fit right in,' I explain, laughing. 'Actually, you don't have that elf outfit in the boot, do you?'

There is something about coming back to places you know that can really reset your soul, that make you feel safe and happy, and this is one of those places. As we park up outside, I can see the faint outline of colourful paper hats, visible through the fogged-up glass. It looks like the cosiest of Christmas parties and I can't wait to get inside.

Joe, however, looks up at the building, confused. 'Your dad owns a restaurant?' he asks me.

'Not really. The people who own the restaurant open it up and my family are part of a group of who cook Christmas dinner for people in the community – people who maybe don't have family. To give them somewhere to be.' I look up at the restaurant, memories of the parties we've held here making my heart sing.

'That's amazing,' he mumbles.

'You should come in, meet everyone, you'll love them.' However, before I have a chance to say anything else, there's a rapping on the car window and someone stands there with a vape hanging out of his hand. He cups his hands looking into the car.

'YOU!' he says, opening the door and pulling me onto the pavement and into a hearty embrace. We stand there for far too long, but I guess that's allowed when it's your brother.

'About bloody time,' he tells me, looking me in the face. 'I was so worried about you. I'm your shitting twin. I don't know when that stopped meaning something!'

'I'm sorry?'

'She's sorry,' he says, laughing. 'I love you so much, you daft girl. I love that you're here. It's CHRISTMAS!' He makes me jump up and down with him on the spot and I join in because it's Noel but also because I'm here, this feels like home, a chance to finally let loose and be myself. Another familiar figure comes out of the restaurant and heads over to me, too, wrapping his arms around me and lifting me a little off the ground. I lied before, this feels like home. Dad. I stand back to look at both of them, tears in my eyes. Oh my life, they're in matching Santa jumpers with little dangly legs.

'EEEEEVVVVVE! Merry bloody Christmas! Look at you, you've gone all fancy on us. You're here,' he says, pushing me back to study my face. 'Noel told me everything. Are you alright?'

'Good news travels fast then,' I mumble. 'I'm sorry I've been so quiet and absent. I just didn't know what to do.'

Dad shakes his head. 'Well, you're here now. You take your time with all of that. We're just glad you're safe.'

'For the record, though, he is an absolute crapbag!' Noel adds, jutting an angry finger into the air. 'I'll kill him. Can I kill him? We can run him over as he comes out of work. I have it all planned out,' he shouts before clocking someone else sitting there in the car, listening to everything. 'Who are you?'

Joe gets out of the car slowly, loitering by the passenger side. 'I am Joe,' he says, waving.

'The friend on the phone?' Noel quizzes him.

'The very one.'

Noel nods at him, his face a cold mask, obviously trying to work him out.

'Just to clarify, my dad is a tiler and plasterer, and my brother works in an optician's, they're not hardened London gang lords,' I say, trying to lighten the mood. 'Dad, this is Joe. Joe, this is my dad, Nick, and my brother, Noel.' He heads over and shakes both of their hands.

'Did you steal him from a hotel concierge?' Noel asks, eyeing him curiously.

'No, don't be rude.'

'Please tell me you've done some harm to Chris on my sister's behalf?' Noel asks Joe.

Joe shrugs. 'I haven't. She did that pretty well all on her own.'

Noel beams at me and hugs me again.

'I also come bearing gifts,' I tell them, opening the door, and putting the seat forward to show them the turkey still resplendent in his foil jacket, sitting on the back seat.

'That's my Christmas gift?' my dad bellows. 'I'm more of a Toblerone man.' His laugh echoes down this quiet street. 'Bloody glad to see it. Where on earth did you get this?' he asks me.

'Don't ask,' I say, winking at Joe. Joe helps deliver it to the kitchen with my dad as I follow into the restaurant, the doors opening and the familiarity of that place hitting me all at once. Inside there are dozens of people, some I know, some I don't, all in different states of inebriation and merriment: Mr Callaghan, masterful on a piano in a corner, his daughter, Lucy, belting out some Christmas tunes. The restaurant has a wonderful line in foil garlands, and a glowing LED tree, everyone in various states of Christmas fancy dress. I was right, Joe's jingly shorts would have gone down a treat here.

'How's it gone today?' I ask Noel.

'A treat – the U3A put the word out so a few extra faces. Everyone's just been asking about you. You've been missed.'

'I missed it,' I say, watching as Lucy gets everyone in that room to sing along. This is why we make sure Lucy's here, that and she also flirts with all the old men and makes their year. I

think about previous years, sometimes dragging Chris along
against his will after his family do, memories of him sulking in a
corner with his phone being absolutely useless, and suddenly it
feels good to know I can ride this party solo and can stay for as
long as the fun times continue. That's a good feeling. Another
familiar face bounds out of the kitchen and runs towards me.
Josie.

'ABOUT BLOODY TIME! Come here, you big lemon!'
She wraps her arms around me. I met Josie at university and
ever since I found out her family do this sometimes at Christmas, I've joined in and made it our family thing, too. It's always
warmed the cockles to spread some festive love and it's become
a highlight of the season so despite all that's happened with
Chris, I'm glad I'm here. For all I've lost, I'm glad I get to
submerge myself in all this joy, amongst all these people I love
and trust so dearly.

'I have to be quick because there's a turkey to carve but first
things first, who is the turkey boy? And second, Chris is a
wanker. Humungo wanker of serious proportions. I officially
hate him.'

I turn to Noel who obviously spread the word for me. I
don't know whether to be grateful that I don't have to re-tell that
story again.

'He *is* a wanker. The turkey boy is Joe.'

'You moved on fast?' she says, her wide eyes telling me she's
also been indulging in a Christmas tipple in that kitchen.

'He's a work colleague. Where is he?'

'I left him with your dad. They're chatting now.' She points
towards the kitchen where I see them both sharing a joke
through the glass panels of the door. 'I have to go but I want a
drink later, yes?' she says, running off in her holly headband.
'Tell Lucy to stop sitting on people's laps, too.'

She runs back to the kitchen as Noel and I stand here to

take all of it in for a moment: the music, the lighting, the low-level party chatter that makes a room come to life.

'I'm glad you're here,' Noel says, perching his head on my shoulder. I turn and embrace him tightly. 'I'm sorry I was mean to you when I thought you weren't coming today,' he tells me.

'Well, now you know why. I'm sorry I didn't tell you at the time. It'd just happened, I was all over the place.'

He winces and shakes his head. 'So do Dad and I have you for the rest of Christmas?' he asks me.

I nod, swaying with him to the music. 'Almost. I have one more ring to deliver and then I'm all yours.' And suddenly I love the idea of a quiet Christmas with Noel and Dad, huddled inside our family home, seeing out the season with TV and copious amounts of cheese. That will be all the healing I need. Noel does a little happy dance and I grab his cheeks, kissing him on the forehead. 'I was worried for a while that strong jawline was going to steal you away,' he teases, looking across at Joe. I'm not sure why but someone in the kitchen has him on service duty. Some much for a quick pop-in.

'His name is Joe. Behave. He's just a friend,' I remark.

Noel raises an eyebrow. 'I don't have friends like that. What's happening there, by the way?' he asks, his twin senses tingling. 'I've never seen trousers fall so well on a man.'

'I don't quite know,' I mumble.

'So you've spent the last few days together. You've stayed at his place. This is interesting,' he tells me.

I pull him close. 'We kissed yesterday,' I say out of the side of my mouth.

'WHAT?' he cries.

I elbow him in the ribs to remind him to watch his volume. 'Shush yourself! It was mistletoe, it was mandatory kissing. And there was a drunken kiss, but he quickly put a stop to that.'

'I will not shush. That's a good thing. A Christmas

smoochy. I get good vibes off him, too. I should tell you, we were never one hundred percent sold on Chris.'

I push him playfully as Noel steals us a couple of glasses of festive bubbles. 'Why am I finding this out now?' I tell him, clinking his glass.

'Because we loved you and respected your choices.' He watches Joe again as he returns to the kitchen. 'I can think of worse people to have a rebound fling with, you know?' he says casually, sipping his drink.

'I just get the feeling he doesn't want that at all. And I get it. A fling wouldn't be fair on him. I don't think being flung by a mate and then losing him in the aftermath is the best way to heal.'

'I see you looking at him though.'

'Shush.'

'Evie. Love doesn't have timing. Plus, it's Christmas. It's the season of—'

'Secrets?'

'Love. Giving. New things. That sort of shit...'

'They should put that on cards,' I chuckle.

I see my dad standing at the kitchen door, waving at Noel for assistance. 'Duty calls. I love you,' he says, kissing me on the cheek before taking his leave. The singalong is still in full resounding effect at this point and I look around the restaurant, at the glow of everyone and thing around this place.

'Would you pull a cracker with me?' a man says, standing next to me. He's well dressed in chinos and a blazer with a Christmas bow tie, his silver beard smartly groomed for the evening.

'Why, of course,' I reply and I take a well-balanced stance as we pull it together and he wins the treasures inside. I pout.

'Please,' the gentleman tells me. 'All yours.'

I bow my head to thank him and empty the cardboard roll to find a green paper hat, a giant plastic ring and the customary joke inside. 'The hat matches my dress, it's perfect,' I say, arranging it on my head. The man then takes the plastic purple ring and places it on my engagement ring finger. The action raises some emotion in me thinking about the events of the last few days, but I'll take this plastic purple one over any other fake ring, any day of the year. I hold my hand up to admire it.

'That is stunning,' I tell him. 'I reckon at least twenty-four carats.'

He smiles, making his whole face crease up. 'Merry Christmas. Is that a yes then?' he asks me.

'It's a definitely. You should probably know my name though. I'm Eve.'

'Clarence. Tell me your joke then?' he asks.

I unfold the piece of paper in my hands. 'What's the difference between a snowman and a snow-woman?'

He shrugs.

'Snowballs?'

We both laugh heartily, him putting a hand to a nearby table to support himself. 'Apparently someone put in an order for rude crackers by accident. Audrey had a joke about Santa's Hos that made her spit out her soup,' he tells me. I like the cheeky glimmer in Clarence's eye. He puts a hand out asking for a dance and I can't refuse as it's Bing Crosby. I love how he sings along with the music then pushes me out for a twirl under his arm.

'You're a good dancer, Clarence,' I tell him.

'Oh, that would be my Felicity. She loved a dance and trained me up.'

I sense the emotion in his eyes shift, the change of tense and work out why he may be alone this Christmas.

'She sounds like fun.'

He beams proudly. 'She was.'

'How long has she been gone?'

'Six years. But the time makes no difference, she is very much missed, every day.'

I grab his hand a little tighter and I smile at him silently. I know that feeling. That's my mum all over. She came to a few of these evenings before she passed but she loved them, completely. She loved sitting with people and hearing their stories, she'd wear the brightest jumper and do her nails. I can picture little moments – seeing her sharing a kiss with my dad at the kitchen door, her arm over my shoulder as we sang along with the piano – moments that are so clear it's like they were yesterday, and it makes my heart ache to remember them.

'Kids?' I ask Clarence.

'I'm a little old for that now but we can try...'

I laugh loudly at his cheekiness.

'So, I know I just proposed, but are you dating anyone?' he asks.

Instinctively, I gaze over at Joe and Clarence follows my eyes.

'Well, I'm not sure how I can compare,' he tells me.

'Oh, no. That's nothing. He's just a friend,' I tell him. 'I'm a single pringle this Christmas, all on my lonesome,' I add without divulging too much about my recent heartbreak.

'But not really, hey?' he replies. I look around this room, glancing through to that kitchen, to all the people in here who'll remind me of that fact. I look over at Joe placing a turkey dinner in front of an old lady and admiring her hair. He looks over at me and smiles. Not alone, not at all.

Joe

Is it bad that I forgot there was a whole turkey in the back of my car? A proper mega turkey in a fancy roasting pan, that probably would have remained in my car until New Year if I hadn't earwigged into Eve's conversation with her brother. I would have only realised a few days later when I started wondering where the smell was coming from.

'You come with me straight through to the kitchen,' Eve's dad tells me. Now it's gone from a stolen turkey to an almost forgotten turkey to one I'm gifting to her family in a restaurant where the most wholesome yet liveliest of parties seems to be taking place. There's a girl singing at a piano. I say singing, she's now sat on top of it encouraging everyone to sing along, dressed as a Christmas tree, flashing lights wrapped around her. This is what Eve does at Christmas, well, of course it is. She needs to stop revealing things like this to me, things that reveal her kindness and compassion, things that make it harder for me to break the habit of her.

I carry my turkey through the crowd of people and into the kitchen where there's a bizarre mix of people who don't seem to be chefs. People are dancing and chopping carrots haphazardly, stirring massive pots of gravy and drinking, picking at plates of nibbles.

'Are you the DJ then?' someone asks me from one side of the kitchen.

'Oh no.'

'He's brought a turkey,' Nick announces, and everyone cheers, coming over to inspect it. Now is maybe not the time to tell them I stole it. There's a collective 'ooh' as I unwrap it on the counter to see it still bronzed and crisp, remnants of bacon rashers hanging off its legs. I'm glad my petty theft will feed the masses, this feels like good karma. Someone shakes my hand.

'Is that bay and orange I smell?'

I nod. 'I brine it beforehand to keep it succulent,' I blag, trying to avoid saying the word 'moist' to a room full of people I don't know.

'Thank you so much. And who do I have to thank for this?'

'I'm Joe.'

'Well, snap. I'm Josie and this is everyone...'

I raise my hand at all of them, as someone takes the turkey away. 'So how do you know Nick?'

I used to be and possibly might still be in love with his daughter?

'Oh, we've just met. I'm mates with Eve.' I point out towards the restaurant.

'EVE'S HERE?' Josie screams and runs out of the kitchen, and I look through the glass of the door to see her run up to her and embrace her tightly. I watch them closely as they chat and I realise Eve hasn't just invited me into any party, many of them are people she loves and trusts, she's brought me into her fold. Nick watches me as I look on.

'That's a quality bird,' he tells me.

'The turkey or Josie?' I ask.

Luckily, he finds that funny though he doesn't reply so I will assume both. We watch the interaction from the kitchen, but I can spot the moment when Chris is mentioned and the mood of Josie's face changes. Be angry on her behalf please, I encourage it. I'm not sure what to do now. We've supplied the turkey. There's one final ring to deliver. We should go. But I watch as Nick looks out towards Eve, with a look of protective pride but also awe, as if he's surprised that she's his daughter and she simply exists. I like that someone else looks at her like that. I guess we can stay for a moment.

'So, I realise I don't know you, mate, but give me the gist... Is she alright?' he asks me.

'She's had a rough couple of days. She caught Chris in the act, but she's dealing with it, possibly coming out the other side.' He stops for a moment to take on his daughter's pain, trying not to let his anger consume him. He turns and places two hands on a countertop.

'Well, I hope he gets a severe case of knobrot.'

'I think we can both agree on that much.'

He looks at me, and I feel as though we've bonded instantly in that moment.

'And she didn't think to tell us?' he says despondently.

'She didn't want to ruin your Christmas,' I say.

'That sounds like something my Eve would do. Poor girl. When I met him, I knew he wasn't the one for her, but I thought she'd work that out for herself eventually. Just a shame it took her three years.'

'You weren't keen on him?'

'He looked down his nose at me, shifty looking eyes. I could tell. Her mother would have probably told her sooner, but I never had the heart... She always deserved better. Her mother always knew what to say.'

'What was your wife's name?' I ask.

'Angela.' He gets out his phone to show me a picture of the family as a screensaver. 'Isn't Eve the spit of her?'

'It's the way her smile hits her eyes,' I say, studying the photo. That was a bit much. 'Hold up... Angela, Nick, Noel and Eve. Those are some proper Christmas names. I applaud the theming.'

He laughs, exuding a jolliness and warmth that feels familiar. 'She bloody loved Christmas. I liked it less before she came along. She helped me believe in the magic of it all. The fact that anything could happen, seeing the surprise etched in the kids' faces, she just went above and beyond to make it special, you know?'

'So Eve is like her in a lot of ways then,' I mention.

He stops to study my face, to watch my gaze that keeps dipping out into the restaurant.

'Remind me how you know my Eve again?' he asks me.

'We work at Caspar & Sons. The jewellers', where she works at the weekend. We've just been doing some last-minute deliveries for them for Christmas. It's been good, I think, taken her mind off things.'

'Noel mentioned the rings. Well, thank you for looking after her,' he tells me, putting a hand to my arm. 'I've been told there's one more ring to go out tonight?'

'One more ring and then I'll get your girl back to you,' I tell him. 'Is that OK?'

'More than OK. Just a shame you have to shoot off again. Here, before you bounce, how are you with carving? Give me a hand?' he tells me, handing me a carving fork. I do as I'm told. I did a surgery rotation at medical school, so my carving is not awful. I place slices of turkey and ham on the festive themed plates, looking around the kitchen at everyone busying around trying to make Christmas great for others. I don't know, having played Joseph literally an hour ago and now with all this good energy in the air, this finally feels like Christmas. Suddenly, someone storms into the kitchen, reindeer antlers on her head.

'No one's dentures can deal with the roast potatoes. I think we need to whip up some mash,' she declares, eyeballing me. 'You? Who are you?' she barks.

'I'm Joe.'

She looks me up and down. 'I have a nephew called Joe. I'm Meg. Seeing as you look the part, grab those plates, will you?' she tells me.

I shrug my shoulders. Hell, why not? Meg leads the way out into the dining room, and people cheer as food is served and placed in front of people. Eve and Noel are chatting, but she puts a thumbs up to me and asks if I'm OK. Given my hands are otherwise occupied, I wink. That was a dodgy move, possibly a little mis-aimed too as an older woman winks back at me from across the room.

'Merry Christmas,' I tell a man as I place his dinner in front of him. He holds on to my arm.

'Did you cook this?'

'Yes, I did,' I say, pushing the gravy boat in his direction.

He tucks in and I absorb some of that glow and energy from

the room. This is a good thing, a collection of people just doing something charitable and community minded for Christmas and it's lovely to contribute but also see Eve in her natural habitat. I go back into the kitchen watching through those glass panels as an older gentleman asks Eve for a dance and she agrees, sashaying with him next to one of the trestles.

'Here boy, you got a free hand? Just help me with my belt.' I turn to someone behind the door, bent over, trying to adjust a cushion that should be a paunch.

'Santa?'

'Or Mr Claus. I also go by Father C.'

I grin and do as requested, looping up his belt and tightening it up. This is premium Santa. He's spent some money on the outfit, high quality velour with a fitted trouser, embroidery on the cuffs.

'You look just the part,' I tell him. 'That's quite a sack.'

He stops to give me a look. 'This is a family event, young man... keep it appropriate.'

I freeze but he starts to laugh, a big bellowing roar that echoes through the kitchen. I can't help but join in. 'Don't mind me. How was the laugh? Did the laugh work?'

'It was very authentic, I'm impressed. Is this a regular gig for you then?' I ask him, helping him adjust his hat.

'Only because my daughter dictates it,' he tells me, pointing to Josie. 'I used to be an actor,' he says in RADA tones.

'Wow, stage or screen?'

He pauses. 'Screen,' he says, still chortling, still a bit drunk, as I hand him a wiry pair of glasses to perch on his nose. He stands back from me and poses, joy lighting up his face, the music from next door accenting his moves. He's certainly a different version of Santa, far more fun than any I've seen this Christmas. Is it possible he's my favourite Santa I've ever met? The faint whiff of whisky radiating off him makes me think he's going to be a fun Santa, too. Do we stand there and have a dance moment while the kitchen rushes around us? We do. It's Christmas, after all. It's allowed.

'So, who are you again?' he asks me as he fluffs out his beard.

'I'm Eve's friend.'

Friend. I guess that's the point we've got to now with my relationship with Eve, and even though that stings a little, I try to tell myself it's better than nothing. I take a peek out of the kitchen door again. She's there, in the centre, still dancing with that old man, looking in a far better place than when I found her in the Caspars' shop. Feel good you got her to this place at least, Joe. That's what a friend would have done. Feel good that's she here amongst all these people who love her so unconditionally and that she gets to enjoy the rest of the season.

'Aaaah, the lovely Eve. Brilliant girl. Love her,' Santa says.

'She on your good list?'

'Every year – top of that list.'

'Good.' She deserves to be there. I smile. She's starting to shine again, to look like the girl I remember, and it's a relief. Deep down, I'm just glad she's still standing. It really is a gift to hear her laugh and see her so relaxed and indulging in all that family banter and love. I can go and see my family and I know she won't be wallowing in the sadness of what happened with Chris. That at least gives me some peace of mind. She's here, in the safest of spaces, with people who will look after her. I've done my part. And then I realise, quietly if a little reluctantly, that maybe this is where it should end. Maybe we've come to a point now where I move on, where I can let her stay here instead of rushing off with me again.

An idea slowly comes to me, and I take a deep breath. 'Can I ask a favour, Santa?' I say, turning to him.

'Sure thing.'

'Do you have gifts you're giving out to everyone?'

He goes to retrieve his massive hessian sack that he shakes, trying to find a way to sling it over his shoulder. 'I'm laden with chocolates, socks, scarves and shortbread. My wife went on a bit of a mission.'

I reach into the inside pocket of my jacket and hand him a gift, wrapped in holly-patterned paper and tied with a red ribbon. I've had it in my jacket for far too long and the paper is slightly crinkled. 'If you're going out there, can you make sure Eve gets this?'

'Will she know it's from you?'

'Maybe. If she asks, just say that I've gone to do the last ring and then I'm headed home. Tell her Merry Christmas from me...'

Santa looks down at the gift, stumbling around a bit from the alcohol. 'You sure you don't want to give it to her yourself?' he asks me.

I look out at the dancefloor where she's sharing a joke with Lucy, singing along. 'It's all good.'

He looks down at the gift then puts it in his sack. 'Well, I am sure you have also been a very good boy so I will do this for you.'

'Thank you, Santa.'

And from out of nowhere, he reaches around me, possibly a little too merry and gives me the biggest of hugs. He'll never know how much I need that, right now, right in this moment. I hug him back. Thank you, drunk Santa. He then reaches for quite a large bell on the floor and gives me one last pose before disappearing behind that door, ringing it loudly to announce his appearance, yelling Merry Christmas to the room. I hear the crowd cheer in response. I watch as Eve's face lights up to see him, so incredibly happy. It's time to go. Merry Christmas, Eve. It's been my absolute pleasure.

EIGHTEEN

Eve

'GO SANTA! GO SANTA! GO SANTA!'

Josie's dad is Santa every time we hold this event, mainly because he has the big voice and laugh but he also seems to have a lot of costumes in his locker that I suspect he and his wife wear for different types of festive fun. I love watching how he works a room, double air kisses all the older ladies and poses for photos. However, he is also fond of breakdancing when he comes out on the dancefloor. Not real breakdancing – they are body popping, robot moves, all intended to make the crowd roar with laughter. I stand there and clap and chant as he does his thing, laying his sack to one side.

'God, he's so drunk,' Josie says as she filters past with more bottles of champagne but also filming on her phone, capturing all the action.

'But a complete ledge. My hero,' Lucy tells us as she goads him on. She'd join in but I don't think her dress is made for that sort of movement or it might catch alight. Lucy is someone I know by association. She went to school with the wonderful

Josie. Every three months, Lucy would come visit us at university and the girl taught us how to party and not just party, she would raise the merriest of hells. I don't remember any of it, I just remember the aftermath of some of those epic benders, including one where I actually phoned Noel and gave him my last will and testament via voicemail. She takes my hand and we half dance, half twerk inappropriately to the music.

'Josie told me about Chris. Can I egg his house?' she tells me.

I laugh. 'Tonight?'

'It can be arranged. Josie, we can get eggs, right?'

Josie nods. 'I can get ones past their sell by date, too?' The problem is they probably would do this, all in my honour and for that I grab them in a collective hug.

'So where to after this, girls?' Lucy tells us. 'I can get us into a club in Mayfair with Christmas drag bingo, all-night buffet and trance DJ?'

Josie and I look at her in confused horror.

'So dull. I'm going to ask your turkey friend, I bet he'll be up for it.'

'His name is Joe. Actually, he won't be around tonight. He's headed home,' I inform her, slightly sad to say that out loud, to know that the end of our adventures is just around the corner. That said, I stop for a moment at the mention of his name. Joe and I have been here for a while, such is the lure of these parties, but it's been longer than intended and I've realised we've stayed a moment too long. There's another ring we need to deliver this evening and then we can come back here. I say, we. I really hope Joe may come back, for a drink, so we can celebrate Christmas properly together and raise a mince pie to all we've done in the last three days and pat ourselves on the backs. I owe him that much. More, to be honest, than a crumby Christmas pastry but it's a start.

I look around and realise I can't see him anywhere. 'Do you

know where he is?' I ask them. Both girls shrug as Santa gets down on the floor and Josie rushes over to stop him doing the Worm and possibly breaking his back. Where is Joe? I scan the room and the people coming in and out of the kitchen. Noel comes out of the doors, platters of pigs in blankets in his hands. I see Meg, I see Dad's figure still standing in the kitchen, carving fork held in the air, possibly dancing.

I walk over to Noel. 'Hey, have you seen Joe? We'd better make a move.'

He peers around the room. 'Kitchen? Last thing I saw he was chatting to Dad.'

I head into the kitchen, waving to a few familiar faces and see Dad hacking away at some turkey thighs, his bottom half moving to the Christmas music. I can't help but laugh because I know how much this man is Christmas people, through and through.

'That's some jumper, by the way.'

He looks up and grins. 'That's all your brother. I think he may have got one for you, too. How's it going in there?' he asks.

'Oh, it's all good fun as usual.'

He pauses for a moment to study my face.

'You alright?'

I nod.

'So, this may have been a bit presumptuous but when Noel told me what happened, I cleaned up your room. Just in case you wanted to hang out with us for a bit over Christmas? I didn't know. No pressure.'

My heart glows to hear him ask, as if I'd consider going anywhere else. 'Only place I want to be.'

He puts a hand to my arm and grabs it. I'll overlook the turkey juice. 'Your new mate is welcome, too,' he says, smirking.

I shake my head at him. 'He's a friend.'

'He's a handsome friend.'

'Stop stirring. Stir your gravy instead.'

'He likes you.'

'No, he doesn't...'

Dad shrugs his shoulders, sniggering to himself, and I frown for a moment, wondering why.

'Have you seen him? I thought he was back here? We need to go deliver another ring.'

Dad looks around. 'Anyone seen the lad who brought the turkey?' he bellows through the kitchen.

'He headed outside. I assumed he'd gone out for a smoke?' a voice pipes up.

But he doesn't smoke. I pop my head out of the kitchen door. He's not there.

Dad's gaze follows me. 'He was chatting to Santa before he went out, maybe ask him?'

I nod and head back out to the party in full swing where Santa has stopped dancing and has started to give out gifts to all attending. An old lady waves around socks that look like cashmere. I think I may want to get in on that.

'Santa?' I say, tapping him on the shoulder.

He turns round to clock me and beams. 'EEEEEEVE!' He gives me a huge hug and then realises something. 'I have something for you, hold up...' He rifles through his sack and pulls out a gift, wrapped in holly paper and hands it to me. 'This is because you've been so good this year.'

'Thank you, Santa,' I say, putting the gift to one side. 'Just checking, have you seen Joe?'

'Was he wearing a dinner jacket?'

'Yes, that's the one.'

'He had to go make a phone call and then he had to go home.'

I stand there glued to the spot for a moment as the party happens around me. He's gone? Home?

Noel stands nearby, noticing my expression and comes over. 'All OK here?'

'Joe's gone. What do you mean, a phone call?' I ask Santa, worried now that something has happened with his family.

'Something about giving someone a ring,' he says, shrugging. 'I'm sorry. Open your gift?' he tells me, but socks don't feel like the answer at the moment. 'You should...' But before he has a chance to finish his sentence, an old lady pulls him back into the party. I should do what?

Noel stands close to me, his arms around me. Joe has gone? Without me? I'm not sure what happened. Maybe Joe was worried about the final delivery, the fact that we were running late. But even then, I just thought he would wait, not leave. This was our thing. We deliver these five rings together. I didn't know how it was going to or supposed to end but it wasn't destined to be like this. I have things to say to him. Should I go and find him? Has something happened where he's had to rush home? None of this makes sense. I get out my phone and scroll through texts and messages.

'Eve, talk to me,' Noel says, worriedly. 'Are you OK?'

'Not really... I just...' And I'm not sure why but tears start to fill my eyes. Maybe I just misread the signs. I've been so cruelly dumped that maybe I latched on to Joe unfairly and poured whatever hope I had left into him. He obviously felt differently. We were never that close before this – work colleagues really – so he shouldn't have felt obliged to stick around. That said, I can't help but feel incredibly crap, though, at this very moment.

'Shit, are you crying?' Noel asks me. 'Don't cry.'

'It's just... it's been a manic few days. I haven't even caught a breath.'

'This is why you should call me when you're dumped. Stay. And when we're done here, I'll wrap you in a duvet and you can hibernate with us over Christmas with box sets and a trifle.'

A trifle. And just like that I rewind through all the moments of the last few days. Sharing a trifle with Joe on his sofa, patting his back while he threw up on a boat, mistletoe kisses on a rooftop, grand proposals in Trafalgar Square, stealing an ex's turkey, looking after the baby Jesus – all these distractions, that helped me forget, and that meant something, to me at least. I wish I could thank him for that much. It started off so badly, but somehow, it's turned into the best memorable Christmas ever. Maybe I'll get to tell him in the New Year. Maybe I've well and truly lost him. I really hope I haven't.

Joe

'Why are you dressed as James Bond?' Carrie asks me on Face-time, as I sit in this cold, half-empty car park this early Christmas evening, looking up at the large grey building in front of me. 'Is this part of your stripping thing? Is this why you're not home yet? You're letting some women see your goldfinger?' Carrie cackles down the phone, the sort of laugh that lets you know she's seeing in the festive season with a pint glass of Baileys. 'Everyone, come and see Joe,' she announces to the room and several faces cram into the screen to make fun and point.

'One, I am not a stripper and two, I was actually at a wedding in an actual church so sod off and get your mind out of the gutter. Hello... Hello... Hi!' I say, trying to greet all the nephews, nieces and sisters as they pass in and out of the call in our family living room. And despite any low feeling that sits in my soul, to see my parents' golden Christmas tree in the same corner of the room as always, Monopoly money strewn about the place, and my nephews in matching onesies is suddenly comforting, and I feel a glimmer of happiness knowing I'll be there soon, with all of them, the ultimate Christmas distraction.

'SANTA CAME, UNCLE JOE!' a nephew bellows in a way that tells me we need to limit the sugar intake.

'Did he leave anything for me?' I ask.

'No, because Mum said you were a dick for not being here,' Carrie says.

I hear echoes of laughter and scolding from other sisters as Carrie takes me away from the conversation so she can take the mick out of me from the hallway of the family home instead.

'So I'm a dick.'

'A very tiny dick,' she says, gesturing as much with her little finger. 'You're back tonight? Definitely? In time for cheese and mince pies?' she tells me, as she takes refuge on the stairs.

'Definitely, I'm all set.'

'You sound sad. Have you been dumped by some mystery girlfriend?' she says, unsympathetically. It's possibly the searing realism that I need in this very moment. I need someone to give me perspective and make me laugh but what's sad about all of this is that in order to have been dumped, Eve and I would have had to have been in a relationship first, and that hasn't happened. But Eve is exactly where she needs to be. She's safe, she's with her people, she's happy, and there had to be a point where I let her go.

'In a way...'

I sit there in my car wondering how much to say because Carrie will go one of two ways. She will either mock me or show rage towards a woman she's never met before, and I don't think I want either. But in a moment where I'm deciding to flee, I felt like I needed to speak to my sister, the person to whom I'd be fleeing. I'll never tell her that much.

Carrie senses me being ponderous about disclosing details of my love life to her. 'Then come here, come and be surrounded by people who love you unconditionally. We have so much cheese.'

'Brie?'

'We're not amateurs. Of course.' Carrie spends a moment looking at my face, trying to work me out. 'What's up, little brother? You're giving me sad un-Christmassy vibes here and you *are* Christmas.'

'I am. But I'm just single at Christmas, and a girl I like doesn't feel the same way. I'm allowed to be a little melancholy about this.'

'Why doesn't she like you? Is it your feet?'

'What's wrong with my feet?'

'They kind of smell and you have unusually long toes. Did she get creeped out by them?'

I pause for a moment, adjusting my toes inside my shoes. Really?

'Well, now I'm paranoid about my feet...'

'The rest of you is very loveable though.'

It's a strong line of banter between me and all the sisters that never grows old, that may be the one thing that carries me through Christmas. I always miss it, those sibling bonds because they are like glue; they are part of what raised you and understand you completely. A few years ago, when Dad got ill, those women became the reason I'm still standing. Carrie and I were on the frontline dealing with the emotional impact and trauma of it all. Carrie saw what it did to me, how it broke me, how it made me pull away from a profession I thought was my calling. She was there and present and got me back on my feet. She might just do the same now.

'I just have one more thing to do before I set off,' I tell her.

'It's not to do with the girl who's possibly dumped you?'

'No. I've spent the last two days delivering five last minute rings to people and I have one more to deliver.'

'Rings?' she asks, her face all scrunched up on screen. I shouldn't tell her she has crow's feet when she does that, should I?

'As part of my gig at the jewellery shop. For proposals, weddings... 'Tis the season of last-minute romance...'

She smiles for a moment, and I realise that it's been pretty special, to have witnessed all that love, all those grand gestures of romance, to have been a small part of all these relationships moving into new dizzying heights.

'It's taken you two days to deliver five rings? That's a sucky delivery service. You'd not get a UPS job, that's for sure.'

I laugh loudly and see her glad to have cheered me up.

'Well, I get the dinner jacket now – it's you trying to be fancy. You should have dressed up as Cupid, with a bow and a toga...'

'That's less fancy,' I mention.

'So, tell me, why the hesitancy?'

I look up at the building again. 'I'm delivering it to a hospital.'

Both of us are silent and ponderous. I hadn't even recognised the address when I was driving here. It's not just any hospital, it's one in Hammersmith where I did a rotation for three months, so I feel I know the bowels of this building intimately. However, going into any hospital always feels like trauma to me now. It makes me relive my dad's suffering, the uncertain fragility of life, moments embedded in my mind for an eternity. She's one of the very few who get it.

'You OK?' she enquires kindly, putting her sisterly sarcasm to one side.

'Yeah, but no...'

She looks at me through the screen, my shoulders slumped, knowing there's little she can do sixty miles away. 'Do you know who the ring is for?'

'No. I just have the name of the man who ordered it.'

'Well, I hope it's like an episode of *Grey's Anatomy* where a surgeon proposes to another over someone's open heart,' she says, a little too enthusiastically.

'And then he comes out with some cheesy line about how she has fixed his heart and taught him how to love,' I add.

'Because he was just super career driven before. He was

mean and didn't allow people in and now his heart will be full this Christmas and forever more... THE END!' she announces to the screen, bowing. She's as mad as a box of frogs but the shift in emotion is very welcome. 'Well, get it done and come see us. We'll make it better,' Carrie mutters at me. 'You're also the missing piece in all of this. Christmas will only start when you get here,' she says, the alcohol obviously hitting her in the festive feels.

'That might be the nicest thing you've ever said to me, Carrie.'

'Which I retract immediately. I hope you've bought me a gift.'

'Yes, a picture of me, wine and a comedy fridge magnet. I went all out.'

'I feel so loved. I feel less guilty about getting you socks now. Get it done. Drive safe.'

She hangs up. I look at the ring in its box again. It's the simplest ring I've had to deliver in the last few days but there is something very perfect about that. I rest my head against the glass of my car window. I used to nap in Olive during my work breaks, in this very car park. One more ring. It'll be fine.

I put it my pocket and get out of my car, heading towards the large automatic doors at the front of the building, looking up at all the floors, all the windows. This place offered me one of my first placements in medical school and they weren't awful months, but I do feel some shame being back here. For all the work I did put in, for all that potential I had to just be quashed, still feels like failure on my part.

I walk through the doors, deciphering the signs, amused by the people walking past me with Christmas hats and antlers, gazing upon the corridors and the eighties tinsel hastily attached with blu-tack. It's not somewhere anyone wants to be at Christmas, poorly and unable to enjoy the season, but back when I was a junior doctor, Christmas was the time this place felt more important than ever. It was bound together by sacrifice and some unerring festive spirit.

I read Mr Caspar's scrappy writing on the delivery details and suddenly realise where I need to go. Second Floor. Damn it. You can do this, Joe. Eve would be good right now, if only for her company, her support, a hand to hold. I take strides up the staircase and head for the ward name on the delivery slip, walking up to the reception desk.

'Hi, I'm here to... ummm...'

The nurse behind the desk pauses and looks me up and down.

'Yes?' she barks.

'...see someone?'

'Visiting hours are 2 p.m. to 6 p.m. You'll have to come back tomorrow.'

I look down at my watch that reads 6.09 p.m. 'I know that but I'm hoping you might make an exception seeing as it's...'

'Christmas? Young man, illness does not make an exception for Christmas. It doesn't take a break. I do not take a break for Christmas.'

I scrunch my face up. 'Well, you should. You deserve it.'

She seems taken aback by my reply but then studies my face. 'I know you. James. No, Joseph? Joe Lord...'

'Yes?' I whisper at the nursing sister behind the desk. You know this is a woman who means business because she's got her nurse's uniform on with a flashing Santa hat but she's also in trainers because she has places to be.

'I never forget a face. Or a name.'

'Sister... Drummond?' I say, pointing at her, not knowing whether to smile or cry. She still remembers me? I passed through many wards and hospitals in my training, people started to merge into one, but this nurse here used to shout at me because I wasn't great at labelling blood samples. She quickly put me right. She put us all right. She looks me up and down.

'Why are you here? I don't suppose it's to see me and take me out to dinner,' she jokes in a harsh voice.

'Well, no... Unless you want me to go and buy you dinner?' I say, a little scared.

Her look tells me that was not her intention at all. 'Are you here as a doctor?' she asks me again. A receptionist in elf ears snickers under her breath at her interrogation.

'I'm not a doctor anymore,' I tell her, and she stands there confused at my admission. It was easier breaking this news to my own mother.

'Whyever not?' she asks.

'Ummm...' Personal tragedy and a deep introspection into the meaning of life? 'It's a long story.'

'Then why are you here?' she asks, starting to be peeved that I don't seem to have a use or reason.

'I'm here to deliver something.'

'Deliver what? Is it food? Is it flowers? We don't allow for flowers.' I put my hands in the air. There are no flowers about my person unless I'm going to pull that out of my sleeves like a magician. Christ, does she think I'm a magician?

'No flowers.'

'Patient name?'

'David Peare.'

She stops for a moment. 'How long will you be?'

'Two minutes.'

'Well, as it's you, and I vaguely know you. Room Four,' she tells me solemnly. 'Turn right, past the curtains.'

I nod, not before feeling my phone vibrate in my pocket. I retrieve it and see Eve's contact on the screen. I reject the call, writing a brief message, and put my phone back in my pocket.

'Thank you, Sister Drummond. Merry Christmas.'

'Indeed.'

NINETEEN

Eve

> I'm sorry, had to run to make the last delivery then headed straight home. Stay, have fun – Merry Christmas.

I look down at the text on my phone, my face scrunched into a thousand different lines, a thousand different emotions that don't quite know how to process Joe leaving. I tried to call to say something to him but even then, I wasn't sure what I was going to say. Stay? Come back? I like you? I didn't get much sense out of drunk Santa and no one else saw him leave. Not even a good-bye. I won't lie in saying it stung a little but maybe the wisest thing to do was to put some space between us and not pretend this was anything else but two work colleagues who needed to get a job done. The last ring can be delivered. He can go home to his family. The end.

'I hope this place reeks of alcohol because you threw it at Chris and were going to set him alight,' Noel says, standing there by the door to my flat, his arm around my shoulder. Noel and I have escaped the party to help transport some pensioners home, and we've stopped at my flat now to collect some essentials so I can go and camp at home-home for the rest of Christmas. This basically means I will be packing pyjamas, hoodies and big socks. Maybe my duvet. It will be all I need.

My flat is fast becoming my least favourite place in the world. As I enter the cold, dark living room, nothing has been moved or changed; somewhere that was once a sanctum, my home, now feels sullied. I also worry that all the alcohol on the floor has started to stain the wood. We'll have to put some nice rugs in place so I can get my deposit back. I stand there in the room, lit by the streetlamps, and head over to the Christmas tree to turn on the fairy lights.

'When you came here on Christmas Eve, how did Chris explain all this mess to you?' I enquire.

'He said you'd had a fight about Christmas gifts. I didn't pry. I should have seen through his lies though.'

I shrug my shoulders. 'More like I'd just caught my boyfriend in the shower. I was ragey,' I tell him. 'I opened all the gifts.'

'Not all of them though?' Noel says, nodding towards a parcel by the tree.

It's Mrs Milkov's gift. I collapse on to the sofa and rip the paper off to reveal a massive tin of Quality Street. Noel punches the air in celebration. I prise open the tin and sift through looking for my favourite caramel cups.

'Purple one, please?' he asks, plonking himself down next to me and I hand him over a chocolate. We sit back chewing, entranced by the lights on my tree. Noel tries to put the wrapper back in the box and I slap his hand. He pretends to be more hurt than he is and steals another chocolate. There is something of a much littler brother quality to Noel, but he feels like the right person to be here now, the literal other half of me.

'I'm sorry, sis, that this Christmas has been such a shitshow for you,' he says with a mouthful of chocolate.

'Not your fault,' I tell him. 'We're here now. Together, as it should be.' I reach under the tree and hand him another box. 'Merry Christmas.' I see his eyes light up until he reads the tag on the box.

'You cow, this is labelled to Chris. Are you giving me second-hand gifts? That is both cheeky and rude.'

'They're vintage Stan Smiths, you're both the same size and I can't bear to return them. But I also got you those headphones you wanted, chill.'

He throws his arms around me. 'Then I am grateful, not hateful. Except towards Chris. Always.'

This is the power and joy of having a twin. He'll carry that hate for an eternity. He opens the shoes and feigns shock and gratitude, getting a shoe out and holding it to his chest. They're super rare and I bought them because I knew Chris loved them and I wanted to see that exact same expression when he opened the box. I hope Chris never finds a pair for himself or spends an eternity bidding for them on eBay and never winning that auction.

'So what did turkey boy say on his text again?' he says, kicking his boots off and trying on his new trainers. 'He really just left? Does that not have legs? He had good vibes,' Noel quizzes me.

'I don't know what happened. All I can imagine is the last few days have been fun, but it just ran its course,' I say, lining up chocolates on my knee. 'Maybe in the New Year when I'm less of mess and the air has cleared. Maybe. Maybe it's just veered into platonic. I just don't think he's into me like that.'

'Is it your feet?' he asks me.

'What's wrong with my feet?'

'You have very strange little toes, they're like cashew nuts hanging on at the end there.'

I playfully push Noel but look at my toes in my heels. Am I a freak? What if he was a foot man?

'Call him...'

'I tried. He must be driving. His family are down in Brighton. Don't do this...'

'Do what?'

'Give me hope,' I say, eyeballing him.

'Well, I thought it might go well with the socks I bought you.'

'I feel so loved.'

'They are very fluffy socks,' he tells me, his eyes still shifting around this place. 'What happened to your bed?' he asks, peering through to the bedroom.

'Oh, I dismantled it,' I say casually.

He nods slowly to take that in. His attention is caught by a photo on the floor, crumpled and half torn. A photo of Chris and I in happier times, at someone else's wedding reception, before the deceit, before really understanding what love is or was. 'Did the wanker at least apologise?' he asks.

'He wrote me a note.'

'Really?' Noel says, pulling a face.

'Why really?'

'He never came across as much of a wordsmith to me. Was it song lyrics? Did he apologise with you via Coldplay? Show me the note.'

'It was quite a good note, to be fair. There was some semblance of sentimentality to it.'

I get up for a moment, remembering Joe rolled it in a ball and threw it on the floor. I look amongst all the debris of wrapping paper and half-opened gifts, Noel's attention caught by a set of espresso mugs I bought one of his aunts.

'You can have them, too,' I tell him, looking around the room. Noel fist pumps the air. I find the ball of paper in the corner of the room and open it up, scanning the words. Hold up...

I'll send you the bill because that was all you... You can buy me a new phone, too, and that ring cost me £1K so think about how you'd like to pay me that back... If you want to know why we finished, it's because we got boring. I don't want a life like that... I just want more out of my life.

I can feel my hands grab at the paper, crumpling it, my hands frozen like claws, every inch of my body tense with emotion.

'Eve,' Noel mumbles, taking the paper from my hands then reading it for himself. 'Hun, this is worse than Coldplay lyrics. This is one of the worst things I've ever read. How dare he! You said it was a good note.'

'It was,' I say, trying to think back to being here with Joe, offering him a sandwich toaster and glancing over at a hole in the wall I made.And a letter I made him read to me because I couldn't bear to do it myself. And a tear rolls down my cheek to think of words Joe said to me.

You are the most wonderful person I know... I see it in how you ask people about their days, in how you cry when people tell you about their pets... I love how you stand at countertops and sway to music that no one can hear, that you bite at your thumbnail when you're thinking really hard.

I look down, biting my thumbnail. I think back to a time when a woman came into Caspar & Sons to get a ring refitted and she told us about her arthritic dog who had to be carried up the stairs and I cried. I do sway at countertops. In that shop. Because the Caspars play a lot of waltz music. When I work there. With Joe.

'Evie, I'm so up for this. I can go and fuck up his LinkedIn profile. We can burn stuff,' Noel says, still scanning the letter, fuming. 'I think if I make some phone calls then I can find someone else to do it. I am sure Dad would loan us some money for that.'

Noel assumes my silence to be born from the same feeling so sits me down on the sofa, trying his best to work me out.

'I couldn't bear to read the letter, so I made Joe read it out to me. This is not what he read out to me. He said something completely different.'

'To spare you this?' Noel says, holding the letter up. I nod and he pouts because in amongst all the lovely things he did say, that hinted towards everything he had noticed, to protect me in that moment was a kind thing to do. And the tears start to roll out of me now because he does care. He possibly even likes me? He noticed and remembered all those things about me. I am so bloody confused. Then where is he now?

'Oh, Eve... Please don't,' Noel says, throwing his arms around me. I lean into him and sob on to his chest.

'This is such a mess,' I blub.

'You're telling me... You're snotting all over me.' Noel puts an arm around me. 'Still the messiest crier I know, so much snot. Do you have any tissues?'

'Check my handbag.' He reaches over and puts my handbag between us, taking out keys, a bag of Haribo and my phone, pressing a button by accident to see a screensaver of Joe and I took in the back of his car, glow into life. And then he places a gift next to me. It's wrapped in holly-patterned paper with a red ribbon and a small tag tucked into it. I didn't see the tag before. Santa gave me that gift at the party. He told me to open it. Instinctively, I pull at the tag to read it.

For the very amazing Eve... Because everyone should know your name. Merry Christmas. Joe x

I open the gift and look at it, my mouth open in shock.

'You have a lot of shit in your handbag, you know. You're basically carrying around half a make-up counter in there. Why do you have talc in here, but no tissues?' he says, before looking up.

I clutch the gift in my hand, running my fingers over it. I can't. How? I look up at Noel, overcome by some emotion that takes my breath away.

'Joe. I have to find him. Tonight.'

Joe

Ring 5: Round cut, solitaire, 3ct diamond, yellow gold infinity band. For Natalia.

The door of Room Four is slightly ajar as I approach it and when I enter, I see a man lying there in a bed, staring at a screen propped up on a table, doing his best to laugh but coughing abrasively. I knock on the door and he looks over.

'Jesus Christ.'

'Not quite, I believe he made his big appearance earlier today,' I try to joke.

The man furrows his brow at me, not knowing if that's a decent joke or not. He turns the screen off looking at me suspiciously.

'Please tell me you're not a stripper? Are you a gift? I did tell work I'd be very happy with vouchers.'

I shake my head. 'You're not the first person to think that today. But alas, no.'

'Well, you are very overdressed for a doctor unless that's how they're serving me dinner now, full silver service,' he tells me. It pains me to be able to scan the wires and IV bags, and the pallor of his skin to know that this man is quite unwell but also, sadly, not much older than his thirties. Beside his bed, there are photos, drawings from young children and items from home to provide some familiarity. 'I mean, I'd kill for a steak.'

'How would you like it cooked, Mr Peare?'

'Medium rare, chips – chunky chips, not skinny fries – and a peppercorn sauce if that's on the menu,' he says, smiling. 'Who are you, really?'

'I'm from Caspar & Sons.'

He sighs. 'The ring people. I am impressed. This is quite a service. On Christmas Day. I told Mr Caspar to deliver it for the New Year.'

'It's a special service. I'll assume he just wanted you to have the ring.'

'Before I carked it?'

'Because it's Christmas?'

He pauses, taken aback by the gesture. 'Well, let's see it then...'

I walk over to the bed as he tries his best to sit up. I offer some help, propping a pillow behind his back, then place the velvet box on the table, opening the lid so he can inspect it.

'Crikey. There she is,' he says, removing the ring and looking at it closely. 'I didn't really know what I wanted so I left the old man in the shop to his own devices. It's perfect.'

'That's Mr Caspar for you.'

'I rang around so many jewellers', but they were all trying to flog the most expensive rings in the shop to me. Mr Caspar listened. He understood the assignment. I thought about something else – a pendant or bracelet and you know what he told me? A ring. It will last forever.' His finger traces the circumference of it. 'Like a circle, it has no beginning, no end. I liked hearing that.'

I smile. Mr Caspar uses that line a lot on anyone who comes in the shop, and it never gets old. I watch as he looks at the ring quietly, from every angle, before forming a fist around it and holding it to his heart. I have so many questions but just quietly observe him.

'Can I give you anything for coming here so late?' he tells me. 'I have a whole tin of Quality Street.' He reaches over for the shiny angular tin and wedges it open with his fingers. I sift through the rainbow-coloured confections and take a caramel cup.

'You can take more than one,' he jokes. 'So, is this what you do? Are you a proper lord of the rings?'

'Of sorts,' I reply, laughing. 'In the last few days, I've done five last minute deliveries. It's been quite a few days of proposals and weddings.'

'That's a lot of love.'

It was a huge festive bomb of love; it was humbling and magical, even if none of it was for me.

'I don't even know what hand a ring goes on. Is that terrible?' he tells me.

'Left hand,' I say, holding up my ring finger. 'It dates back to the Ancient Romans who believed there was a vein in that finger that led directly to the heart.' I repeat another of Mr Caspar's lines. 'And then when you do get married, you stick another ring on there for good measure.'

'I've not got that far with my planning yet,' he tells me.

'Mr Caspar can sort you out,' I tell him.

He nods at me and smiles.

'Well, I got the next best thing. Turkey sandwich meal deal – it's got turkey, bacon, cranberry and...' a voice suddenly says, coming into the room clutching on to some takeaway sandwiches and crisps. The lady is in a Christmas jumper, jeans and trainers and stops when she sees me. 'Sorry, I didn't realise we had company,' she says, placing her food haul on an armchair in the room. 'Did my mum send one of those singing telegrams? I told her not to do that.'

'It's all good. I'm just leaving,' I say, but Mr Peare puts a hand on my arm, taking a deep stuttering breath.

'David,' the lady says, rushing over to his bed. I look at his oxygen levels and react quickly, even though I probably shouldn't, offering him a mask.

'Deep breaths, Mr Peare – long exhalations.'

The lady looks over to me. 'I'm confused, who are you? Are you a doctor?'

I'm not sure what to say. Technically, yes, but in this moment, no. I bend down to check on Mr Peare, putting a hand on his.

'Will you stay?' he asks me.

I nod, offering my hand to the lady. 'I'm Joe.'

'Natalia,' she says, eyeballing me, sitting by David's bed. 'You're overdressed, whoever you are,' she tells me.

'He's just making up for my lack of formality,' David tells her. I watch as she kisses his hand and perches her head on his mattress, looking up at him. From the photo on the bedside table, I see both of them flanked by two young children. 'Joe, give me a hand now. Can you sit me up? As far as the bed can go?' he asks me.

Natalia looks over at both of us curiously.

'Now tell me, how do I look? Don't talk about the hair but is there anything in my teeth?' he says, clenching them in front of me.

'You're all good, chief. I will take it this is happening now.'

He nods and looks me in the eye. 'Oh, the one thing I'm learning in life is that you do everything now. No waiting.' And with that he turns away from me, urging Natalia to sit on the edge of the bed next to him. I back away into the shadows of the room.

'David, what the hell are you up to?' Natalia asks him.

'Marry me...' he says, plainly.

'What?' she says, incredulous.

And for a moment, he sits there, his hands on her face, not saying a word but looking into her eyes as they glass over, watching as she affectionately kisses his hand. It's such a quiet admission of love, the complete opposite of everything I've seen in the last few days and the intimacy of it floors me. He just asked the question without a boat, without a band, without calling birds and ladies dancing. Two people who simply live in love, and who know that they may lose that love. I take another step back. David puts his palm out and reveals the ring to her.

'David! How on earth...' Natalia's eyes shift to me then back to him.

'I should have done this when I first met you. After the kids were born. I keep thinking about all the times I should have told the world how much I loved you...'

Natalia starts to weep as his frail hand reaches for hers and he puts the ring on her finger.

'So this is me telling you now. I don't know how much longer we have but for now, let's tell everyone that while I was here, I was yours. We had something really, really great.'

Natalia can hardly talk but nods, sobbing. 'Didn't we just?'

'The most perfect thing.' He puts his hand in hers and squeezes it tightly. 'It's a good Christmas gift, eh?' She laughs through her tears. 'I'm just sorry I couldn't give you a wedding. I know you'd have preferred something in a country house with a three-course dinner...'

'I have a tin of Quality Street and my turkey sandwich meal deal. You're in a white dress of sorts. It's kind of the same.'

'So, is that a yes?' he asks her.

'Of course, you idiot,' she says, grabbing his face and kissing him.

They sit there embracing as I look on in awe at both of them, quietly weeping, a slim perfect line of gold sat on her hand, glistening in the low lights of the room. And I think of all those rings I've handed over in the last two days, all symbols of people saying they want to be forever. They want that love to be forever for however long that may be. That is quite a wonderful thing.

'Time for your medicine, Mr David,' a Filipina nurse suddenly says, walking into the room, and Natalia jumps up from the bed. 'Ruby! LOOK!' she says, showing her the ring and the nurse squeals with excitement, running to the corridor to tell people, all while David laughs from his bed. The room fills with light and Natalia jigs around in that room with the joy of a child on Christmas morning. I may take that as my cue to allow them to celebrate this moment. I head towards the door slowly and turn to look back at the bed, catching David's eye as the room suddenly comes to life in the collective excitement of that very small yet special ring.

'Thank you,' he mouths to me. I don't quite know what to say in return but nod my head and smile, studying his face, his happiness for one last time, before taking my leave.

As I walk down the corridor, I hear a voice. 'You said two minutes, Mr Lord.'

I turn, trying to hold it together. 'I'm sorry, Sister. But it's...'

'Christmas. Yes, you keep labouring that point. Did you get what you needed delivered?' She turns to look at the excitement and celebration coming from that room.

'I did. Thank you for letting me do that, Sister Drummond.'

'You're welcome. One last thing...' she tells me, thoughtful. 'I'm sad to hear you left medicine. You were a very good doctor, Mr Lord.' Her sincerity floors me. 'I only remember the good ones.'

I don't know how to reply. To any of it.

'Enjoy the rest of your evening.'

I smile, before turning away, hoping she hasn't seen the tears in my eyes.

TWENTY

Eve

I can't even remember when it happened. We had both gone for lunch one weekend shift in the shop, and the queue for our sushi had us standing outside one of these tourist shops that sold everything from bottled water to handbags to Union Jack T-shirts. It also had a lovely line of personalised jewellery. Outside the shop was a display that had lines of gold necklaces that spelt out names. He scanned the display.

'They have your name!' Joe said.

'I'm good, thanks!'

'They also have personalised signs for bedroom doors if that's your bag.'

I laughed.

'You have such a good name for a necklace though. It's just three letters. You could have a name like...'

'Marie Antoinette,' I said randomly.

'Yes,' he said with eyes widened. 'Imagine that emblazoned in cheap gold across your neck.'

'I don't think anyone needs to know my name,' I told him, and I remember he looked sad as the queue moved forward.

'Yeah, they do. You're great. Is this just too basic for you? It's only five pounds. Are you just all about the bling?' he joked with me.

'Please! How long have we worked together? Do I look bling to you? Let's make a deal. You can get that for me for Christmas if I can get you a sign for your bedroom door.'

'Deal.'

And he shook my hand.

Because everyone should know your name.

I read the tag again. He thinks I'm amazing? When did he buy this? During our ring quest? Before? If it was before then he thought all those things before. I look down at the necklace in my hands in shock.

'You can say it out loud. I am the best brother that ever existed,' Noel tells me as he manoeuvres his car off the M25 and on to the M23. Over skies, I see planes head towards Gatwick, glowing red taillights for as far as the eye can see, cars beside us crammed with people, gifts and bags, headed home after a day of Christmas festivities.

'You are the best brother that ever existed,' I tell him in his Christmas jumper and new vintage Stan Smiths. Noel's radio blasts out Nat King Cole and I think about someone who refused to sing that song to me once. Noel's car is different to the green Mini I've lived in for the last few days. It's laden with trash for a start and smells like vape but I suddenly miss Joe's flashing lights and mooning Santa on the dashboard.

'So, is there a plan here? Brighton is a big place. Do I just head for the pier?' Noel tells me.

Since I opened that necklace and pieced together what Joe did by protecting me from Chris's shitty note, I've been in a strange state of shock that Noel just seems to be carrying me through. We need to find Joe, tonight. We need to get in your car. Drive. Stop at this shop. I need to buy something really quickly. Brighton. Head for Brighton. The horizon, just head that way. And like a brilliant twin brother, he questions none of it. He drives and seems mildly excited by the adventure. But he has also asked for petrol money and suggested that some super strong coffee may be a good idea.

'Maybe we message him when we get there? I haven't thought that far ahead.'

Noel nods, slightly bemused. This is usually him. It's impromptu road trips in our youth to music festivals and days at the beach where he was always very unprepared and we ended up having to sleep in this thing. But this time, it's me who's unprepared. What am I going to do? Turn up at his family home in the middle of the night? *Hi Joe, I've worked out some things. I think you like me, I like you. Let's see if this has a chance? I'm sorry I've woken your whole family.* This feels as if I need a speech prepared, a grand gesture. Like a brass band? Not a boat, I know that now.

'And Joe never hinted that he possibly had a crush on you? All that time?'

I shake my head. 'He was just a nice bloke.'

'...Who was honourable and probably didn't want to cross that line,' Noel says, voicing his approval at the man's morals.

I think now about little moments in his Mini. Comments where he offered me a hand and pulled me up, kindness, someone who was looking out for me, who made it all about me. I feel a bit blindsided by the fact I never saw any of this. That and a bit stupid. My phone rings and I answer it immediately.

'Joe?' I say, panicked.

'No, it's Mrs Caspar. Merry Christmas, my dear. Is everything alright? I have some missed calls from you.'

I catch my breath. 'I'm so sorry, Mrs Caspar, it's late and it's Christmas – were you asleep? I hope you've had a good day?'

'Oh no, we're still up,' she says in her soothing, warm tones.

'Mr Caspar and I were just talking about you and Joe. Did all the rings get delivered?'

'They did. I think. Joe did the last one.'

'Oh.' She pauses for a moment sounding supremely disappointed. 'So you're not together now? You're not with Joe?'

'Define together...'

'Like, in the same car?' she says, unconvincingly.

I can hear her mumbling something to Mr Caspar in the background.

'Mrs Caspar, I have a question. When I came into the shop, you called Joe to come along, why him? Why not George who works in the week? Or Bailey who works Tuesdays?'

'Because George is in his fifties, and I know for a fact that he goes to bed at seven o'clock every evening because of indigestion issues.'

'Mrs Caspar...'

There is silence on the end of the phone. 'So the rings were our mistake, completely. But yes, I rang Joe because... He is a good boy. And because he likes you, Eve... and, yes, in my infinite years of wisdom I thought it was a window of opportunity for the two of you to get together.'

'MRS CASPAR! You knew all this time and never told me... He liked me?'

Noel reaches over trying to listen into the conversation, urging me to put it on speaker.

'Of course he did! It was little things. He used to stand a bit straighter when you were in the shop, he listened when you spoke, he paid attention to you. It was a sweet and lovely thing to observe. So, when you broke up with that rotter, Chris, I just gave things the little push they needed. I pushed too hard, didn't I? Why are you not with him now?' she asks, sadly.

I am again a little emotional to hear her words, thinking about all those times the three of us would have been in the shop and she would have been watching over us. Shame on her for not letting on to me though.

'He's gone home for Christmas.'

'Are you OK, my dear? You've had quite the week. We are here if you need us.'

I feel tears start to well up in my eyes at her kindness. 'I'm with my brother, it's all good. Please give Mr Caspar a big Christmas hug from me. I think the last few days have been eventful but also done me the world of good. So, thank you. Thank you so much. Merry Christmas.'

'Never thank us. We love you, Eve,' she says kindly before hanging up.

I look blankly at my phone as a screensaver of Joe pops up again. He liked me. Shit. I put my head in between my knees as Noel looks on, chugging his third espresso of the evening.

'Oh, Evie. Deep breath. Is there anything I can do?'

I shake my head. It's a very big mess in my head at the moment but all I know is that it would be good to see Joe tonight. To at least tell him that while he's had a head start, I'm catching up. I'd like to jog beside you now and tell you how I feel, too. What are we doing? Brighton is a bloody big city. I have no idea where he lives down there.

'Well, are we good to take a pit stop?' Noel asks. 'I love you. But my bladder can't take all this caffeine.'

I nod, signalling that a pit stop is allowed. Hell, maybe it's a chance to plan this, to think about what I need to say. Or maybe it's a chance to turn this car around. I don't know where we're going or if Joe will ever pick up his phone or reply to me. It's selfish of me to think he'd come away from his family at a time like this. This was a stupid plan. I've taken up enough of his Christmas Day already. We've left Dad alone, too. I don't want him to be alone. We should go back. Noel takes the turning for the motorway services and finds a space in the unnaturally empty car park, parked next to a van where the driver in a Santa hat sleeps in the driver's seat, like an elf but not.

'You should pee, too,' he tells me.

'Alright, Dad,' I jest.

'No, seriously. If there's no plan and we're driving around Brighton all night, shouting out on to the streets for this Joe then I say pee now. Or you'll have to go and squat in the sea.'

I salute him, undoing my seat belt, looking down at the necklace in my lap and putting it on, catching myself in the rearview mirror of the car. Joe was right, it's three letters but it's a good name. It's kind of perfect.

'Hurry up, it's cold.' I hear Noel outside the car, jigging around to keep himself warm.

I get out, smoothing out the skirt of my dress, and link arms with Noel. 'God, we're a right pair,' I tell him as I look at our party dress and Christmas jumper collab. 'Nice kicks though.'

'Someone really awesome bought them for me.' I pull him closer. 'I love how we're spending Christmas Day in a motorway services – the glamour of it all,' he jokes, casting a hand over the building. 'Oh look, Burger King is open. I think the only time I ever eat a Burger King is at a motorway services,' he says.

And for some reason, I stop. I think about what someone once told me. And just like that, I look around that car park and watch as the van we were parked beside pulls away, revealing a green Mini. I take a deep breath. I believe that car's name is Olive.

'Noel, where are we? What is the name of this services?'

'I think we're in Crawley. Pease Pottage,' he says, reading off the sign.

Joe

'Joe?'

'Hey, Dad... Yep... all good there?'

'How far away are you?'

'I reckon about half an hour, just stopping for a bit. Is everyone asleep?'

'I wish. Can't get the little ones to settle. Little Belle made me put a broom up the chimney in case any of Santa's gifts got stuck.'

I chuckle under my breath. 'Hey, do you remember that time I slept in the living room trying to catch Santa out and I slept through it all?'

I can hear Dad laughing. 'You slept through it all because I drugged your cocoa.'

'Say what?'

'Antihistamine. You were out like a light. We couldn't have you catch us in the act. Mum said I probably gave you too much. That's why if you look at all the photos from that year, you look slightly stoned.'

We both laugh in chorus and that sound is like music to me. 'Just get back. I need help corralling your sisters, too. Carrie had some fight with Holly over the charades and threw a wicker reindeer at her and they're not talking now.'

'Standard then...'

'Wouldn't be Christmas without it. You alright, son?' he asks me.

'Just wanted to hear your voice. Be good to see everyone. Do we need anything? There's a shop here.'

'Milk. Rugrats put most of ours out for Santa. He needed a pint, apparently, to get him through the night.'

'Milk it is.'

'Where have you stopped?'

'Where else?'

'Good lad. See you in a bit. Love you, bud.'

'Love you, too.'

The air gets stuck in my throat as I say that, for reasons I won't say out loud. Not now. But I think of David and Natalia back in that hospital room, thinking of moments in similar rooms with my own dad, the future unclear, and how it broke my heart and the pieces have never quite healed. It did mean I returned to my car in that very quiet hospital car park and cried. I sobbed. I don't know what these last days have meant but all these very powerful shows of love, of people living their lives and moving forward tells me that I'm not. I'm jumping between jobs, avoiding life, not telling people I love them, thinking that is some way to be. And it was now Christmas Day and here I was, alone. I didn't want to be alone, not at Christmas, so I wiped away those tears and I started driving. Back home. I may have a few days of airbeds and endless rounds of Connect 4 ahead of me but at least I will be surrounded by people I love. I thought long and hard about Eve, sat in my passenger seat, moments with her to bank and remember fondly, but I need to move on from her. I really do. I need to move on from all of it. I need to remember to live.

'Can I take your order please?' the elf behind the counter asks me, squinting a little at the emotion still etched in my face. Probably not good form to cry at a motorway services to a man dressed as an elf, is it? I want to tell him he's lucky. I was an elf a few days ago and I had to show chest and the faint outline of my baubles.

'Can I get a Whopper meal, please, with a Coke? Thanks, Kevin.'

Kevin the Elf looks back at me, suspiciously. 'Do I know you?'

'No. But your name tag says Kevin,' I say, pointing at the badge. He looks down at his chest like this is a huge surprise.

'Oh, yeah. Do you want onion rings, too? We're giving them away for free because it's Christmas.'

'Sure.' It's fried, it's free. It will surely help. 'Also, don't think I'm weird but do you have any crowns?'

'You got kids?'

'Yeah. Forgot to get them a present, didn't I?'

He looks a little sad that this is what I may be gifting my children this Christmas, but he hands me a stack of them, and I think about a photo of all my nieces and nephews looking like fast-food royalty that will be a part of tomorrow.

'Quiet today then?' I say, trying to come up with some small talk as my order is prepared.

'Yeah. Some Christmas commuters but not many people want a burger at Christmas. You headed home from a big party?' Kevin asks me, looking at the tuxedo.

'Sort of. What about you? Big man bring you what you want?'

'You calling my dad big?'

'No, I meant Santa,' I say, confused.

'Oh, I believe Christmas is a materialistic exercise in consumerism, excess and greed. Hate it.'

'I'll assume that's why you're working a shift on Christmas Day then.'

He shrugs. 'Triple pay, you know?'

I nod and see my burger sliding down the rack and point towards it, alongside paper bags of onion rings, waiting to be claimed.

Kevin assembles my tray and slides it over. 'Well, Merry Christmas, mate.'

'You, too.'

The services are deathly quiet bar the sound of a man cleaning the floors and some Christmas music echoing in the background. It's Nat King Cole who I never really had any strong feelings about before but now will always mean Eve singing along in my car and getting the lyrics wrong. Whilst I normally enjoy a pit stop, this space has never felt as empty as it does now. Even with the big tree by the entrance and their efforts to put up twinkling lights and garlands across the condiments station, it feels soulless, a place for people to pass through with nowhere else to go. I take a window seat and watch as two men in head-to-toe hi vis down the last of their coffees and nod to me. I really hope you two have somewhere to be this Christmas. I then make myself a crown, pulling the tabs of cardboard through the slits and place it on my head. Kevin looks over, confused, and I think he furtively takes a picture of me on his phone. I look forward to going viral, like the sad case I am, in my dinner jacket, about to enjoy my burger, alone.

I don't notice her at first. In some part of my mind, I wonder if I'm hallucinating her. Eve. She comes and sits beside me at my window seat in this very quiet cavernous room where the music has switched to Elton John. She sits there and smiles, reaching over to take a paper crown and carefully build it, placing it on her head. She then steals one of my chips. I sigh deeply, frozen. You're here. That's actually you.

'Can I just check... is your name Eve by any chance?' I say, pointing to the space just below her neck.

'It is,' she says, putting her hand to the necklace.

'That's some bling.'

'Right? Goes with my new ring,' she tells me, showing off a giant plastic engagement ring on her hand.

'That is classy. You're engaged now?'

'His name is Clarence. We're planning a wedding in a big London hotel. With birds, lots of birds.'

I can't help but laugh. She slides something across the table, wrapped in a white paper bag. I won't talk about the wrapping, but I open up the bag and chuckle softly. It's a name plate with Joe in the middle, surrounded by stars and a rocket ship.

'For your room. In case people don't know you sleep there. That was the deal, wasn't it?'

I take a deep breath, trying to act cool about all this despite everything inside me somersaulting. 'It was. I love it, thank you.'

'I'm glad.'

Why are you here, Eve? To hand over a missed Christmas

gift? I can hardly breathe as she looks me directly in the eye. Please don't be here just for that.

'You left me at the restaurant,' she mumbles, looking slightly hurt.

'You were having fun. It was the right time. You didn't need me.'

'I do need you.'

I glance at her, trying to work out if she's telling me the truth, trying to work out why she might not. How did she know I was here?

'I went back to my flat earlier and I found that note that Chris wrote to me,' she tells me.

'It was a shit note. I didn't want to see you any more hurt than you already were.'

'Because you care about me...'

I swallow hard. I may as well tell her. Here. In this empty motorway services. No more waiting. 'More than you know.'

It's the first time I've said that out loud to her and I see her eyes glass over as she starts biting at her thumbnail, in that way she does.

'But why?'

I take a huge breath. 'Because you are amazing, Eve, and I'm sorry Chris never told you that, every hour of every day.'

'And what if I told you I think the same about you?' she says, nervously, her eyes full of tears now.

I stop for a moment. She has a hand out on the table and reaches for mine. As soon as our fingers touch, I can't breathe, the moment is so potent I have to look at her hand to make sure it's real. 'I mean, I know I carry this crown off,' I say. 'Or is it my singing?'

'That too, obviously... Also, you're very good on boats. I'm attracted to your seaworthiness,' she says, smiling broadly. 'Or maybe it's the fact that over the last few days I've seen someone who will do anything for anyone. He's desperately kind, he's human, he can wear shorts with bells and he's someone who's held my hand at a really awful time in my life. And maybe I don't want to let go of that hand.'

And her cheeks blush as she grabs that hand tighter and says those words, out loud, to me. All at once, they make my being completely still, calm, relieved. The huge storm of emotion settles and she's all I can see. My horizon. I can't move. I never want to. Unfortunately, we might have to because I can see Kevin closing up Burger King, but I think this might be our own version of romance, some gesture and declaration of love.

'I can't quite tell if this is the end of a really long date,' I tell her.

'Or the beginning of something else...' she tells me. I can't wait anymore. I lean over and I kiss her. With hope, without hesitation. And unlike that moment with the mistletoe, or in Trafalgar Square, this feels different. A wonderfully new and intense feeling of love overwhelms me. That feeling of her being so close is an intoxicating type of magic. It really is all I ever wanted.

'YES!' a voice echoes through the room. I turn around to see Eve's brother in a Christmas jumper, cheering from the entrance, a Red Bull in hand, hugging the man who's been polishing the floor. I laugh, looking over at him.

'I don't know what to do now,' I tell her, putting a hand to her face.

'Well, I'm kinda starving. Would you mind if I took a bite of your Whopper,' Eve jokes.

I grin, opening up the box, turning it towards her. 'You are very welcome to my Whopper. I also have onion rings,' I tell her proudly. She acts impressed but I won't tell her I got them for free.

She looks quietly down at the tray and shakes them out on the paper then beams, counting them out. 'Five go-old rings...'

she sings quietly. We both look down and laugh as she takes one and bites into it.

'I can't believe you made that joke,' I tell her.

'I sang that joke because, you know, you can't sing...'

I fake shock at the insult.

'And the joke told itself, really. Though technically it's four gold rings because you bailed on me...'

'I did not bail, I left you with your family. Santa can vouch for me.'

'Oh, Santa was not impressed. He told me he saw you steal a turkey, too.'

'He did, did he?'

'Santa sees everything.'

And as this version of banter goes back and forth, I adjust Eve's crown and sit back in my plastic seat. I don't know what this is, but these last three days have shown us how this could be the beginning of something great. Maybe we go back to London for what's left of Christmas, maybe we descend on Brighton, but whatever happens we're together and the adventure continues. I study her face, the necklace glistening around her neck, the emotion in her eyes. As she speaks, Elton John turns into Chris Rea, the lights on the tree in the foyer continue to dance and scatter, and the clock behind us creeps closer towards the end of the first day of Christmas.

EPILOGUE

'Hello, how can I help you today?' I ask the gentleman as he walks into Caspar & Sons, worried, lost. I know that look. It's a look that says, I have to buy something of incredible worth, as a symbol of my love for a significant other so it has to be perfect and basically, I don't have a clue what I'm looking for.

'Hi.' He's dressed in chinos and a smart light blue shirt. 'I guess I'm looking for a ring.'

'For any special occasion, sir?'

'I was hoping to propose to my girlfriend,' he says, gulping.

'So, an engagement ring?' He nods.

I smile and reach down to the counters, bringing some rings to the top, all embedded in red velvet cushions, small tags all handwritten, glistening in the early spring light that fills the shop.

'Well, let's see. Does your girlfriend have a preference for metal? Silver, gold?'

'Rose gold, I think. I did some research on the internet.'

'Excellent choice. And what about stones? Would you like to go traditional with diamonds or something a little different?'

He looks at me, panicked, the option of choice looking completely overwhelming to him. He has a little notebook with him where he's very neatly written down the findings of all his research.

'I should have brought her along, right? I just want to get this perfect, but I also wanted to surprise her,' he says, his shoulders slumped.

'It's a common problem with engagement rings, don't worry. What's your name, sir?'

'Ed.'

'Well, I'm Eve. Lovely to meet you. Tell me about your girlfriend, Ed.'

'So... her name is Mia. We met at work. We're both teachers. You know I don't think she'd go traditional, she'd like something bright, bold...'

'What does she teach?' I ask.

'English. She's a big Shakespeare fan.'

'Well, we could look at getting something engraved with a quote, perhaps? We have a few really lovely vintage pieces. We can also design something together based on what you think she'll like.'

'Really?'

'It should be perfect and reflect who she is. Tell me more about Mia.'

'She's hilarious, kind, smart, the sort of woman who just helps everything make a bit more sense. My best friend really.' I like how talking about Mia puts him at ease, completely.

'What colour eyes does she have?'

'Blue.'

'Then maybe a sapphire? They represent honesty, purity, and traditionally are supposed to bring good fortune to a marriage.' I show him an example of a vintage one in a cabinet and his eyes light up.

'Or perhaps a more modern piece. This one is made of virgin gold – it has a unique raw texture.'

He freezes, biting his lip, not knowing what to say. His gaze shifts to my left hand. 'Your ring is stunning. May I?' he asks. I put my hand out on the counter.

'Is that an emerald?'

'It is.'

'And that shape is quite unique,' he notices.

'It's called a pear cut.'

'The thin gold bands look like lots of different rings.'

'Oh, yes... It's supposed to represent five different rings. It's called a stacked ring.'

'Your fiancé obviously put a lot of thought into it.' I look down at it. He did. Though I suspect there was an older couple in the building who may have given him a hand. 'Does he have a name?'

'Joe.'

'And what does he do?'

'He's in medical school,' I say proudly.

'Wow. How did he propose?' he asks. 'I bet he went with the grand gesture. Restaurant? Did he skywrite it? Hire a boat? Any tips?'

I laugh for reasons he'll never know. 'It was Christmas Eve.'

'Like your name.'

'Exactly. He proposed on a rooftop terrace of a hotel. First place we ever kissed. There was mistletoe because he can be a cheese ball like that. Have you thought about how you may propose?'

'Well, we first kissed on my sofa over a takeaway so maybe not that.' He blushes hard as if recounting the memory. 'I did have an idea of making her a PowerPoint.'

I don't know how to tell him that's a terrible idea but I'm sure he can see that from the horror in my face.

'Oh, I mean... I was going to make it and pretend to give an assembly at school and then drop on one knee.'

'In front of all the kids...?'

'Possibly.'

'I like that,' I say, grinning. 'Well then, Ed, a proposal like that deserves a proper ring. Let's see what we can do for you.'

A LETTER FROM THE AUTHOR

Dear lovely reader,

Hello, there! You're bloody marvellous! Merry Christmas! Or if you're not reading this at Christmas then who cares? I see you. I watch Christmas films in the summer, too. They're like the best comfort blankets, aren't they? Thank you from the bottom of my heart for reading *Five Gold Rings*. If we've met before then hello again but if you're new – welcome, take a seat... it's a pleasure to meet you. I'm Kristen.

I hope you enjoyed reading Joe and Eve's festive tale. If romcoms, banter and willy jokes are your thing then you're in luck. Stick with me! You can keep up to date with all my latest releases and bonus content by signing up at the following link. Your email address will never be shared, and you can unsubscribe at any time.

www.stormpublishing.co/kristen-bailey

And if you enjoyed *Five Gold Rings* then I would be overjoyed if you could leave me a review on either Amazon or Goodreads to let people know. It's a brilliant way to reach out to new readers. And don't just stop there, tell everyone you know on social media, gift the book to your mates, drop WhatsApp notes to everyone you know.

I started writing this book this time last year, and I'll be frank, I wasn't quite sure where it was going. I thought I could write a Christmas book because I quite like Christmas, but I wrote a scene about someone waking up on Christmas Day next to a man dressed as Santa and well, that just felt a bit wrong. There's a time for raunch and Christmas just doesn't feel like that time. Anyway, the book went through a couple of different versions until after Christmas, when I went into my loft to put away some decorations, and I saw the table plan for my wedding. I got married on 6th January and we named all the tables after the *Twelve Days of Christmas*. I went through the song and the story for *Five Gold Rings* came to me as I climbed down the loft ladder. Why rings? Why not turtles doves or partridges in pear trees? Well, reader. It's the best part of the song, no?

And as the story transformed and Eve and Joe came to life, I found myself writing a super warm, cheesy festive romcom. This makes total sense to me – I'm a HUGE fan of a good brie. It's a little less cynical and bawdy than my usual books but at the heart of this novel is a very sweet love story between two of the best people, set in my favourite city. We get to peer into five other relationships, too, bask in their glow, witness their joy, and learn about the power of love. (I am aware I've just quoted a *Frankie Goes to Hollywood* Christmas song and I encourage you to sing it now.) Love is the best thing, especially at Christmas, and it will always be my greatest honour to be able to write about it. I hope this book made you smile, laugh, and made you believe in all that is magical about this time of year. I hope you've had trifle this Christmas, too. If not, go out and buy one now. Eat it on your own. I won't tell.

I will leave it here. For anyone who's possibly a fan, you get top marks for spotting all the previous book references. Yes, that's Josie Jewell and the Callaghans in the restaurant, and that's Ed Rogers buying a ring at the end. Remember it's a KB universe and that's where all my characters live. As always, I've spent a lot of time on my surnames, too. You're welcome to go back and guess the theme. I'll give you a hint, it may have to do with Christmas.

I'd be thrilled to hear from any of my readers, whether it be with reviews, questions or just to say hello. If you like retweets from Fesshole, then follow me on Twitter or whatever that tosser is calling it these days. Have a gander at Instagram, my Facebook author page and website, too, for updates, ramblings and to learn more about me. Like, share and follow away – it'd be much appreciated.

With much love and gratitude,

Kristen

xx

www.kristenbaileywrites.com

 facebook.com/kristenbaileywrites

 twitter.com/mrsbaileywrites

 instagram.com/mrsbaileywrites

ACKNOWLEDGEMENTS

I'm going to start this by acknowledging my husband. I first met Nick in 2004 and on our first Christmas he gifted me an iPod and a copy of *It's a Wonderful Life* on DVD (both of those things existed in 2004). They were both magical gifts so you can imagine my surprise when he told me, 'I don't really do Christmas.' That's funny, I thought. Because I do. I bloody love Christmas. This should be interesting. Since then, it's been nearly twenty years and four kids of this – our very own Christmas grumpy-sunshine romcom. Pure comedy moments like the time I volunteered my Grinch to be Santa for our kids' preschool, and he was made to wear a beard of cotton wool balls and a highly flammable suit. But also romantic moments, like when I married him on the twelfth day of Christmas, the day of my epiphany. He'll argue he went for that date because we got it cheap, but I think he secretly knew it was the perfect time of year to get wed. He even let me walk down the aisle to *Winter Wonderland*. So, Saint Nick, thank you. I love how, ironically, we don't wear rings. We're just not bling like that. I'll eat my Christmas hat if you read this book but know you are the inspiration for everything – all the laughs, all the love and everything in between.

Second round of thanks go to the kids. I love how you love Christmas (despite your dad). I love how you're suspicious of fake Santas and I love that you always ask for random things like a salmon and bags of Werther's Originals. Thank you for always finding joy in the smaller things in life, and making me laugh every single day whether it's Christmas or not. I don't sound like a crow when I sing though, that's just rude.

My love for Christmas came from quite an eclectic and multicultural background which means I've seen this season through lots of different lenses, and it's certainly inspired how I wanted to express Christmas through this book. I have Guyanese and Singaporean roots, so Christmas has always been about huge amounts of joy, food and celebration. All my memories are of houses, hearts and plates always full, as it should be this time of year. So a huge thank you to the brothers, sisters, aunts, uncles and cousins I remember so fondly around Christmas. It's impossible to name you all but I hope you'll see how some of you have featured in this book. A special mention to my Aunty Sandra who sadly passed away this year but who loved Christmas. She used to work in Harrods and when we were kids, we used to visit every year to see her work in Santa's Grotto. I will miss the cards you used to send in November. And thank you to my mum. I learned how to be Santa from the best. My favourite year was when you'd obviously forgotten a gift and shoved Leanne's Gordon the Gopher sleeping bag in the fireplace, trying to convince us that it must have got stuck in the chimney.

Huge thank you to Helen Williams, Kelly Adey, Anna and Baptiste for their help with the French in this book especially as the French I needed to know was less than orthodox. *Merci beaucoup*.

Thank you to all at Storm who continue to champion my books. This was a bit of a jumble of a manuscript, but Vicky Blunden unravelled it, fixed it and said, let's get this out there in time for Christmas. She's not only a miracle worker but just a godsend of an editor. Anyone who writes comedy will tell you, it's not just about finding someone who edits like a mofo but also about finding someone who gets the joke. Thank you getting me but also having such belief and confidence in my stories. A massive thank you to all behind the scenes at Storm, too, who are responsible for getting my books out there, I appreciate you all.

This is my random list of people who keep telling me to keep on. THANK YOU. Bronagh McDermott, Danielle Owen-Jones, Elizabeth Neep, Natalie Johnson, Gabi Code, Sharon Crawford, Leanne Paul, Javier Fernandez, Geraldine Taylor, Nikki Clayton and Morgan Mepham. Finally, for the last three years, I've also had an awesome community of book bloggers and Instagrammers who offer me and my books their support and love. I don't deserve you. I hope you all have a bloody lovely Christmas.

Made in the USA
Middletown, DE
08 January 2024

47445266R00168